ANXIOUSLY ENGAGED

THE SUDDENLY SINGLE SERIES
BOOK 3

SALLY JOHNSON

Copyright © 2023 by Sally Johnson

All rights reserved.

No part of this book may be reproduced in any form or by any electronic or mechanical means, including information storage and retrieval systems, without written permission from the author, except for the use of brief quotations in a book review.

❦ Created with Vellum

To Trisha Luong
Since you are the other half of my brain
And you've loved Sophia as much as I have from the very beginning.

1

VANITY

"Hi, I'm Travis," he said and my life was never the same again.

My breath caught in my throat and my heart hammered against my ribs.

He was the most gorgeous, absolutely beautiful guy I had ever seen.

My roommate, Gretchen Clark, and I giggled. We'd had a conversation about him literally thirty seconds before when we first noticed him. We stood against a wall of the Garden Court, where a new student dance was being held. "Do you think he's coming to talk to us?" she'd whispered.

"I sure hope so," I replied as he headed in our direction.

As much as I liked my new friend and roommate, I secretly hoped he'd pick me. Don't get me wrong, Gretchen was cute—a round face, long, beautiful dark brown hair, big brown eyes and a sprinkling of freckles on her face. But I hoped tall and blonde was more his type. I *wanted* him to choose me. Besides, Gretchen was going on a mission in a couple of months.

"I'm Sophia," I said.

He flashed a drop-dead gorgeous smile. I swear he had to be a model for Abercrombie and Fitch. He was *that* good-looking. Was there a six pack under that t-shirt? But, since I'd probably never see his abs, I'd have to imagine that a creature with such a beautiful face *had* to have a body to match. Yummy.

He leaned in close. "Nice to meet you," he shouted above the thudding beat of the music.

I could smell his aftershave. Or maybe it was his hair gel. Whatever it was, it was woodsy and delicious.

I was smitten in an instant.

He really could've been the model on Abercrombie's shopping bags. He had sandy blond hair, gelled to perfection and slightly tousled. His hair was longer than a missionary haircut, but short enough to satisfy Brigham Young University's grooming standards. He had the whole package look-wise: square jaw, a slight hint of a cleft in his chin, cheekbones that defined his face, but not high enough to look bony. His eyes were a deep, intense blue, but it was hard to tell the exact shade in the dim lighting. And his lips. His lips were full and kissable. Not that I was lusting after him or anything. But Travis didn't need mood lighting to make him look any more attractive. He was nothing short of perfection. He was definitely not a "sweet spirit."

"I'm Sophia." I smiled back.

"You mentioned that."

My cheeks grew warm. I motioned beside me. "This is Gretchen." He didn't as much as nod in her direction.

He cocked his head a bit and looked at me intently. "My grandmother was named Sophia."

I giggled, giddy we had something in common. Surely, he'd loved his grandmother. "That's good for me, right?" I smiled so wide I probably looked like the Cheshire Cat.

He squinted a bit. "My mother never liked her. So, I'll call you Fifi."

It sounded like a pet poodle, but I'd be his pet.

"Would you like to dance?" he asked.

Would I? Of course! But I had to keep calm, play it cool. "Yes, but I'm not the most graceful person in the world."

He laughed. Laughter of the gods, surely. "I don't believe it."

You'd be surprised. "Consider yourself warned." I turned to Gretchen who had busied herself checking her phone. "You'll be okay?"

She forced a smile. "Sure. I'm going to find a guy to ask to dance." She looked out vaguely over the crowd.

I gave her the thumbs up as he took my hand and led me to the dance floor. I paced myself, hoping luck would be on my side, the song would end and the next would be slower. *Much* slower. It would also give me a chance to ~~touch him~~, I mean, hold his hand.

We hung off to the side, yelling over the music, until a slow song started. He was a perfect gentleman when we danced: his hand lightly on my shoulder, the other firmly on my waist.

As we swayed to the music, he maintained constant eye contact. It made me a little uncomfortable. "What?" I asked.

He angled his head slightly and stepped in closer, like he was trying to see me better. "You look familiar. Have we met?"

I knew what he meant. "People always say I look like Barbie." I might as well just say it. Yes, I looked like her. I was tall (5'10" to be exact) and slim, and had long blond hair, green eyes, a pert nose and full lips. I'd heard it all my life, but unfortunately had yet to receive any royalties. People might think it was a compliment, but believe it or not, it got old.

"Barbie. Yeah, maybe. I don't have any sisters, and since I didn't play with Barbies myself..." He slowly smiled this smile that I dare say was seductive. In a clean, non-sexual, seductive way, of course.

"And what about you?" I flirted back. "How long have you been modeling for Abercrombie and Fitch?"

He did that slow smile thing again. "I can't meet a beautiful girl like you if I'm too busy being on shopping bags."

He's a model!? "You model?"

"No," he whispered.

I giggled. I was being ridiculous, but I couldn't help it.

While the music played, the conversation lulled. Travis continued with the intense staring.

"Really, what? Why are you staring?" I blushed.

"I'm waiting for you to start talking like a man or something. You're so amazingly beautiful I'm worried you're not real."

I playfully swatted him. "I hope that's a joke." I *really* hoped I didn't look like a man. I better do a mustache check in the bathroom, in better lighting.

"I don't want anything to ruin the beautiful snapshot I have of you. You are the most breathtaking girl I have ever met."

Breathtaking. I liked that. My cheeks flushed once again. "You're embarrassing me."

His gleaming white teeth almost looked blue in the lighting. "It's true."

I could've stared at him all night, even more smitten than before, if that was possible. I loved that he was dancing with *me,* despite my own self-consciousness about dancing. If he noticed, he didn't act like it.

Small talk was a challenge because of the music. It was hard to come up with something to say after he announced I was breathtaking.

Wow.

I tried anyway. "So, um, you go to BYU?"

That was a stupid question! Obviously!

He chuckled and tightened his hold on my back. "Yeah. And how about you? You're not crashing from a local high school, I hope?"

I raised an eyebrow. "No, no. I'm legitimate. High school was last year. I can show you my student ID."

The music changed to a fast-paced song and I stopped. "Can we go..." I didn't know where. I didn't want to dance once and then say goodbye. But I also didn't want to embarrass myself fast dancing. It might take his breath away in a not-so-good-way, so I hurried off the dance floor and back to the safety of the hall.

"Walk?" he suggested, motioning toward the door. "Do you want to go for a walk?"

Yes, I did. But...I'd only met him ten minutes ago, and didn't know anything about him other than his name. "Okay," I said, making a rash decision.

"Or I could walk you home." It wasn't a question. It was a suggestion, an invitation. "If that's okay? Unless you want to stay at the dance."

I looked at the full room, heads bobbing, music booming and knew what *I* wanted to do. But what about him? "Do *you* want to stay?" I hoped not. I didn't want to lose my opportunity to spend more time with him.

He threw his head back and laughed. "Fifi. I'll do whatever you want to do. If you want to dance, I'll dance. If you want to take a walk, I'll walk. If you want to go home, I'm going to delay that as long as I can."

I looked around the immediate area to see if Gretchen was close by, but I didn't see her. A quick glance of the dance floor proved useless; it was so packed there was no way I could ever pick her out from among the mob. "Let's take that walk," I decided.

We made our way from the crowded hall to the stairwell. As a precaution and a courtesy, I texted Gretchen and asked her to call me in fifteen minutes. That way she'd know where I was, who I was with, and if he totally ran out of charm, I'd have an out. But I really hoped his charm continued.

As we left the north entrance of the Wilk, he turned left, walking west, away from my dorms.

I pointed in the opposite direction "Um, I live in Heritage Halls." If he ever wanted to track me down after this evening, I'd given him a huge clue.

"Okay," he said and kept walking in the same direction.

Maybe he misunderstood and thought I'd said someplace else. Or maybe he was confused about which side of campus we exited on. "We're going the wrong way."

"I know. Let's take the long way around; make the night last a little longer. I'm not ready for it to end."

If I was going to be alone with him, I'd better ask some important questions. "Are you planning on attacking me in the bushes?" I gave him my best critical eye, half-joking half-serious. As if he'd really tell me of his bad intentions.

"Not if I want to see you again tomorrow."

Mmm. Tomorrow. Why yes, I did want to see him tomorrow.

"Here," he said, holding out his phone. "Text your friend my number so you can feel safe."

I sent his contact info to my phone and then forwarded it to Gretchen's number. That way I had his number too.

"Feel better?"

"Yes." I was slightly embarrassed, but not willing to mess around with my safety.

"Now that you have my contact info, can we go?"

"Okay." I slid my phone into my pocket. I'd walk around the whole campus three times if it meant spending more time with him. I liked him.

He took my hand (*yes!*) and led me away.

I smiled flirtatiously, holding on to his arm with both hands. "I don't even know your last name. I don't normally walk around strange, unfamiliar campus areas with guys I only know on a first name basis."

"Duck," he said.

Was there a stray branch about to poke me in the eye? Or ruin my perfectly wavy hair I'd spent an hour on? I ducked my head and looked around.

"What were you saying?" I asked.

"Duck," he repeated.

Not again. I checked around me. I didn't see any insects. "Is there a bee flying around my head?" I sounded impatient.

"No. My last name. It's Duckk."

I stopped and looked directly at him. "Like the bird?" How could such a beautiful creature end up with a last name Duckk? I guess he couldn't be *completely* perfect.

He nodded; his face expressionless. "Yeah. D-u-c-k-k."

Sophia Duckk. I tried it on for size.

"So, Travis Duckk, tell me about yourself. All the pertinent stuff."

"Okay." He smacked his lips. "I'm from Salt Lake City. I'm twenty-two years old, I've been home from my mission for just over a year."

"You didn't go out when you were eighteen?"

"No. I did some college first. I didn't feel completely ready immediately out of high school."

Nothing wrong with that.

"I served in the Bolivia, La Paz mission, my major is pre-med—"

"Are you studying podiatry?" I broke in and then giggled. A foot doctor named Dr. Duckk would be pretty dang funny.

He didn't smile. "No. Not podiatry," he said slowly.

I'd better stop making ~~quacks~~, I mean, cracks about his name or he wasn't going to like me anymore. "I'm sorry. You were saying?" I pressed my lips together to smother the laugh threatening to escape.

"That's about all. What about you, Fifi? Tell me all about you."

I blushed and wondered if he could see the heat burning in my cheeks. He stared at me so intensely it was hard to concentrate and string a sentence together. "Um, I don't know." I bit the edge of my lip. "What do you want to know?"

"Everything."

He did the cock-his-head-sideways-and-look-out-the-corner-of-his-eye thing. It was so attractive I seriously lost my train of thought.

"Let's see..." I wasn't sure where to begin, what to tell, how to appeal to him.

My phone buzzed in my pocket.

"Hold that thought," I said, pulling out my phone and glancing at the screen.

Gretchen: you okay?
Me: I'm good

I sent it and put my phone away. Then I smiled at him. "Where were we?"

He smiled back. "You were telling me about yourself."

"I'm eighteen. I'm a freshman. I'm from Las Vegas."

His eyebrow lifted slightly. "Vegas? Oh, like Henderson?"

"Nope. Vegas."

"Sin City. Really?" It sounded like that piqued his interest.

I tried to decipher his reaction from his expression. I got nothing. "Have you been there?"

He smiled a wicked grin. "Yes." Then he winked. "But don't tell my mother. She doesn't like Vegas."

Was I going to meet his parents? That was a good sign.

He did his half-smile grin that stopped my heart for a second. "What's your major?" he asked.

We reached the edge of campus by Maiser Hill. We followed the sidewalk around the building and northward. I wondered if our night would end when the loop ended by the dorms. I sure hoped not.

I swallowed hard to catch my breath, then shrugged. "I don't know. Right now, I'm undecided."

"What do you like to do in your free time?"

"I like shopping, watching movies and reading. My mom was an English teacher, before having kids, so she always read to us."

"I like reading. What do you read? Classics? Poetry? Shakespeare? Fan fiction?"

"Lots of stuff. Harry Potter, when I was younger, but I've kind of grown out of that. I liked Young Adult romance in high school. Now that I'm in college, teenage stuff seems so...teenage." I was rambling, so I tried to be more concise. "And since I'm not a teenager, theoretically, anymore. . ." I shrugged, then let it all out. "That's the problem."

None of that made any sense.

"What's the problem?"

"I don't know what I want to do. I'm a little lost here. Everyone seems so sure of who they are and what they want to do with the rest of their life, and I don't."

I didn't realize it had been weighing on me so heavily, but here I was, blurting it out to a complete stranger.

"Fi." His voice was soft. "No one has it all figured out. I don't have it all figured out."

I tried listening to his reasoning, but I was too focused on the fact that he now had a nickname for my nickname. Loved it.

"At least you have a major. You have some direction. Me," I

frowned, shaking my head, "I don't know what I'm doing here." I took a deep breath, trying to not be so emotional. He probably thought I was a crazy, weird, emotional girl with PMS. A far cry from my mother's PMA (my nickname for her ever-present Positive Mental Attitude).

He laughed.

"What?" I asked. Why was he laughing? I hadn't said anything funny. But when I *did* think I had said something funny, those were the times he *didn't* laugh.

Travis put his hand on my arm. "Fifi, don't be fooled. Having a major does *not* mean someone has life all figured out. It might mean they *think* they know what they want to do for a job."

"Really? Because it seems to me to be the same thing."

"It doesn't mean they know their passion in life. My roommate, he's a music major, but it's because he's good at it. He's not *great* at it because he's not passionate about it. It comes easily to him, so he does it. His parents want him to go professional, but he doesn't. He wants to major in Botany, but his parents don't approve, and the science doesn't come as easily to him as music does. So, does he have it all figured out?"

I shrugged. Was his roommate any better off than me? Majoring in music made his parents happy but not himself. At least he was doing *something*. Me—I had no clue what to do with myself. I changed the topic back to Travis, since finding out about him was so much better than analyzing myself. "What about you? Is medicine your passion?"

He nodded. "Yes. I find it fascinating."

"See." I pointed an "accusatory" finger at him. "You know what you want to do."

"But I came to BYU before my mission. I served my mission, had that time to think about things, and then I've had time after my mission. You just got out of high school. You haven't had a chance to figure things out."

"I just want to find something I'm passionate about," I concluded.

He leaned in a little closer. "I've found something I'm passionate about."

I nodded. "I know. Medicine."

"No. You."

"No, you what?"

"You, Fifi," he said.

I stopped rambling. Obviously, I missed the cue. "Me...?"

He leaned in closer. "I'm passionate about you."

His eyes met mine before he glanced at my lips. He leaned in closer.

"Me?" I continued rambling. Wasn't that a little premature? We just met tonight...Whoa. He was going to kiss me. That's what I was missing.

As he swept my hair off my shoulder, my heart fluttered like hummingbird wings. My stomach tightened in anticipation as he took my face in his hands.

"You are the most beautiful girl I've met in my whole life. You may not know why you're here, but I'm sure glad you are."

And then he kissed me.

His fingers wove into my hair and his lips met mine, soft and gentle. My lips parted and I breathed in his scent, my heart ping-ponging around in my rib cage. Kissing him was something I could be passionate about.

When we broke apart, he cradled my face in his hands. "You're too beautiful to be worrying your pretty head about that. You'll figure it out soon enough," he said quietly and then kissed me again.

And I believed what he said. Because I wanted to believe what he told me was true. Because it sounded good.

∞

"Tell me everything!" Gretchen demanded the moment I walked in our bedroom. If I didn't know any better, I'd think she was waiting up for me.

She sat crisscross on the t-shirt quilt that covered her bed, wide awake. With four other girls sharing our apartment, I lucked out getting Gretchen as my room-roommate.

In the few short weeks since school had started, Gretchen and I had become instant friends. Even more so than the friends I had grown up with or had in high school. We had a lot of fun together. Plus, she had some really cute clothes and knew how to accessorize. The only downside to borrowing her clothes was she was five inches shorter than me, so not everything worked.

I squealed.

Gretchen inched closer to the edge of the bed. "Oh, my gosh. Did he...?" Her mouth hung open.

I squealed once again. "He kissed me!"

We both screamed in unison.

"Nuh uh." Gretchen's eyes were wide.

"Yuh huh." I nodded fervently.

"NUH UH!" she said even louder.

"UH HUH!"

"Could you two quiet down over there?" a voice from the other side of the wall yelled. It was our roommate, Ruby.

We probably could have if it my news hadn't been so dang-*Oh-My-Gosh*-Unbelievably-Earth-Shattering. We screamed again, in unison.

Ruby banged on the wall.

Gretchen's eyes were huge, her mouth gaping. "Tell me everything." She patted the bed.

"Okay!" I said, sitting down next to her. I misjudged the edge of the bed, or was simply not paying attention, because I completely missed the mattress and landed hard on the floor. We busted up laughing.

Ruby's stern voice came again. "People are trying to sleep."

"Oh my gosh, Gretchen," I said in a loud whisper as I pulled myself up off the floor and carefully flopped on her bed. I didn't want to crack my head on the cinder block wall behind me. In my current state of twitterpation, who knew how else I could unintentionally injure myself. "He is amazing. He is gorgeous. He's sensitive.

He's intelligent, caring, and interested in me." I giggled. I couldn't help it.

I had never been in love before.

"And a kisser? Is he a good kisser?" Gretchen prompted.

"Of course!" I said, although I really had no experience. It wasn't my first kiss, but it was my most meaningful kiss. I had dated a couple of guys in high school, but always on group dates. The "relationships" involved texting, hand-holding and hanging out and were inevitably short-lived and not serious.

"What was it like?" she demanded. "Like the *Princess Bride* kiss or *Pride and Prejudice*? How would you describe it?"

The kiss replayed in my mind as I searched for words. "Perfect."

"Really?" Gretchen asked. "It was that good?" Gretchen screeched.

"SHUT! UP!" Ruby yelled again.

She scowled at the wall in Ruby's direction. "She's so serious," Gretchen whispered. She turned back to me and we broke into laughter again. Her hands shot up as if she were stopping traffic. "Okay, start from the beginning. I want to hear everything: every detail, every thought, every second."

As if I wouldn't tell her everything? I was about to explode with the details of my romantic evening.

We stayed up past midnight, examining every detail, considering every aspect of the conversation, deconstructing his looks, expressions, and body language. I could've stayed up all night I was so excited. It took me until almost dawn to fall asleep.

I felt so blessed. I'd just met the most amazing guy, who had everything I'd ever wanted. I had a roommate who had instantly become the best friend I'd never had.

Maybe it was okay that I didn't know what I wanted to do with my life. Maybe meeting him meant things were starting to fall in place. At least I had some great people in my life. That could be enough for now, right?

2

SMITTEN

I stared at the computer screen as I sat at my desk in my dorm room.

"Major," I said out loud, to myself. That was my goal for Monday after school: make a "major" decision.

With a list of almost two hundred majors offered, I didn't know which one to choose. I *should* know what I wanted to do with the rest of my life before choosing a subject to study for the next four years. But it wasn't like throwing darts at a board and hoping I'd hit on the right major.

I liked reading. English? My mom was a teacher and would love it if I followed in her footsteps, but I didn't want to teach. I didn't have patience for little kids, medium kids or even big kids.

General Studies seemed like a good option. It was nice and... general. Recreation Management sounded fun. I was good at having fun, but not so good at being coordinated.

My mind wandered.

What Travis is doing right now?

How did he decide on his major?

I squinted at the screen, reminding myself to focus. Not that I had to decide my major *right now*, but I wanted to have something declared by the end of the semester. It was easy to skate by on freshman level classes that fulfilled General Education requirements, but I couldn't do that for too many semesters. I'd eventually have to decide on something.

Maybe he likes chocolate chip cookies. It was one of the few things I could bake. Since I wasn't great at most kitchen-related things, I eliminated Food Science from my list of potential majors.

I could make cookies and drop them at his apartment.

I don't know where he lives.

But I *did* have his number.

Should I text him? I inhaled deeply. The thought was a little intimidating.

The bedroom door opened and Gretchen walked in. "What're you doing?"

I shut my laptop with a *snap*. "Trying to decide on a major but not having much luck."

She put her hand on her hip and raised an eyebrow at me.

"What?" I protested. "I really was. I wasn't doing anything bad."

"I wasn't worried that you were doing something bad. I'm more curious about your smile. I don't think you were exactly getting all dreamy about majors."

My cheeks heated up. "I was," I protested, getting flustered. "Then I started thinking about Travis—"

She sat down beside me. "Have you heard from him?"

"No. But if I made him cookies, I'd have a reason to text him."

Her face brightened. "Cookies. The perfect excuse. What guy doesn't like cookies?"

"Exactly," I readily agreed. "But I don't know where he lives."

Gretchen held up her index finger. "Text him and ask him for his address."

"I could," I said.

"You should," she said.

I spun my desk chair around and stood up. "Feel like making cookies with me?" A smile overtook my face.

"Let me grab an apron," Gretchen said.

"Cookies are done," Gretchen said. The extra cookies were piled on a plate in the center of the kitchen table where we were seated. The other plate, Travis's plate, she pushed across the surface until it was right in front of me.

She had helped me package them up cute in cellophane wrap (because I had to impress him) and a tag and curling ribbon. After all, presentation was everything.

The next move was on me. I pulled up Travis's text and stared at it. It loomed in front of me. The blinking cursor made my heart race and my palms to become sweaty.

"It shouldn't be this hard," I said.

"It's not. It's pretty simple. Just text him."

I had hoped he would've reached out to me over the weekend. But he hadn't. What if he was in class? Or studying? I didn't want to disturb him.

Gretchen pushed the plate closer. "Do it. You made him cookies. Who can say no to cookies?"

"A diabetic," I said.

"Is he diabetic?" Gretchen asked without an ounce of concern in her voice.

"Not that I know of."

She pointed at the phone. "Okay. Problem solved. Text him."

I could've come up with a ton more excuses. It was now or never. I pulled my hair up out of my face and secured it in a scrunchie. I could do this. I took the leap and touched the chat box with my thumb.

Me: Do you like chocolate chip cookies?

I waited, my heart literally in my throat.

Of course, I wanted an immediate answer. I checked the time. It was after three, which really didn't mean anything. Just because I was done with classes for the day didn't mean he was. He could still be in class, at the library, at work. He could be anywhere.

The bubbling dots appeared on my screen.

"He's typing!" I screamed.

Gretchen hopped up and rushed to my side. "Did he respond?"

We stared at the screen, as if willing the words to appear. "Not yet."

The dots stopped and disappeared.

"Oh," Gretchen said.

"No," I said. All that energy and excitement to have it turn into nothing.

My phone vibrated.

Travis: My favorite!

"He responded," I said, suddenly feeling a little sick to my stomach.

"Okay. Your turn," Gretchen said.

I took a couple of deep breaths.

Me: I made some for you

Travis: Thanks!

"Man, he's not making this easy," I said. I put the phone on the table and pushed it away from me.

Gretchen pulled it back. "It's not that hard, Soph."

I wiped my sweaty palms on my pants. "I know, I know. It's just nerve wracking." I shook my hands in the air to dry them.

"Make arrangements to meet," Gretchen said.

"Okay."

I grabbed my phone.

Me: Where should we meet?

I dropped my phone back on the table top like it was a hot potato.

"Are you like this with every guy you date? Or just the super gorgeous guys?" Gretchen asked.

I undid my hair and then re-did it in a messy bun. "I haven't ever really had a boyfriend," I said. "Not that Travis is my boyfriend," I quickly corrected.

"I know what you meant," Gretchen said. "I just find that surprising."

"Because?" I truly wondered why. There had been many comments made by friends, relatives—strangers even—about my looks. It was usually about how pretty I was or that I probably had the guys lined up. But it hadn't been like that. Ever. And it wasn't that simple. Sure, I'd gotten a lot of male attention—some good, some bad—but somehow had never been in a relationship.

"Because you're gorgeous and gorgeous girls always get the guy." She said this like it was fact.

"Maybe for others, but not for me." Although this time I hoped to prove that wrong. I *wanted* to get the guy.

She smiled in way of encouragement. "Well, how can he say no when you come offering cookies? Now take your hair out of that bun and march up to school and find him."

"He hasn't texted yet," I said. I was buying time to calm the anxiety in me, but it was also the truth. Where would I find him?

Gretchen stood. "Act like he has and be ready to go. When you hear back, you don't have to waste any time meeting up.

I did as I was told and brushed my hair out.

I hurried up just to wait.

Finally, four long minutes later he responded.

Travis: I'm at the library.

Me: Is food allowed in the library?

I was pretty sure it was only in certain areas. Would we meet there?

Travis: Who cares? I want to see you.

Who cared? Not me, suddenly.

Travis: And try your cookies

Me: omw. Where should we meet?

Travis: 4th floor SE corner

That was a good piece of knowledge to put away if I ever needed to "accidentally" run into him.

I cradled the plate of cookies in my arms. I didn't want anything to happen to them. It wouldn't do to pull out crushed cookies if I was to impress him with my baking.

"I'm off," I called to Gretchen as the door slammed behind me, muffling her response.

I stopped at the bookstore and bought two bottles of water mostly to get the bag. I couldn't walk into the library carrying a plate of cookies and needed something to hide them in. As carefully as I placed them inside the bag, it didn't matter. As soon as I grabbed the handles, the plate slid and my presentation went to waste.

Oh, well.

The cookies would have to speak for themselves.

I found Travis right where he said he'd be. He was leaning back in the chair, with a couple of books piled on the side of the desk, his backpack zipped open on the floor by the wall. I pulled a chair up beside him and realized how impulsive I'd been.

Now what?

He angled his chair so he faced me. "Hi," he said in a quiet voice, leaning in.

I smiled. "Hi."

"I was thinking about you when you texted."

I'd thought about him since the moment we said goodbye. And here we were, together again. "Obviously, me too."

He pointed to the bag. "Are those the cookies? Let's eat."

I emptied the bag as quietly as I could. I probably should've brought napkins. The wrap crinkled and rippled as I removed it. Surely, everyone on the floor heard it and knew we were eating because it was *that* loud.

He took one and bit into it. As he chewed thoughtfully, I watched, waiting for his reaction.

"It's good," he said. "Perfect. How did you know I needed a treat?"

"The secret is real butter," I said, then realized he probably didn't care. "I mean, I'm glad you like them."

He ate another one. Then opened his water bottle. The plastic crunched like only a water bottle can, disrupting the quiet one again.

"What happens if we get caught?" I asked. I hadn't spent much time here, preferring to study in my bedroom. Maybe I'd have to start coming to the library.

"If it's a lady security person, I'll handle it," he said. "If it's a guy, you handle it. I'm sure we can smile and talk our way out of it somehow." He winked.

I wasn't a strict, by-the-rule kind of person, but I wasn't a total rule-breaker, either. I tended to side with the spirit of the law, seeing reasons for accommodations and justification for sometimes "bending" the law. If we didn't spill and didn't leave any crumbs, it wasn't so bad that we were snacking in the library, was it?

After a third cookie, his rubbed his hands together and pushed the plate off to the side. "Thanks. I had that afternoon slump. You saved me from falling asleep and drooling all over my notebooks. I'd wake up with pen transferred to my cheek."

He'd still be attractive.

"Glad to help," I said.

"Did you bring anything to study?" he asked and looked around me as if searching for text books.

I shook my head. "Nope. I didn't think this was a study date." I said "date" without thinking and silently scolded myself.

"Speaking of dates," Travis said and leaned in so close I could smell his aftershave again. "Are you busy this weekend?"

"I'm not," I said. Even if I was, I would've canceled all my plans and rearranged my schedule to accommodate him.

"Wanna go out? Friday night?"

Yes! My heart jumped and I had to make a conscientious effort not to sound breathless. "I'd like that."

His smile lit up his whole face, all the way up to his bright, blue eyes. "Cool. I'm excited."

"Me, too," I said.

We talked a little longer, discussing date ideas and making tentative plans. After a slow, soft kiss, we finally said goodbye.

I practically walked on air back to my dorm, mentally reviewing the visit. Although I had a bunch of studying ahead of me, I wouldn't get much studying done tonight.

3

TWITTERPATED

*O*ur first "official" date was a momentous occasion for everyone. Well, okay, for me and Gretchen. She was as involved as I was getting ready for my date with Travis. We hopped on the UVX bus to University Mall to do a little shopping. I wanted to look and feel amazing. I wanted to make an impression. I wanted to be perfect. I wanted to exude confidence. I wanted to be...*breathtaking*.

I loved any excuse to go shopping. Looking great on a first date, especially with Travis, was nothing to skimp on. We found a great pair of jeans to go with a knit top and a pair of booties I already owned. Then I found a must-have color of lip gloss at the makeup counter. It was must-have because my lips had to look perfectly kissable. It was almost twenty-five dollars for that must-have tube, but if I ate ramen noodles all week, I could afford the lip gloss. Besides, looking good tonight was much more important than what I'd be eating for the next week. In my mind, there was no competition: lip gloss vs. groceries, I'd choose the lip gloss.

I had the perfect Kate Spade wristlet to match the outfit. I was going for the sophisticated and stylish look.

"How about a frozen yogurt before we go?" Gretchen suggested.

Although I was anxious to get home and start prepping for my date, we had forty minutes until the next bus. "Sounds good."

Gretchen ordered first and paid first.

"And what can I get for you?" The guy at the counter smiled.

I flashed him a smile. "Chocolate with gummy bears, please."

He not only put one scoop of gummy bears on my yogurt, but added a second and third. Clearly more than the normal serving size.

"Here you go," he said, returning the smile. As he handed me the cup, he didn't immediately let go as I took it from him. He tried to catch my eye, but I wasn't looking to full-on flirt.

"Thanks." I doubted there would be an extra charge for the extra bears.

"You're welcome," he said, deliberate.

I set the cup down and pulled out my debit card.

He smiled once again. "Don't worry about it," he said and looked me straight in the eye. "It's on me."

Delighted for the freebie, I returned his smile. "Thank you!"

"Come back soon," he said to us, but looked at me.

Gretchen didn't miss it and her eyebrows shot up. How could she *not*? It was so blatantly obvious.

"Oh, we will. Especially if it's free for both us of next time," she said, then walked off.

I had a wave of remorse for enjoying the extra attention. I kind of momentarily forgot Gretchen wasn't given the same consideration. It wasn't like she wasn't pretty—she was. And it wasn't a competition between us. She was a real friend even though we'd only been friends for three weeks.

I hurried to catch up to her, struggling to carry the bags in one hand and the cold yogurt in the other. Gummy bears fell to the floor, casualties of the awkward hold I had on my cup. "I'm sorry, Gretchen," I said quickly.

"For what?" she mumbled.

"That wasn't very nice of me. I should've asked him to comp yours as well."

She shrugged. "Comes with the territory, I guess."

"What do you mean?"

She sort of "harrumphed". "I've had pretty friends before. I'm just the sidekick."

I had a second dose of remorse. "I'm really sorry it made you feel that way." I found a bench so we could sit down. I chewed on my lip for a second before I launched into the ugly truth. "I feed into that attention from insecurities I had in high school. I guess I'm still licking my wounds." That didn't justify it. And seeing the look on Gretchen's face minutes before reminded me I didn't want to be that way.

"What happened?" Gretchen asked so sincerely I had more guilt over my moment of gloating.

"I rezoned to a different school my junior year in high school. All my old friends stayed at my old school, and I didn't make many new friends in the new school."

"That sucks," she said.

"It did. Some girl thought I was trying to steal her boyfriend. I didn't even know who her boyfriend was. She and her friends made life kind of miserable. Ironically, I was barely sixteen and my parents didn't even let me date." I snorted at the irony.

"That's not very nice of them." Gretchen consoled me.

"Nope." I could feel the emotion building up in my throat, making it feel tight. It'd been a lonely time and my self-esteem took a major hit. "And sometimes that insecurity rears its ugly head again."

"Those girls obviously didn't know you very well because you're super nice. I'm glad you're my roommate. I've been having a blast with you. And," she leaned in close and whispered, "I'm so glad I'm not stuck in the same room as Ruby. She snores."

We hugged it out *and* cleared the air all before the bus arrived.

∼

TRAVIS WAS in charge of the plans for the evening and picked me up in a white BMW.

"You look breathtaking," Travis whispered in my ear as he greeted me with a hug.

If he only knew how much *he* took *my* breath away.

I caught a whiff of his now familiar scent. I loved how he smelled.

"Are you hungry?" he asked.

"Yes," I said.

He opened the door and waited while I got in.

I tucked my hair behind my ear and willed myself to relax. I didn't know how I'd manage to eat when my stomach was rolling with nerves. Despite our library visit and talking and texting every day, being on a date—in real life—was different. It was easy to present a completely different person when you're talking and texting, but face-to-face, actions can so easily speak louder than words. I wanted to make sure that we clicked in person

I peeled off all my fingernails on the ride there.

He went to a restaurant by The Riverwoods. The restaurant smelled like steak and garlic, warm and savory. The lighting was dim, but perfect, and there was soft piano music playing in the background. It was so romantic.

Once we were seated, the waitress approached our table. "Hello, my name is Juliet, and I'll be your server this evening."

"Hello, Juliet," Travis said, his voice smooth and low.

I glanced over at him, surprised by his tone. *Was he flirting?*

He continued. "Did your parents name you after Romeo and Juliet?"

She tipped her head to the side for a split second, then smiled. "Actually, they did."

Then *he* smiled. "I bet you get that question all the time."

"Actually, I do," she said.

Was she about to giggle? It sounded like she was about to giggle to me.

Why was he so *friendly* with the waitress when he was on a date with me? I was a teeny weenie bit jealous.

"Can I start you off with drinks?" Juliet asked us, but smiled at Travis. "Or an appetizer?"

My earlier trip to the frozen yogurt place came screaming back. Is this how Gretchen felt when that guy flirted with me? Because I didn't like it. *At all.*

"What do you want, Fi?" Travis looked at me, his expression seemingly oblivious to the effect he had on Juliet.

Did he realize she was flirting with him? How could he not? Especially when it sounded like he'd been flirting with her. Or were people flirting with him something that happened to him all the time?

"Diet Coke, please," I said.

"And I'll have water," he said, looking back at Juliet.

"Got it. I'll be back with your drinks and to take your order." Juliet turned and walked off.

I played several different scenarios in my mind how to broach the *flirting*. I was a little afraid to bring it up to him. I didn't want to sound catty or jealous, but I wanted to address it.

"You have quite an effect on our waitress." I glanced over and caught her looking at Travis from behind the kitchen partition. She quickly turned and walked into the back. I didn't want to outright accuse of him of flirting, because he wasn't (*was he?*), but he didn't have to be quite so...*charming*.

He leaned across the table, as if taking me into his confidence. "I always say their name. It makes it more personable. Plus, you get way better service. I want everything to be perfect. Poor service would ruin dinner."

My mom's constant PMA and always looking on the bright side of everything, drilled into me growing up, shaped the words that popped out of my mouth before I could curb the enthusiasm. "Even if the service was bad, or slow, I'd still get to be with you. That's good, right?" I desperately wanted him to confirm my hope.

He reached over and took my hand. "Even if I got food poisoning, being here with you would definitely be the best part."

And with that, I was a goner. Hook, line and sinker.

"Here you go," Juliet said, interrupting our moment.

She set the drinks on the table in front of us and the smile returned. "Are you ready to order?"

Travis looked at me. "Ready?"

I ordered lasagna.

Travis looked at the menu and then at Juliet. "What do you recommend?"

She blushed. Blushed! "If you're a meat and potatoes kind of guy, I'd suggest the pot roast."

"I do love a good pot roast," he said and smiled at her.

"Is that part of the good-service plan?" I asked.

Travis directed his smile at me and winked. "It works like a charm."

During the conversation, I made sure I smiled and looked engaged. I ate slowly, chewed with my mouth shut and used my napkin frequently. His manners were impeccable: he didn't talk with his mouth full, chew with his mouth open, wipe his fingers on his jeans or slurp his drink.

Juliet returned at least three times with refills, constantly popping in to "check on us." It got to be a little bit disruptive to our conversation.

"How is it?" he asked, pointing to my plate with his fork.

I bobbed my head. "Really, really good. Want to try a bite?" I stabbed my fork into a noodle.

Travis leaned in. "You got a little something here." He used his nail and pointed between his two front teeth.

I regretted my food choice. It must've been a momentary lapse of reasoning. It tasted really good, but now I was paying for it.

I stood. "I'll be right back." I hurried to the bathroom. There was a lot more than just a 'little something' between my teeth. It was a big, green piece of parsley. I was so embarrassed!

I returned to the table after scraping out every last trace of evidence of my dinner. I made a mental note to pick up some of those tiny disposable tooth brushes to keep in my purse for emergencies such as this.

"I was saving that for later," I said. "In case I got hungry later." I laughed nervously.

He gave me a strange look and didn't join in my laughter.

My smiles slowed and I ordered boring vanilla ice cream for dessert, just to be sure nothing else would cause me embarrassment.

"How are we doing?" Juliet returned. "Do you need anything else? Drink refill? Coffee?"

Travis again looked to me. "You good?"

I nodded.

"Just the check, thank you," Travis said, and his beautiful smiled appeared.

Was he flirting with Juliet again?

He had his credit card ready when she returned, and she immediately scampered off. When she returned, she placed the check holder in front of Travis and tapped her finger on it. With his award-winning smile, he thanked her.

I pulled out my phone. "Do you want me to pay for half?"

He waved his hand. "No. It's my treat. I'm just figuring out the tip. What do you think? Twenty percent for a job well done?"

Sure, it was a job well done. With the smiles he was throwing at her, she was very attentive.

I shrugged. "Whatever you think." He was, after all, the one paying his credit card bill. I didn't know what his budget was. With the car he drove, I assume his budget was healthier than most college students. But I also knew it wasn't always safe to assume.

He looked at the several strips of paper, thought for a moment, smiled, filled in the tip and signed it, tucking away the receipt in his back pocket. Juliet waved goodbye, with her stupid smile plastered on her face.

When we arrived back at my dorm, he parked in a no-parking zone. I wanted to invite him up, but it was approaching midnight and visiting hours ended soon.

"Thank you for the incredible night," he whispered, his eyes meeting mine and then glancing at my lips.

He was going to kiss me!

"It was," I said, then realized that made no sense. But it didn't matter as his lips brushed against mine. I melted into him as his lips touched mine again, this time more determined. I lost track of time as we kissed.

We broke apart, breathless.

He swept a piece of hair out of my face and tucked it behind my ear. "Take care, my beautiful Fifi. See you soon." He kissed me one last time before I let myself out of the car.

I think I was in love.

4

SWEET DREAMS

I floated up the stairs to my apartment. *He is perfect! He called me beautiful! And he said he'd see me soon!* We'd definitely have a second date, even if I had to ask him. My phone *dinged*, disturbing my reminiscing.

Travis: Thx for the great night, sleep well Trav

He is so sweet!

I tiptoed into the apartment and over to my bedroom. The light under the door was just a sliver, but let me know Gretchen was still up. As I entered, she was propped up by pillows, holding a book. The little reading lamp perched on the edge of her desk cast a yellow glow on her.

"Don't let me disturb you," I whispered.

Gretchen snapped her book shut and frowned. "For a book called *Pilgrim's Progress*, I'm not making much progress in it."

"Ugh, my mom tried to get me to read that once. It was so boring."

Gretchen straightened and stretched. "The only thing I can relate to is the slough of Despair. Like when you hit a spot in life that is overwhelming. I'm sure your evening was probably a lot more interesting than mine." She patted the bed signaling me to sit.

I settled on the end and smiled to myself as I thought about the evening.

She giggled. "You have it bad."

"Have what bad?" I pretended to not know what she was talking about, but I totally knew.

"For Travis. You got this dippy smile on your face and your eyes are all dreamy." She imitated my expression on her face.

I blushed.

Gretchen pointed an accusatory finger. "See. That! You totally do!"

As hard as I tried to suppress my smile, I couldn't. "I do," I agreed, grinning. "I can't help it. He's perfect," I declared, then thought a moment. "Well, except for the part where he seemed overly nice to the waitress."

Gretchen slapped both her palms down on her comforter. "Wait! What happened?"

I chewed on my bottom lip as I chose my words. "Maybe I'm making too big of a deal about it, but he made a point about knowing the waitress's name and chatting her up."

Gretchen set her hand on my forearm. "I'm not defending him. I'd probably feel the same way as you, but he was like that with your name when you first met. It makes him endearing to others. By saying their name, it makes people feel important and like him."

I nodded. "He said he gets better service that way."

She flipped her hand. "See, it's just part of how he is."

"And he is endearing," I added, then giggled.

"Shut up!" Ruby yelled, as if on command.

Gretchen and I talked some more, but much more quietly, so as not to disturb Ruby.

When Gretchen finally said she was about to fall asleep and we had talked through the date, step-by-step, we both agreed Travis and I were meant to be.

Long past when Gretchen fell asleep, her breathing creating a rhythm, I laid awake, my mind buzzing from my overly-excited thoughts about Travis.

My phone buzzed.

Travis: Are u still up?

Me: Yes! I can't fall asleep

Travis: I can't stop thinking about you

Oh! My! Gosh! It took all of my willpower not to scream out loud right then! I was keeping him up at night! It was almost as romantic as him telling me I was *breathtaking*.

But because Gretchen—and Ruby—and my other roommates were sleeping, I controlled myself.

Me: I can't stop thinking about you, either

Travis: When can I see you again?

I wanted to say *right now*. I was willing to get out of bed and dressed so we could make that happen. But I was tired enough to admit to myself I didn't *really* have the energy.

Me: Tomorrow?

Travis: Can't. Working. Sunday?

Me: Sunday's good! Where do you work?

Travis: What time do you have church?

Me: 9. You?

Travis: 11:30. Then I have to go to my parents

Would he invite me to his parents? I'd totally take that as a sign that this relationship was going somewhere. I waited for him to text more. When he didn't, I sent one.

Me: Where do your parents live?

Travis: Salt Lake

Duh. I knew that.

Again, I waited for an invitation to come along with him. After a few seconds, I realized it wasn't coming.

Me: What time should I plan on Sunday?

Travis: 5?

Me: Great!

Travis: Sweet dreams

Me: You too!

How could I *not* have sweet dreams when I could (hopefully, finally) fall asleep thinking of him? Sunday was so far away.

～

When he picked me up Sunday night, he was in jeans, a t-shirt and a long-sleeved flannel. I hoped we weren't going hiking, because I was not a hiker. In fact, I was horribly uncoordinated, and was not ready to have him see me in a bad light yet. If we were hiking, he wouldn't see me in any light, because it'd be dark, which would make it an even more treacherous adventure. I checked out his shoes, which were Birkenstocks. I relaxed, decided that wasn't what we were doing. Besides, it was Sunday. He wouldn't take me hiking on Sunday, would he?

"How do you feel about going up to Provo Canyon?" he asked.

I paused, caught off guard, feeling like he had read my thoughts. "It depends on what we're doing up there." *Please don't be hiking! Please don't be hiking! Besides, I don't have any hiking gear. I don't have the right shoes, my sweater isn't warm enough, and I'd need a flashlight or a headlamp to see the trail. It didn't make sense to go hiking.* "I don't like hiking."

He chuckled. "Hiking? I'm not talking about hiking. I'm talking about driving up the canyon."

Driving. I sighed in relief. I could handle driving.

"Have you ever seen the view from Squaw Peak?" he asked. "It's amazing."

"I've never been there." It must've been a public park or something like that.

Squaw Peak was not a *public* park. It was more like a *place* to park.

And while the view was amazing, we didn't look at the view much. And there definitely wasn't a whole lot of talking going on.

～

My mom had called four times while I was ~~making out~~, I mean, out with Travis. I had accidentally left my phone in my apartment, but it was a good thing I did.

After I filled Gretchen in on all the details of the evening, I called my mom back.

"Where have you been?" she asked, sounding impatient. Optimism, not patience, was my mother's virtue.

"I was on a date, mom, with the most amazing guy," I blurted out.

"That didn't take much time, did it?" My mother didn't sound exactly happy, but maybe it was our connection. My mother *always* found something to be happy about in *every* situation.

"What do you mean?"

"You don't have to marry the first guy you meet."

"Who said anything about marrying him?" I asked. I might not have said it, but I was definitely thinking it.

"Just be reasonable about it, Sophia." She sounded like her normal self. "You just started dating and you just started school. Try and keep a balance. There's plenty of time to date."

My parents had been very strict about my dating in high school, sticking to the Church guidelines: no dating until I was sixteen, and then only group dating. At eighteen, I could finally have single dates. I turned eighteen in August when I started school. So far, my dates with Travis had been the only single ones I'd been on.

"His name is Travis and just wait until you meet him. I think you'll really like him," I gushed, knowing she'd be won over soon enough. How could she not? He had so many good qualities, he was hard not to like.

I really had it bad for Travis if I was telling my mother about him. Once she liked something—whether it was an idea, an opinion, or just about anything—she tended to get enthusiastic. One of her favorite sayings was, "If it's worth doing, it's worth over-doing."

"Does that mean you're bringing him to visit?"

"If things keep going the way they're going, then probably yes."

"How many dates have you been on?" she asked.

"Two," I said.

"Just remember, Sophia, don't rush into anything. Take your time. Date a variety of people. Go out with friends, experience college and life. This is the time to spread your wings and become an adult. Don't limit yourself by only dating one guy."

Mom had given me a variation of this same talk when I left for college. It was basically have fun, but not too much fun; study hard, but not so hard that you don't have any fun. She also mentioned it was a time to meet new people and have new experiences. It was a balancing act that sounded like it could easily get off-kilter. And why would I want to meet other guys when I really liked Travis? He was the one I wanted to have fun with, and get to know better, and have new experiences with. Even after two dates, I already *knew* this.

I also knew my mom. And if she didn't like something, she could be just as enthusiastic about *not* liking it. I didn't want my mom deciding she didn't like the idea of Travis, or me dating exclusively, so early in the relationship. So, instead, I quashed my enthusiasm and played along. "Who knows, though, if it'll turn into anything."

"That's right, honey. Focus on school and keep things casual when it comes to dating. You're barely eighteen."

I didn't want mom to become hyper-focused on my love life. "Okay. Sounds good."

"Have you seen Dan this week?"

Dan was my older brother who was also at BYU. I hadn't seen him since we drove up from Vegas. He was a senior and had his own life. Every couple of days he would text to check on me, but that had been the extent of our interactions since we'd been in Provo.

"No, I haven't."

"You two could go on double dates together. That would be fun."

That didn't sound *fun*. It sounded *awkward*.

He was a good guy, but we didn't hang out together. He was super smart and a little bit nerdy, tending to lean toward the computer nerd/technology geek and interested in things I wasn't. He had a passion for anything to do with *Star Wars* which I didn't share. Don't get me wrong, *Star Wars* was okay and everything, but I'd rather go shopping or hang out with friends than watch *Star Wars*.

"I don't know. I'll talk to him and see." I doubted we'd double date, either. Personality-wise, we were completely different people.

He was introverted, I was extroverted. You'd never think we were siblings since we didn't look much alike, and didn't seem alike. We were both the same height, 5'10", but I was tall for a girl and he was average for a guy. That was where the similarities ended. I was thin, he was stocky. I had my father's build; he had my mother's build.

"I'll mention it to him."

My mom had good intentions, but no matter how much she tried to "encourage" us to follow through on her "suggestions", it wasn't going to happen.

I quickly ended the conversation before more great ideas were birthed. I vowed to slow the information I gave my mom about Travis and me.

"Are you thinking maybe he'll join us at Thanksgiving?" she asked.

I smiled to myself. I hoped so. He could meet my family then, maybe get engaged over Christmas, married by April. I really hoped things kept going the way they were going. "Yes."

"Let me know. There's always room for your friends," she said, emphasis on the word *friends*.

By Thanksgiving, I hoped we'd be more than just friends. *Much more.*

By the time we said our goodbyes, she didn't seem convinced.

Dan called less than an hour later. Chances were, she called him as soon as she hung up with me, then he called me as soon as he hung up with her. It was a vicious cycle that perpetuated in my family.

"Who's this guy you've been dating? Mom talked my ear off for the last forty-five minutes about it and couldn't believe I didn't know about him. What's going on?"

"I just met him."

"Rumor has it you sound pretty serious about the guy. Is it serious?"

"I hope so," I said, then realized I was gloating too much. Dan was graduating in December and wasn't dating anyone. He tried to brush it off that it wasn't a big deal, but he talked about it enough to show it bothered him. A guy leaving BYU unmarried, by BYU's unofficial standards, made him old.

"How about you?" I asked, hopeful. Maybe things had changed since the last time we talked. "Any prospects?"

"Nope." His tone of voice made me think Dan had resigned himself to the fact that he was leaving college unmarried.

"Don't give up hope, Dan. In fact, I could set you up with my roommate, Gretchen, and we could go on a double date."

Dan snorted. "When did this become about my dating life? I asked about your boyfriend."

"I know, but then you could meet him. But Gretchen is thinking about going on a mission."

"Why are you setting me up with a future missionary, Soph? There's no future in that."

"Why not? You never know when you are going to meet your future, eternal companion. And, you'd have a year and a half to get to know each other through letters. Besides, she can always change her mind about the mission if you're *The One*." I would love to have Gretchen as a sister-in-law.

"Do you think this guy is *The One*?" Dan asked, steering the conversation away from himself. "Is he going to have to talk to dad soon?"

I stood and paced the room. "It's not exactly official. We've only been on a couple dates."

"How often do you text?" he asked.

"Everyday." *All* day.

"Uh-huh." Dan continued firing the questions. "Just once a day? At night? Constantly?"

I cleared my throat. "Um, pretty much all day." Texting, selfies, GIFs, memes and links.

"Do you see each other every day?"

At least.

We spent most of our waking hours and non-class hours together. "Usually." I tried to sound nonchalant.

"Have you posted pictures together on Instagram?"

"No." But we did follow each other. Posting something like that seemed to announce to the world that we were official, and we weren't official. *Yet.*

"Are you going to church with him?"

Ah, a true statement of relationship status: attending your boyfriend's ward.

"No. I haven't even been invited. We haven't even talked about being a couple."

Dan snickered. "You guys are a couple."

I silently celebrated, hoping Dan was correct. I really wanted it to be official between Travis and me.

Travis and Sophia. Sophia and Travis. Travis and Fi. It definitely sounded like we were meant to be.

5
COMMITTED

I had just finished classes for the day when Travis texted.
Travis: Hey Beautiful
When he said things like this, I didn't know how to answer.
Me: Hey Gorgeous. I was just about to text you. How are you?
Travis: I'm at the flower store. What's your favorite flower?
I giggled even though he couldn't hear me.
Me: I'd like anything from you
It could be a dandelion, and I'd still be happy.
Travis: But I want to know what makes my Fifi smile
Me: *You* **do**
What really made "his Fifi" smile was hearing him call me that.
Travis: I'm not a flower
He didn't need to point that out. But he always smelled good.
Me: I know. Kissing you is *way* better than kissing a flower
Travis: So what is your favorite flower?
Me: Um...

I hadn't ever gotten flowers from a guy before, other than a corsage from the guy I went to junior prom with. But I tried to forget about that night.

Travis: Then I'll choose. I'm going to get you an orchid, because you're exotic

Exotic? I didn't think so, but okay. I'd be exotic for him. I was going to have to up the gift-giving ante from my usual cookies and candy bars. Maybe Gretchen could help me come up with something romantic.

I liked being in love. It was fun.

Whoa. Did I just admit to thinking that?

Me: What are you doing tonight?

Travis: It's Monday. FHE, of course

I couldn't tell if he was being sarcastic. Family Home Evening was a standing event, and I didn't want to lessen my spiritual credibility with him by suggesting we skip it to hang out. Gretchen planned on us going together to our apartment's FHE group tonight. But I really wanted to see him. Mondays and Wednesdays were his busy days, so I didn't get to spend much time with him on those days. What could I suggest that would get me some Travis-time? Maybe a romantic candlelit dinner.

Even though I couldn't whip up a romantic, candlelit dinner at the moment, I immediately changed direction and headed to the bookstore. My mission was to find something to relay the message of just how much I thought about him without coming right out and saying it.

Me: Want to meet up on campus for a little bit before you go home

Travis: I was about to suggest the same thing. Then I can give you your flowers

My stomach did a little flip in response to our spontaneous plans.

Me: Where?

Travis: 4th fl. library

Me: Okay. About twenty minutes

Travis: Can't wait

Me, neither!

The situation was doubly good. I got to see Travis and I had an excuse to stop at the bookstore.

I loved wandering the bookstore. It was relaxing. I loved reading the cards and looking at the cutesy trinkets. It was all stuff I really didn't need, but was easy enough to convince myself to buy. And the books. I loved to peruse the bookshelves, especially the "Newly Published" section. I always loved reading. My mother had been an English teacher during her early years of marriage and constantly read to my brother and I while we were growing up. But reading had taken a bit of a back seat since I had met Travis.

Today's trip wasn't for wandering; there was an end goal: find something for Travis to let him know he'd been on my mind. Maybe even a little obsessed. But I didn't want to come off as the psycho/stalker type. Psycho tendencies could quickly kill a relationship, pun intended. I didn't want anything to ruin my chances of a relationship with him.

I sided with safety. I bought a pound of fudge and added a tag that said, "You are the sweetest." It was cheesy, but I didn't have time to be more creative.

I found him in the same area he'd been last time. I sat next to him.

"This is for you," I said, handing him the fudge.

He looked in the bag. "Thanks! I love fudge!" Then he handed me a tiny, potted orchid. "For my exotic girl."

I took the delicate plant and smelled the sweet scent. We kissed—probably longer than was appropriate at the library—and then I brought up something we needed to discuss.

"This guy in my Book of Mormon class asked me out today," I said cautiously, trying to pull off a casual, *oh-by-the-way* tone. I was slightly nervous to bring up the subject since I didn't know how Travis would respond.

"What did you say?" Travis asked.

"I said no—I had a boyfriend." I held my breath, waiting for his answer.

I didn't really know *what* "we" were. Were we exclusive? Had I assumed too much? Was this a casual thing for him? Was he seeing other people but I didn't know it? Did he have a missionary girlfriend he was waiting for?

It wasn't casual for me, but I wasn't sure how Travis classified our "relationship." I couldn't imagine he was dating other girls since we spent so much time together. But I felt it was time to have the DTR (Define The Relationship) talk. I considered him my boyfriend, but I wanted to make sure we were on the same dating page. I didn't want any "misunderstandings" in the future.

He laced his fingers in with mine and smiled at me. "Good."

I waited. Was there more? Like a confirmation that we were, in fact, boyfriend and girlfriend. Did I have to spell it out to him?

I looked at him, expectantly.

He shrugged his shoulders. "What?"

"Am I right?" Did I have to make him say it?

"About what?"

My eyes met his. "Are you my boyfriend? Am I your girlfriend? Are we a couple?" This wasn't how I imagined the conversation would go. I didn't think I'd have to straight-out ask him.

He grinned. My insides melted, but I was still anxious about his reaction and nervous about his answer.

He leaned forward and gently pressed his lips to mine. "I've thought of you as my girlfriend since the day after we met. There's no one else, Fi. You're my everything."

The breath I'd been holding rushed out, along with my anxieties.

"So, you're not dating other girls? Or have a secret missionary girlfriend?"

He chuckled. "No," he said. "Nothing like that. How about you? Do you have a missionary you're emailing?"

Tyler Powers came to mind. He wasn't my boyfriend—more like a friend who wanted to be more. He was currently on his mission, and might think I was waiting for him. I wasn't and had clarified that before he left. We emailed—he more than me—but that was the extent of our interactions. But he was definitely into the "relationship" (if that was the appropriate thing to call it) than I was. Being on a mission had to be tough, and I wanted to be a listening ear and a supportive friend. But I never led him on. For me, when it came to Tyler, it'd be more like stepping back a step. Or on Gretchen's gauge, going from "a little more than friends" to "just friends." Not much difference in my mind.

"No. I have a guy friend on a mission, but we're not in a relationship."

Travis leaned forward, genuinely interested.

"Is he someone I have to worry about?"

Tyler's face flashed in my mind. Compared to Travis, he was... well, there was no comparison. Tyler was a nice guy, but not someone I wanted to date. I shook my head, amused. Travis would win over any guy. "No competition at all."

He pretended to wipe sweat from his forehead. "Good to know. Now, c'mere." Once I was close enough, he bridged the gap and kissed me softly.

∽

"Are you coming to Family Home Evening tonight? I feel like I haven't seen you lately" Gretchen asked. She closed the bedroom door behind her and sat on her bed, propping herself up with a pillow.

I'd only been dating Travis for two weeks, but it felt longer. At least relationship-wise it did.

Even though Family Home Evening, or FHE, was supposed to provide a "family" away from home during your college experience, I didn't need a surrogate family. Travis and I spent so much time together I wasn't missing home.

But I was missing a bunch of classes.

I pushed away from the desk and swiveled my chair to see Gretchen better. "Probably not. Travis and I were going to grab dinner and then study at his place."

His place was a condo, was newer than our dorm and with only three other roommates. More room and less people equaled more appealing. Although anything including Travis seemed better.

"Studying, huh? How much actual studying will be getting done?" Gretchen quirked an eyebrow.

Not much. A silly grin crept across my face. "I'll be studying."

"I'm sure you are. But what are you studying?"

Him. I found him fascinating.

If he was auditioning for an eternal companion, I wanted to be his top candidate.

∼

TRAVIS TOOK me to his condo for the first time.

I was apprehensive about meeting his roommates. Travis only mentioned Jake, so I got the feeling the others weren't important in his social life. I felt like bringing me to his apartment was a statement that we were in a relationship.

My emotions ran the gauntlet from feeling like I was arm candy to wanting their approval because they were Travis's friends. What if they didn't like me? Would that have any effect on Travis's opinion? I wasn't sure if they were going to be social, friendly, completely uninterested, or joking and immature that we were dating.

His condo was quiet.

"Where is everybody?" I asked.

"FHE. We've got the place to ourselves."

Which meant there was plenty of time to make out.

"Do you like your roommates?"

He shrugged. "They're fine. Jake's cool."

"He was your mission companion, right?"

"Yeah."

I sat on the couch, which was a little firm for my liking. "Tell me about your mission," I said. I only knew he'd gone to Bolivia.

He sat beside me. "You know how everyone says it's the best two years of their lives."

"So, it was your best two years?" I asked.

"I wouldn't say that," he said. "Right now is *way* better than my mission."

He leaned in, his eyes focused on my lips.

My stomach did little flips as our lips met.

Being with Travis was like feeling all the feels. He checked every box: gorgeous, charming, smart and just wow, wow and wow.

I was in love.

Whoa, did I just admit that?

6

SIGNS AND WONDERS

It was Sunday afternoon and Gretchen and I were hanging out in our bedroom. She sat on her bed, propped up against the wall, while I stretched out on my bed.

"You are completely smitten with Travis," Gretchen accused.

"Guilty!" I was absolutely, positively, completely smitten with Travis. (Although I still hated his last name. Why did it have to be Duckk?)

Gretchen and I constantly talked about Travis, discussing every detail of every date, action and conversation.

She persisted. "You are in a constant state of twitterpation." She batted her eyes and pasted a dreamy look on her face. "Oh, Travis," she murmured.

We laughed and giggled and examined again all the details of what was going on with Travis.

We went through tests in magazines meant to clarify one's feelings and or possibilities and/or chances of being and/or falling in love. We took those tests repeatedly.

If Gretchen didn't know about it, I don't know if I would have ever admitted it to anyone else. But she was as caught up in the love taking tests as I was—it was fun.

"What if he asked you to marry him tomorrow?" Gretchen asked. "Would you say yes?"

Playing the "*What If*" game became one of my favorite pastimes.

I rolled onto my stomach and nodded emphatically. "Yes."

"What if he had to move to Iceland for medical training? Would you go with him?"

I knew very little about Iceland. Did they even speak English there? "Absolutely."

"What if he was diagnosed with some tragic disease? Would you live out the rest of your life taking care of him?"

No question. "Of course."

"What if he was in a car accident and was paralyzed?"

My answer to every scenario was the same. "Still a yes," I said. "What about you? Same questions."

Gretchen laughed. "I'd have to be dating a guy first, of course, to even consider these scenarios. Going to another country wouldn't be easy, but it might be easier than living with a debilitating disease or a chronic condition."

"But love should be unconditional," I said. *Right?*

"I totally agree," she said quickly. "But I've never loved someone enough to consider marrying them, never mind dealing with extenuating circumstances. I've never had my love for someone tested to find out if love really does conquer all."

It had only been two weeks, but I couldn't imagine Travis not being in my life. He was already a part of my every day and I wanted that to turn into every day for the rest of my life. Even if something life-altering happened, I'd still want him to be a part of my life, no matter what.

"I truly believe love *can* conquer all," I said.

"Especially if your relationship was meant to be."

Another one of our favorite pastimes was analyzing just how "meant to be" Travis and I were. So many things could be considered a sign that we were destined to be together. In fact, Gretchen had a gauge for guys we dated: S.S. for Sweet Spirit, meaning the guy did nothing for me; M.M. for Marriage Material, because the guy had potential; and E.C. for Eternal Companion, because you could totally marry the guy. I'm not sure how she came up with it, but it was close to being gospel to us when analyzing my relationship with Travis.

I measured things by relationship milestones, such as meeting friends, meeting family, establishing you're in a relationship. We had DTR-ed the relationship as "exclusive" *and* I had almost met his roommates. I don't know if they could be considered his friends.

"I hope when I get back from my mission, I find someone as perfect for me as Travis is for you. You're soulmates," Gretchen said.

"Isn't that supposed to be one of the blessings of serving a mission?" I asked. Although I'd never wanted to serve a mission, I'd heard stuff like this all my life. I considered Travis and my relationship to be one of the blessings that came from his missionary service.

"Maybe. I don't know if there're certain guarantees that come from serving a mission. I think I'll get out of it what I put into it. I plan to work hard and serve the Lord and hope I'll be blessed because of it."

"Sounds like most things in life," I said. "You'll be great and get lots of blessings."

"I hope so," Gretchen said.

"How'd you *know* you wanted to go on a mission?" I asked. I was curious how Gretchen got her answer. How would I *know* if Travis was *who* I was supposed to marry?

"I thought about it a lot, prayed about it a lot, and it just felt right."

That sounded like exactly what I was doing with Travis, and everything felt right. Very right.

"All the pieces fell into place."

So many things with Travis fell into place and I took it as a sign our love was meant to be.

Travis and I both had 1:00 o'clock off on Monday, Wednesday, and Friday (it's a sign!) and usually met up for lunch on those days. We both loved Chinese food (it's a sign!). We both loved chocolate (it's a sign!), but not the same type. I loved milk chocolate; he loved dark chocolate—the darker the better. That may have been his only other flaw, other than his name.

My focus shifted from school to Travis without realizing it. We texted constantly. We talked for hours. On campus, on the phone, any chance we could get. I even contemplated if I could still officially drop a class or two, and still have enough credits to be a full-time student. Less classes meant more time to spend with Travis. It was perfectly logical to me.

∽

ON WEDNESDAY MORNING, he unexpectedly slid in next to me in American Heritage. Not that anyone would notice a stray, errant student who wasn't enrolled in the class. It was a huge class held in an auditorium.

"Hey there, beautiful," he whispered.

I jumped, but was delighted by the surprise. I leaned in close to him, catching his scent. My heartbeat quickened. "What are you doing here?"

He nuzzled my ear. "I wanted to see you."

"Don't you have class?" I whispered and giggled.

He pretended to frown. "You don't want me to be with you?"

I was thrilled I took priority over his class. "No, no. You make this class less boring."

He dropped his chin and leaned in close. "So, I should start coming every class?" His voice was husky and his breath tickled my ear.

I tried to regulate my racing heartbeat. "You'd do that for me?"

"Definitely."

"I wouldn't complain." I also wouldn't get any work done. And he might fail the class he was supposed to be attending.

"Good to know," he said.

As you could guess, I didn't get a whole lot out of class that day. My notes consisted of a written conversation back and forth between us I that had absolutely nothing to do with the heritage of our country.

There was a slight breeze as we walked to the food court at the Wilk. I had snagged some chocolate chip cookies Ruby had whipped up last night in hopes of meeting up with Travis at some point that day.

"Was it lonely growing up as an only child?" I asked.

"Maybe a bit when I was younger, but I got used to it. We did everything as a family and were always together and always had fun. We traveled and took a lot of vacations."

"Sounds like you enjoy spending time with your family. Your parents must be so cool."

"They're okay. Back then, I didn't have any choice but to spend time with them."

"You got all the attention."

He shrugged. "I did, but I never felt like my mom was happy. I realized in high school how sad she always seemed."

I passed him a cookie. "Did you know why?" I didn't want to seem too nosey.

"My mom would've liked more kids, but had fertility issues. It took almost ten years to have me, with many miscarriages before and many after me. That always seemed to be in the air. You could tell when she had had another miscarriage. My dad would overcompensate with gifts to try and make her happy and take her mind off of things. That's when we'd take a vacation, and inevitably my mom would seem happier. And if mom was happy, everyone was happy."

I squeezed his hand. "I'm sorry. They must be so happy to have you."

"I always felt wanted, that's for sure. I was my mother's world growing up. She was the classroom mom, the soccer mom, into all my activities. She was the Uber-Mom. She's still the most incredible woman I know."

I dramatically cleared my throat. "I thought *I* was the most incredible woman you know."

"You are. Trust me, I don't want to kiss my mother the way I want to kiss you."

I giggled. "Prove it."

He did and he *definitely* should *not* kiss his mother that way.

"Okay." I took a breath once we parted. "I believe you."

He ran a finger down the side of my face. "Your turn."

"For what?"

"Tell me about your family. What was it like for you growing up?"

I checked my watch. "Are you going to be late for class?"

"Very late. So late I'm going to miss the whole thing."

I wasn't going to argue. "Okay. So, my family." I giggled.

"What's so funny?" Travis asked.

"My family. We're an interesting bunch, always unintentionally having a good time."

He cocked his head; his piercing blue eyes held my gaze. "How do you manage to always unintentionally have a good time?"

"My mom is the queen of PMA."

"PMA?"

"Positive Mental Attitude. And sometimes, in her quest to find the silver lining, she ends up looking, or being, or saying something completely ridiculous. She provides many unexpected moments of…I don't know, surprise? Comic relief? She's funny without meaning to be."

"My mom's not funny. She's more…proper."

"Proper? Like her upbringing was proper?" I tried to think what he meant by proper. "Or like the Queen of England?"

Travis shook his head. "No. She just likes things to be done the right way."

That could be interpreted so many ways. Did the right way mean her way, or a particular way? Someone's right way could be someone else's wrong way.

I continued. "My dad is a little less intense and my older brother, Dan, is graduating in Computer Science here in December and is a huge *Star Wars* fan."

"Is that all I need to know before I meet your family?"

He wanted to meet my family. We'd be taking a trip to Vegas!

I asked a question I'd been wondering about for a while now. "I got the impression your mom doesn't know you've been to Vegas. How come?"

"She doesn't like it," he shrugged.

"Why not? Too touristy? The immorality? The gambling? What Vegas stands for?" Despite it all, I still loved the city I grew up in.

"All of the above."

"Bad experience? Did you go there on vacation and lose all your money or something?"

"No. Her dad gambled. I don't know all the details because she didn't talk about it much, but it caused a lot of contention in her family. Her parents fought about it and they wouldn't have money for food sometimes because her dad had gambled it away. It was very traumatic for her."

When I met his parents, I'd be sure not to mention Vegas. I wanted them to like me.

7

EXPECTATIONS

*T*ravis had to go to the International Cinema for his Humanities class. I hadn't ever seen a foreign film, but was more than willing to go. Anything to have more Travis time. Somehow, I didn't realize we'd have to read subtitles, which was too much work. Instead, we whispered and kissed. Needless to say, we didn't see much of the movie.

It wasn't a complete make-out session—we did *try* and watch the movie. The beginning at least. It was a Chinese movie about a firstborn son defending his family honor and was boring. I preferred paying attention to Travis's lips.

"What'd you think?" Travis asked as we walked out of the dark theater into the light.

I squinted, trying to adjust my eyes to the light.

"Well?" Travis persisted. Why was he so interested in what I thought? He was the other half of the lips involved in all the kissing. It left little time to watch the movie and form an opinion.

I grabbed onto his hand and swung it in step. We walked toward the bookstore. "It was too complicated and I couldn't relate to the whole defend-your-family's-honor-at-all-cost theme. Isn't that more of a cultural thing? My dad doesn't lecture me or my brother about the Davis Family Honor. If anything, my parents lectured me about my own honor and not to make stupid choices and decisions that would affect the rest of my life."

Travis looked at the sky when he answered. "I get it."

"What? The idea of defending family honor, or the pressure to defend your family honor?"

I pictured a group of ducks, parading down the street, their heads held high. *Why* did his last name have to be Duckk?

He shrugged, ever so slightly, as if to suggest it wasn't a big deal. "You know, making my parents proud, living up to their expectations—"

"Oh, come on," I cut in, genuinely surprised. "Your parents have *got* to be proud of you. Look at you."

Yes, just look at him. Creating such a beautiful creature was reason enough to be a proud parent. I hadn't met his parents (yet), and hopefully I would (it's a sign!), but couldn't imagine them not being proud of him.

I continued on with my gush of uplifting compliments. But the more I said, the quieter he got. Finally, I stopped. "It really worries you?"

He nodded. "My parents expect a lot. Not in a bad way. It's an unspoken understanding that I need to be as successful as they are. It's a lot of pressure."

I felt that pressure dating him. I really wanted to impress him—so he'd *like* me. But when it came to parents, they were supposed to love you no matter what. Did his parent's love come with conditions?

"You're impressive, and I'm not just saying that because I like you," I said. "Every time I see you, I swell with pride." I hoped I wasn't exposing too much of my true, in-way-too-deep feelings, but I couldn't help myself. "You're amazing, charming, confident and charismatic." I ticked off my list of positive attributes, just like I had to Gretchen. "You have this way of making every person feel good." Okay, I had to admit, that bothered me sometimes. For example, Juliet, at the restaurant. I thought it bordered on flirting.

Yes, I was a little jealous. I didn't mind him making other people feel special, as long as I was the most special person to him.

He grabbed my hand and quickly kissed me. "You're amazing, gorgeous and such an inspiration."

Swoon!

I melted.

I inspired him!

"So, let's put it in context of your life. I know you're struggling with figuring out what you want to major in. Why does that put pressure on you?" Travis asked.

"It's like peer pressure. Everyone around campus seems to know what they're doing. They have a major and they're focused. I don't have that same clarity, that same drive or direction."

Travis gave me a pointed look. "How do you know everyone has a plan? Have you taken a poll? Stopped and asked people?"

"Well, no." It was just an observation.

"What do your parents say?" he asked.

"My parents, and *you*—" I wanted to make sure I included his opinion so he realized how much I valued it, "—tell me it will come soon enough."

"It will. Even though I know I want to be a doctor, there is the pressure from my parents that I'm their only son and need to make them proud. That I need to impress them no matter what, that I need to be the best of the best."

Things were feeling a little intense. "Well, don't go and join the Olympics," I joked lightly.

A scowl briefly appeared. He didn't find it funny.

He continued. "Take my parents for example. My dad is not just a lawyer, but a prominent judge. My mom doesn't work, but everything she does is amazing. She's an amazing cook, an amazing housekeeper, an amazing mother, an amazing wife."

"I guess when you're surrounded by so much 'amaze', it's hard to see how amazing you are," I said. "You'll live up to your parents' expectations, if not exceed them. I know it. You have it all together. You're amazing."

Although, sometimes, it made me wonder if I was amazing enough.

"Thanks," he said, and kissed me.

"It's like you told me the first night we met—no one has it all figured out. It's really about passion. I've thought about that a lot," I said. And about him, *a lot*. "And whatever you're passionate about means you'll be amazing at it. You'll be an amazing doctor, Dr. Duckk."

(Okay, still hated his name.)

He laughed, his straight, beautiful teeth glinting in the sunshine. "Nothing better than having my own logic used on me."

I put my hand on his forearm. "Seriously. I've thought about passion. And you're right, being good at something is different than being passionate about something."

He leaned in, pretending to take a bite out of my neck. "I'm good at being passionate about you."

I batted him away, suddenly passionate about the kick I was on. His nibbling my neck like a wild baby animal distracted me from my *aha* moment.

"I know what I'm passionate about," I said.

"Me?" he suggested. He still nuzzled in my neck, but I could tell he was smiling.

I fought him off a little more. "No. Seriously."

He backed off, his eyebrow raised, his lips in a tight, thin smile. He seemed irritated that I interrupted his moment of passion. "What?"

"Being thoughtful," I said, proud that I had figured something out.

Travis rolled his eyes. "That's not a major, Fi."

I nodded. "I know. I'm still trying to figure out how to turn that into a job."

He went in for my neck again. "Be a nurse."

I leaned away, wanting to finish my thought before reverting to a mindless make out. "I don't want to wait on people or take care of them. I like letting someone know I'm thinking about them." Besides, the blood. And the bodily fluids. And the needles. I wasn't cut out to be a nurse.

"Why don't you let me know you're thinking about me by bringing those beautiful lips over here and letting me kiss them."

I gave in to his ability to make me feel special.

After indulging in a quick make-out session, we got back to our conversation.

"When I was in high school, I was very social and did student council. Then my junior year, they changed the zoning for the high school. I got sent to the new school that had opened the year before."

"That sucks. Really?" Travis said.

I nodded. "Yeah. It was a matter of living on the wrong side of the street. All my friends lived on the east side of a major road; I lived on the west side. So, all of my friends, including friends at church, went to the old high school. I went to a new school where I knew no one."

Travis shook his head. "That must've been hard."

"I was really upset about it—I cried and carried on. I tried to get a zone variance and appeal to the principal at my old school, but nothing worked. It felt so unfair—I felt left out of everything with my old friends."

Just thinking about how hard it was still made me a little emotional. My throat tightened.

I cleared my throat and hoped to sound normal. "School was rough. My schedule was terrible. Groups had already been formed the year before and no one wanted to be my friend. I mean, in the popular crowd. They didn't like me and were actually mean to me. I was chosen last in gym, although that could be understandable with my lack of ability in sports."

It was like back in grade school where I wanted to run home to my mom crying.

"I made a few friends in various classes, people I could eat lunch with, and they were okay and nice enough, but I wanted to be part of a group again. I wanted to be popular again. I thought it was important to be important."

Travis rubbed my arm gently, then kissed my forehead. "Everyone wants to be important. It's human nature."

"Then, to top it off, our ward divided in December. Again, I lived on the wrong side of the road and we got sent to a new ward. It slowly got better and I made new friends, but it was hard. It really taught me how one person can make such a difference to someone else."

"I can't believe that people wouldn't instantly like you. You're smart and so likable. You're beautiful," he said.

"That seemed to be an issue. One girl came up to me and told me to stay away from her boyfriend. I didn't even know who her boyfriend *was*."

"Sounds like she was jealous of how pretty you are."

I pushed back the emotions. "I wouldn't have ever done that. But she wouldn't have known that unless she got to know me."

Travis continued to soothe me. "Sometimes people are intimidated by good looks. It makes the other person feel competitive."

I scoffed. "Again, if they had gotten to know me, they would have known I am so *not* competitive. But I learned perseverance. As my mom says, it's either sink or swim, and I swam. There was nothing else I could do."

Travis hugged me hard, then kissed me lightly on the lips. "I'm sorry they were so mean to you. Do you want me to go beat them up?"

I smiled and looked at him sideways. My knight in shining armor. My protector.

"Sure, at my ten-year high school reunion I'll point them all out and you can take care of them for me out in the parking lot." I laughed. "Although, I hope by then I've gotten over it and forgiven them."

But right now, even though it had been two years, my emotions about the situation were still a little raw.

"Okay, ten-year reunion, I'll take care of them." Travis winked, then kissed me gently on the lips.

8

BIRTHDAY WISHES

"HAPPY BIRTHDAY TO YOUUUUU! HAPPY BIRTHDAY TO YOUUUU!" Ruby belted out.

It was Travis's birthday and I'd invited him over for dinner. When Ruby found out, she insisted on singing to him.

"HAPPY BIIIIIIIIIIRTHDAY DEAR TRAAAAAAVIS!"

Ruby had a very powerful, very untrained voice.

Travis's lips twitched.

"HAAAAAAAPPPPPPY BIIIIIIIIRTHDAY TOOOOOOOOO YOUUUUU!"

Travis stood, clapped loudly and gave Ruby a half-hug. "Whew! That was something else!" he said.

She beamed. "Thank you!"

"Cake?" Travis asked, pointing to the German chocolate cake I'd baked. Not my first choice, since I felt the coconut ruined the chocolate, but it was for him, not me.

She grabbed her backpack and slung it over her shoulder. "Can't. I'm already late for class."

As soon as the door shut, he burst out laughing. "Was she serious?"

I shushed him. "Travis! She probably can hear you!"

"So? Maybe someone needs to be honest with her about her singing."

"Being honest and hurting someone's feelings are two different things," I said. Ruby wasn't the perfect roommate and had her list of faults, but so did I.

Travis shrugged. "Just saying."

I didn't want to get into a fight on his birthday, so I slid the cake in front of Travis. "Let's have cake."

"This looks great, Fi! My mom never baked my birthday cakes."

I felt special that he recognized the effort I put into it. But why didn't his mom bake his cake? My mom always baked my cakes. I thought she was too cheap to buy one.

"Why not?"

He shrugged. "She said the bakery did such a great job. I didn't care, I just wanted cake."

Bakery cake was good.

I grabbed the biggest knife we had. "How big do you want your slice?"

He put his hand on my wrist, stopping me from making the first cut. "Can we wait a while?" He asked. "I'm still full from dinner."

I had made dinner too. Well, I kept the take out warm. But I didn't tell him that. Made, kept warm—that was just semantics. I wasn't the best cook and I didn't want to bake a casserole. That screamed frumpy housewife to me. I wanted to make a good impression so he'd realize I was a good, capable catch.

"Sure," I said, a little disappointed. While I had cheated on the dinner, I hadn't cheated on the cake. I worked really hard for several hours to make the cake. Granted, it looked like something on a cake wreck website or a bad baking show competition, but it was made with love.

"But I'm not too full to open presents," he said cheerfully.

Ugh. Presents. I had agonized over what to get him almost more than I'd agonized over making his cake.

I'd made a playlist and overthought what songs to include and the message they sent. Good thing Gretchen was there to help me. But a playlist wasn't nearly enough.

His birthday had given me an excuse to go shopping—and not just at the bookstore. After checking out many stores, I settled on a gift card to The Brick Oven, in hopes he would use it to keep asking me out.

***

I HAD a study group that I needed to go to before Travis and I could go out and finish his birthday celebration. My freshman English class had to do a group project. I was frustrated because I'd tried to schedule it for a different night, but this was the only time that worked for the majority of the group.

"I'd skip, but my grade is horrible in this class and this project is a big percentage of my grade." My current GPA in the class had a lot to do with Travis, but I didn't want him to feel like it was his fault. I was the one making bad choices.

"I've got a couple of classes like that. But I also have this breathtaking girlfriend who I'd rather hang out with than go to class."

I giggled and blushed.

"I hate this class. I feel like I'm back in high school. Like I'm excluded. No one wants to listen to my ideas and all their ideas are stupid," I confessed.

His solution was to join me for the study group.

We met in a study room on the fourth floor of the library, and the other five people were already gathered around the table when we arrived. Everyone looked up as the door latched shut.

I made introductions. "This is my boyfriend, Travis."

"I just took Freshman English," he explained.

He had? I didn't know that. But it wasn't like we sat around discussing what classes he had taken his past semesters. It wasn't his transcript I was interested in.

He continued, easily taking charge. "We had to do a group project. Every Freshman English class does the same thing."

"We were thinking of doing a talk show forum," one of the girls (whose name I couldn't remember) explained, her cheeks turning pink as she spoke. She looked everywhere but directly at Travis.

"Everyone does that. You know, get the characters from the story up there, and interview them. But how about making a short video clip? Like a movie trailer or a product ad. Or if your topic was discussed by a social media influencer."

With that, everyone was convinced. And the girls were mesmerized, as was I. He was truly amazing.

We hammered out ideas, divvied out assignments and agreed to meet up in two days to finish the project. It took less than an hour.

I exited the library swollen with pride. "Wow. How did you do that?" I asked.

"Do what?" By his expression, I could tell he didn't know what I meant.

"That. You are like a natural-born leader. You took a really boring topic and somehow convinced them it could be fun. You had them eating out of the palm of your hands, wanting to do your suggestion." Almost wanting to make him happy. Maybe wanting his approval. I knew I did.

He shrugged off my compliment. "I recycled what my group did in class. It wasn't even my idea. Some really smart girl came up with the idea. I'm glad she did, because I hated the assignment."

His enthusiasm while explaining the idea had me fooled.

"How did it go?" I asked.

He threw his arm around my shoulder. "We got full credit."

The way he explained it, he also took full credit.

"You made them think…"

"You tell people it's great and they believe it's great. For that group, when you present. Tell people what they're supposed to think and they think that."

I didn't need anyone to tell me how great Travis was. I already knew. And moments like this reinforced it.

After we left campus, we drove up to Squaw Peak to make out.

9

MEET THE PARENTS

Our relationship was taken to the next level when he invited me to his weekly tradition of going to his parents on Sunday afternoon for his birthday dinner. Meeting his parents definitely meant our relationship was headed toward marriage, didn't it?

I smoothed my skirt again as I sat in his car, hurtling our way toward Salt Lake and nervously chattered about inconsequential things.

He looked over at me and grabbed my hand. "Relax."

My heart hammered in my throat as I said the words. "This is kind of a big deal, meeting your parents."

Was he nervous at all? What if I made a bad first impression? What if his parents didn't like me? I had never dated anyone serious enough before that meeting their parents felt like a significant event. I hoped it was going to be a good experience and not horribly awkward.

He laughed it off. "They're normal people, Fi. There's nothing to be nervous about."

His words didn't calm my nerves, but I forced myself to repeat them as a reassurance.

Since Travis was such a great guy, surely his parents had to be great. Right? But as the number on the highway exit signs decreased, my doubts increased.

Travis reassured me as we pulled up to his house which was large and stately, complete with pillars, a portico and topiaries on the front porch.

The Goliath-sized front door was made of heavy, carved wood and did nothing but intimidate me.

His parents greeted us at the front door.

His right arm wrapped around my waist. "Mom, Dad, this is Fifi. Fi, this is my mom, Maxine, and my dad, Boyd."

Travis's parents were different than I expected. In my mind, I pictured his mom as a tall, thin, blonde, blue-eyed woman, who wore jeans and turtlenecks. I pictured his dad as a golfer, with a full head of salt-and-pepper hair, wearing golf apparel around the house.

I was completely wrong. Maxine was probably in her early fifties. She had bright, red hair that most likely came from a bottle. It was cut in a bob and had the life teased out of it. Her face was smooth and tight—not a laugh line in sight—and her skin was unseasonably tan. Pretty, but thin and angular. She was not in jeans and a turtleneck, but in a coordinating houndstooth skirt and suit coat. A tan, linen-looking apron covered up most of her front.

I stuck my hand out. "Hi, nice to meet you."

She extended a smooth hand with nude matte acrylic nails and a bunch of bangles on her wrist. "Maxine," she said and smiled broadly. She placed her other hand over mine, holding me in place.

"Fifi."

"Fifi," she repeated slowly. My name rolled over her tongue as if she were sampling an appetizer, deciding what she thought. To me it sounded like maybe...disapproval?

"Is that your real name, or were you named after a cat?" Then she laughed loudly.

Was that Karma paying me back for all my duck jokes?

Even if it was payback, it was a little...odd. Maybe even borderline inappropriate. I would never ask her if she was named after a maxi pad.

It was tempting to kick into dumb blonde mode. That way, I could say something totally mean or stupid, and blame it on being dumb.

I opened my eyes wide. "No, no. That would be my brother, Dan. You know," I shrugged, "as in, Daniel in the Lion's Den?"

Her cackle cut short, as her head quirked and she stopped to process my comment.

Maxine threw her head back in laughter. "Oh, honey, I didn't mean anything by that. I'm trying to figure out if that is your given name, or a nickname."

Travis's hand tightened around my waist, which I was grateful for. "Her real name is Sophia, mom. But since you and grandma never got along, I call her Fifi. Besides, I think Fifi is more suitable." He cocked his head and slid his eyes sideways and caught my eye. Then he gave a little half smile.

He was so beautiful. It would be okay as long as he was by my side.

Her manicured hand went to her throat. "Well, Travis told us you were gorgeous. And you are. It truly is a pleasure to meet you. Travis can't stop talking about you." She shrugged and lifted her chin a little bit.

I blushed a little.

Boyd stepped forward. "Nice to meet you, Fifi." Boyd was about the same age as his wife, or maybe slightly older, but still good-looking for being old. Kind of like a good-looking James Bond, but without the accent, the build, and (hopefully) the womanizing tendencies. Travis had obviously gotten his good looks from his dad. "Like my wife said, Travis has told us a lot about you."

I never knew how to respond to that statement. Should I say I hoped it was all good? (Did he have anything bad to say about me yet?) Or that Travis had told me so much about them (because he hadn't)?

"Where are you from, dear?" Maxine asked.

"Las Vegas," I said quietly, remembering the conversation I had had with Travis that first night. Dang! I hoped to avoid that.

"Vegas? Real-ly?" The words came out real slow and her gaze shifted to Travis.

Was that another strike against me?

"What do you think about living in Vegas?" she asked.

"I love it. The weather's great, the church is strong, everything is convenient. What's not to love?"

"I can think of plenty," Maxine said and turned. She waved for us to follow her. "Well, come on in. Dinner will be ready shortly and it'll give us time to get to know each other better."

I looked to Travis for reassurance. He motioned with his head to follow, so I gripped his hand and went in.

The questions continued as we ate dinner. It was sort of what I expected.

"What are you studying, dear?" Maxine asked.

"I don't know, yet." I said it with as much confidence as I could muster.

"Are you taking time to find yourself?"

I pinched my lips together, thinking. "No. Just taking time to make an informed decision."

"Don't waste too much time. You might end up paying for classes you'll never use."

"True," I said. I wasn't sure if she was offering advice or being critical. I decided I was nervous and over-analyzing everything.

Boyd cleared his throat. "So, Fifi. Have you been a member all your life?"

"Yes," I said.

"Were your parents converts?"

Weren't we all converts?

"Nope. Second-generation members."

"Do you plan to serve a mission?"

So I wouldn't marry their son?

"It's not in the plans."

"What are the plans?" Maxine asked.

"I don't know yet. But I've never felt strongly about serving a mission."

"Did your Patriarchal Blessing say anything about serving a mission?"

None of your business.

The last thing I expected from my boyfriend's parents was an interview. "Travis told me about his mission."

Travis quickly changed the topic and I went into silent mode. I wanted to get out of there. Should I text him? Whisper in his ear? Say it under my breath? We should've decided on a signal beforehand just in case this exact scenario happened.

I excused myself to use the bathroom, needing to regroup. I felt like Travis's parents were grilling me. Actually, tag-teaming me. Could I take anything they said at face value? It always seemed like there was an underlying meaning or insult or jab with every comment. What did it mean? Was I back to reading too much into things? Maybe I had PMS—Para Maxine Syndrome.

Once I was safely behind locked bathroom doors, I called for "backup."

"Gretchen?" I whispered into the phone.

"Sophia? Why are you whispering?" Gretchen whispered back. Maybe it was contagious.

"I'm hiding in the bathroom at Travis's parent's house. I'm freaking out. It's not going well."

"Why?"

"It's mostly his mother. I can't tell if she means what she says. It's like she says something, but that's not what she means."

"Like irony or sarcasm?" Gretchen was an English major. A girl after my mother's own heart. "She's an evil mother-in-law and she's not even an in-law yet?"

I sat on the toilet and breathed slowly. "Something like that."

I rubbed my hand on my temple. I wasn't even sure why I called her. I needed to tell someone, get some sympathy, and feel like someone was on my side. I wasn't sure it'd be smart to say anything to Travis. I didn't want him thinking I hated his mother upon first meeting. She was his mother and he loved her, which was obvious by the way he talked about how wonderful she was. Was I just not seeing it?

"Smile, nod and be agreeable. That will get you through dinner. When you get home, you can tell me all about it." Gretchen said.

Her words did little to reassure me. "Alright, I'll try."

"I'm sure it will work."

Was she sure? I wasn't.

I sighed. "I guess I'll go." I was dismayed about how much longer the meal might go on.

"I'll be praying for you," she said. I could tell she was smiling by the sound of her voice.

"Thanks," I said, and hung up. I was reluctant to return to dinner.

I was sweating so profusely, so I stuck wads of toilet paper under my arms to absorb the extra sweat. I didn't want them to see me sweat.

I didn't think they'd be so intimidating.

I hurried and used the bathroom, thinking they were going to be wondering what was taking so long.

As I was leaving, I longingly glanced out the window where I had a perfect view of Travis's car. I couldn't wait to get away.

I went back to the *lovely* dinner party.

∽

"WELL, THAT WENT WELL." I said sarcastically as we backed out of the driveway.

Travis missed the heavy sarcasm. "It did. My parents like you."

"I'd hate to see how it'd be if they didn't like me."

We'd reached the end of the driveway and he put the car in park. He looked at me, his brows pulled together. "What do you mean?"

"Really? Your parent's *liked* me? It didn't *feel* like they liked me."

He reached over and squeezed my knee. "Of course, they did."

"Are you sure I'm worthy of you?" I asked. Maxine openly showed her disapproval and his father basically interviewed me. If they were trying for welcoming, they failed. They were intimidating.

"Worthy? What?"

"Your dad asked very personal questions."

"Don't worry." Travis glanced over me with a smile. "He does that to everyone. It's habit. He used to be a bishop."

"That doesn't make it okay that he does it." I hoped my expression didn't give away my anger. "Do you bring a lot of girls home?"

He didn't answer immediately and I couldn't read his face.

Finally, he shrugged his shoulders, but didn't look at me. "They've met a couple of girlfriends. None of the relationships were serious. Not like you."

Everything I had pushed down bubbled dangerously close to the surface. "If you like me, don't they trust that you would choose wisely?" Tears filled my eyes and my throat choked with emotions.

"Fi, Fi," he said slowly, as he looked over and realized I was crying. We weren't even out of the driveway and I was already in tears about meeting his parents.

"Really, they didn't mean anything. They would never intentionally make you feel bad. They're a little overprotective. I'm their only child. They want me to be happy. Besides, how could they not like you, Fifi?"

Then he showed me how much he liked me by kissing me. And then kissing me some more. We had even fogged up the windows a little bit. We were (I'm ashamed to admit it) still making out when there was a tap on the driver's side window. We had even fogged up the windows a little bit.

Travis wiped some steam off the glass. Maxine stared at us. Talk about embarrassing! Being caught making out by his mother!

He rolled down the window enough to speak with her.

"You had better not be defiling each other in my car."

She accused us of defiling each other?! What did she think we were doing here? Would she be a mother-in-law who's knocking on the door of the honeymoon suite checking on us?

Whoa, did I just admit to thinking that?

It wasn't until she marched back inside, that I realized she must have been watching out that bathroom window. It was the perfect view of exactly where we were parked.

I cleared my throat and brushed my hair out of my face. "Uh, that was embarrassing."

Travis gripped the steering wheel until his knuckles turned white. "Sometimes she goes too far," he said through clenched teeth.

"Has she done this before?"

"That's not what I mean."

I waited for an explanation. After a few beats, I realized there wouldn't be one. So, I continued trying to make sense of what just happened.

"What did she mean by her car?"

I seemed to have pulled him from deep thoughts. "Oh, yeah, um, my parents pay for my car."

I could've guessed that. They certainly couldn't expect Travis to pay for a car like this and be a full-time pre-med student.

I was silent on the way home, rehashing the visit in my mind, coming up with better comebacks for their probing questions. The good thing was, though, if things worked out with Travis, we'd have our own lives.

10

WHAT'S THE VERDICT?

A text from Travis interrupted my ~~studying~~, I mean, daydreaming in the library.

Travis: you free tonight?
Me: Yes! Why?
Travis: Nothing. Just want to talk. Pick u up at 7?

Uh. Oh. I got a weird vibe from his text. What did he want to talk about? Was something wrong?

My imagination took over and my thoughts spiraled out of control.

It *had* to be about the visit to his parents. They hated me. Or, more specifically, his mother hated me. I didn't measure up to her standards.

Or, he was breaking up with me.

What else could it be? It'd be the "we need to talk" conversation, followed by the "it's not you, it's me" line.

But why? Other than meeting his parents, everything seemed to be going so well. We got along great, had a lot in common, and had an amazing time together. Didn't he feel the same way about "us"?

I struggled to concentrate through classes. Anxiety kept my stomach in a knot all afternoon.

When Travis texted he was on his way, I waited outside my dorm. I was anxious to get this over with.

He pulled up and I jumped in.

"Hey," he said with a smile. He seemed cheerful and not pensive.

"Hi," I said, trying to keep my voice neutral.

"Are you hungry?"

No, not really. I was anxious. Really, really anxious and wanted to get this conversation out of the way.

He continued. "We could get something to eat."

I exhaled. That was a good sign, right? He wouldn't pay for a meal and then break up with me. Or he was putting off the inevitable.

I picked at my cuticle. "I'm not really hungry," I said.

Travis rubbed his knee.

It gave me bad vibes.

"Is everything alright?" I finally asked with trepidation. My cuticle was now a hangnail.

He nodded. "Yeah. There's just something I want to talk to you about."

"What is it?"

He shook his head. "Let's eat first."

"Is it something bad?"

He broke into a smile. "No, nothing like that."

If it wasn't bad, maybe I *could* manage to eat something. Although, his words didn't completely banish my anxiety.

"Dine in or dine out?" he asked.

"Out." Definitely. I worried there was still a small chance he'd break up with me, and I didn't want to cry in front of an audience.

Travis ordered Chinese takeout on his phone and by the time we got to the restaurant, it was waiting for us. We drove in silence to a park nearby, but he kept tapping his thumb on the steering wheel.

Despite his reassurances, I was still worried. It was like being on death row, knowing you're going to die and it's the waiting that's killing you (figuratively speaking.) Only this was breakup row, I guess.

Travis spread a blanket out under a tree.

The meal only came with chopsticks. They must've forgotten the plastic silverware. That, coupled with a (possible) break up, suggested the evening could turn into one big, sloppy mess.

I couldn't wait any longer. I gave in. "What's up, Travis?" I blurted. "Is something wrong? You're acting weird and it's freaking me out."

His expression was blank. "There's nothing wrong."

"Then what do you need to talk about?" And it had preoccupied my mind since ten o'clock this morning.

He chuckled. "Are you worried, Fi?"

That seemed a little callous. "Yeah. Only cause you're acting so weird."

He smiled gently at me. It made my heart melt. I would miss his beauty. I would truly be heartbroken if he broke up with me now.

He reached out and brushed my hair over my shoulder. "It's not a bad thing," he said softly.

Had he gotten an internship and wouldn't be here next semester? Was he moving? Transferring schools? Those were the other worst-case scenarios I could come up with. "Tell me," I insisted.

"We'll talk about it later."

My throat choked with emotion. "No. No more stalling. If you're going to break up with me, just do it. Don't put it off or sugarcoat it." I said and started crying.

He frowned. "Break up with you? Oh, Fi." He put down his food and put his arms around my shoulders and hugged me. "It's nothing like that. It's good, really. I'm worried about what *you're* going to think." He pulled away a little, but didn't let go of my shoulders. He ducked his head trying to catch my eye.

I finally met his look. "I've already thought of every bad scenario there is."

He pulled me close enough that our foreheads were touching. "I'm falling in love with you, Fi," he said softly.

What?! My heart thudded in my chest, accelerating as I mentally repeated his words.

Our eyes met. "You are?"

"Yeah." He nodded. "That's what I wanted to tell you. I'm falling in love with you."

I gave way to my emotions—the anxiety, the happiness, *the relief*. In reality, I was blubbering—tears ran down my face. I swiped at them and cleared my throat, which was thick with emotion.

"Why is that bad?" I asked. I was actually really, *really* happy.

He shrugged. "You might think we're moving too fast."

I couldn't contain my smile. "We're not moving too fast," I said. *We're moving in the right direction.*

"You're not upset?" He pulled me back into his shoulder.

"No," I said.

He hugged me tightly. "I'm so relieved."

"You scared me," I managed to say, being muffled by his shoulder. "I really thought you were going to break up with me."

His eyes widened with surprise. "Why would I do that, Fi? You are the most beautiful girl I've ever met."

"Your mom doesn't like me."

He interlocked his fingers with mine. "Don't worry about her."

"You don't care what she thinks?"

"Nope. I'm dating you, not her. And I'm in love with you."

I blushed as I admitted what had been continuously going around in my head. "I love you too," I said, the words rolling off my tongue. It felt strange and new actually saying the words out loud.

He brightened. "You do?"

"Yes," I said. "I love you!"

His chest visibly decompressed. "I haven't told you this, but I'd been praying to meet you. I didn't like the girls I'd been dating. They all seemed fake and insincere. But you, you are so sincere. I like who I am around you. You make me want to be a better person. And I have fallen in love with you."

His lips found mine.

Making out was *so much better* than breaking up.

11

NO WAY!

The next night we went shopping at the mall. Imagine my surprise when he asked if I liked jewelry. I was so shocked, I had to duck into a bathroom quickly to make a can't-catch-my-breath phone call to Gretchen.

"Guess what?" I whispered fiercely into the phone. I was afraid if I yelled, like I really wanted to do, it would echo and Travis would hear it outside the door where he was waiting.

"Sophia. You have got to stop calling me this way," Gretchen whispered back. This was starting to be a habit.

"He asked if I wanted to look at jewelry." Was he hinting at a wedding ring? Or asking about gold and gemstones in general? I hoped it was a ring, but either way, I'd be happy.

"NO WAY!" Gretchen screamed. I held the phone away from my ear. "Are you getting engaged?"

I didn't dare speak the "E" word out loud. I didn't want to curse it.

"I don't know," I panted. Someone walked into the bathroom and I immediately went silent. I didn't want them to think I was a weirdo heavy breathing in a stall. What if they called security? That would be embarrassing!

"Text me as soon as you can and tell me what happens," Gretchen commanded.

As if I wouldn't. "Okay!"

"Oh. My. Gosh!" Gretchen screamed before she hung up.

My thoughts exactly!

I exited the stall calmly, smoothed my clothes and my hair and then splashed water on my face. I took a deep breath and went out to meet my ~~mate~~, I mean, fate.

Travis waited by a pillar. Fate was not always a bad thing. In fact, it was a very attractive, sexy thing.

We walked hand-in-hand as we entered the first jewelry store we came to. We were immediately greeted by an over-enthusiastic salesman with bleached blond hair and a spray-on tan.

"What can I help you with tonight?" he asked, his too-white teeth gleaming in an extra-wide grin.

"We'd like to look at some jewelry," Travis said, still being vague about what item we were looking for.

"Great. I can help you with that." He directed his look at Travis. "Are we getting ready to pop the question?"

Travis laughed and I gulped. This was the moment. One "yes" from Travis and we'd be starting on the path to happily ever after.

"We're not quite there yet. But I would like to look at some options."

Hope deflated. *Options?* What options? Something other than a ring? Options for a ring? Options for the stone in the ring?

The salesman nodded as if he understood. At least between the two of us, someone did.

"Let's start with bracelets," Travis suggested.

"We have a fine selection over here." The salesman directed us to the other side of the store. We sat on two velvety stools and stared into the clear cases; the jewelry sparkled back at us.

But we didn't look at rings at all. We looked at bracelets and earrings and necklaces. We discussed if I preferred gold over silver, yellow gold over white gold, platinum over silver.

What was my favorite stone? Did I like diamonds? Rubies? Emeralds? Opals? Did I like my birthstone (I was born in August, and the green color of peridot didn't do much for me), or something else? Did I prefer the square cut over the round cut, or oval, or emerald cut. Square cut? Round cut? Princess cut? Emerald cut? So many questions, so many answers given with the hopes of a surprise engagement ring at the end of the night.

Of course, I liked the idea of buying jewelry. But were we really buying jewelry? Was Travis really planning on spending that kind of money on me, or just having fun playing pretend?

I felt selfish, as if I was guilty of coveting all that sparkled and glittered in the glass cases in front of me as I sat on those velvet padded stools. Was it inappropriate to accept such an expensive gift so early on in our relationship?

My phone buzzed in my pocket.

Gretchen: well??????????

I twisted sideways and slipped my phone out by my hip, trying to read it discreetly.

"Who's that?" Travis asked.

I wasn't as stealthy as I thought.

I tried to dismiss it. "Gretchen wants to know when I'll be back."

"Do you have plans with her?" Travis asked.

"No," I said, then quickly texted back.

Me: nothing yet

Gretchen: what does that mean?

Me: no ring

"Gretchen sure seems to be concerned about you," Travis commented.

I would've died if he saw the texts. "Gretchen's chatty right now. She doesn't realize I can't talk," I said.

Travis seemed satisfied by that answer and didn't pursue the conversation any further.

"Why don't you go window shopping? I want to look around a little more," he said. The grin he gave me made my insides melt like a popsicle. I was a little puddle of giddiness.

"Okay," I managed.

Was this really happening?
Was he going to buy an engagement ring?
Was he going to propose?

Eek! Could I really be engaged by the end of tonight? Could he be buying the ring right now?!

I made myself walk out the store without looking back. Once I was at a safe distance, I hid behind a huge fake plant in it and peeked around the edge. Could I see him from this angle? Could he catch me spying on him?

There wasn't much to see. Travis was chatting with the guy. After five minutes, I gave up my *Mission Impossible* tactics and reached for my phone and called Gretchen. She was probably dying to know what was going on as much as I was.

"Gretch?"

"Oh my gosh, Sophia!" Gretchen was literally breathless. "Oh my gosh, Sophia! Does this mean what I think it means?"

"I don't know," I squeaked.

"Did you look at engagement rings?" she asked.

"No."

"Dang."

"I know," I said.

"Did he buy anything?"

I shook my head. "No. But...he sent me away...."

Gretchen sounded like she was choking. "Oh, my gosh! Oh, my gosh!"

"I know."

"Let me know as soon as you know!"

"I will," I said.

Travis appeared around the corner. His gait was casual, as if there was nothing pressing happening, as if we hadn't just been jewelry shopping together. "He's coming," I whispered to Gretchen.

And then I noticed it.

"He's holding a bag!"

Gretchen was still screaming when I hung up.

"Hey." I smiled at Travis as I walked up to him, trying to ignore the shiny gift bag in his hand.

Was this really happening?

"Hi there, beautiful." He kissed my forehead and pulled me into a hug. "What do you say, are you hungry? Maybe some In-N-Out burger?"

I tried to continue ignoring the bag.

I tried not to picture the little velvet box that was probably inside of it.

"Sounds great."

The tiny bag perched in the console between us, a tiny elephant in the car. We drove a few minutes to get our food.

If he proposed, I'd probably lose all bodily function (which would *not* be attractive).

He handed me the bag. Inside was a small cardboard box. Inside the box was a small velvet box.

I broke out in a little ~~sweat~~, I mean, glistening, and my heart beat so fast I could feel it in my throat.

This is it!

He was proposing.

I slowly opened the hinged lid of the velvet box.

Inside was a …pair of earrings.

Oh.

They were beautiful, but they were not a ring.

I had to control my reaction. I was happy, but let down. I was surprised, but not in the way I thought I would be. The earrings were gorgeous, but not what I wanted. Had I really been so stupid as to think we were anywhere near the point of getting engaged? We had barely told each other we loved each other. I silently chastised myself for being so silly and foolish. For being so caught up in the ways at BYU that I thought or even wanted to get engaged. It had been barely a month. Really? What was wrong with me?

"Happy one-month anniversary," he said softly, and smiled at me. His words snapped me out of my self-pity and brought me up to speed and in the moment. He leaned over and kissed me, slowly. "I love you."

Those three words resulted in heart palpitations.

"I love you too," I managed through short breaths while kissing.

12

INSPIRED

Travis insisted we go to Temple Square and attend the Sunday morning session of General Conference in the Conference Center. I worried we'd have to stop in and see his parents for Sunday dinner afterwards. He assured me his parents wouldn't be any part of our day and that he wanted to have a spiritual experience at conference together.

I don't know what it was, whether it was the crisp autumn morning, the trees changing colors, the excitement in the air, or being in the presence of so many other members and the Spirit, but I felt high, giddy and happy. It was a hard feeling to describe other than happiness.

Or maybe I was in love.

I loved Travis. I loved being with Travis. I loved everything about him. I loved his confidence and his charming personality. He had a way about him that made everyone like him instantly. Travis and I could possibly be heading toward having a future together. I didn't know when, or how long it would take to come to that point, but I thought we were heading in that direction.

During the third talk, Travis leaned in. "Would it be inappropriate to make out during conference?"

I looked at him, surprised. He had a wicked, mischievous grin on his face, but at the same time was completely serious.

"Of course." I rolled my eyes at him. "We're in the same room as the Prophet and the General Authorities and thousands of other members of the Church. Yeah, it might be a little inappropriate." I playfully chastised him.

His lips brushed my ear lobe. "Dang, because I really want to kiss you."

I nudged him away, trying not to giggle. "Well, you're going to have to wait."

"Don't you want to kiss me?" he teased.

Seriously? He had to be joking.

"Babe," I whispered. I tried to be stern, but he was so darn irresistible, it was hard. "I'd love to kiss you, but really, we should wait. Waiting will make it that much sweeter." I sounded cheesy, but making out in Conference was completely inappropriate. How could he not realize that? Any other time, any other place, I'd give in. But with my luck, I'd kiss him and it'd get caught on the TV broadcast during a sweep of the audience.

Travis whispered all through Conference, making it hard to hear. As much as I wanted to spend time with him and listen to what he was saying, I also wanted to listen to the speakers. It left me slightly frustrated.

After, we walked to the fountains. He took a small velvet bag from his pocket and handed it to me.

"What's this?" I asked. I peeked inside and saw it was filled with pennies.

He smiled this slow, seductive smile. "I thought we could make some wishes." He nodded toward it but did not look at it. He kept staring at me. My heart started pounding. Wow. I really did love him.

"I love that idea! Okay." I was impressed. He was so romantic! And he came up with it all on his own.

The falling water was relaxing and romantic. I could've sat there with Travis, with my eyes closed, forever. I loved it.

He pointed to the bag. "You go first."

I took the bag.

His hands lingered on mine. "Go on." He nudged me. "Make a wish."

"Okay." I turned my back to the fountain, and tossed the penny over my shoulder.

I wished that Travis and I would get married.

"What'd you wish for?"

I swatted his shoulder. "I can't tell you that. Then it won't come true."

"What if I tell you what I wish for?" He looked at me with a sideways glance, then took a penny and tossed it over his shoulder. "I wish that you love me as much as I love you."

I slid my hand up his face and turned it so we could kiss. "You know I do."

"Your turn," he said.

"What? You still want me to tell you my wish?"

"I want you to tell me everything." His voice was husky as he leaned into my neck to nuzzle my ear. It made me giggle. "What are you going to wish for?" He continued nuzzling, but it just made me giggle more.

I suddenly felt shy. I didn't want to tell him everything I wished for because my imagination was way ahead of reality in this relationship. I was sure I was way more serious than Travis was at this point.

I reached in again, but instead of feeling the cool metal touch of a coin, I felt something else. I felt velvet. A hard velvet box.

Could it be?

I took the box out. A white satin ribbon came out of it and on the visible end, was a penny. When I opened the box, I saw the most gorgeous diamond ring I had ever seen in my life.

"I wish that you...would marry me."

OH. MY. GOSH! Was he really proposing to me? Really? I sat down on the edge of the fountain, feeling a little bit faint.

Travis took the ring from the box, untied the ribbon, and got down on one knee.

This is happening!

I almost couldn't catch my breath.

"Sophia Davis? You are the most breathtaking woman I have ever met. I love you more than words can describe. Would you marry me and make my wish come true?"

"I will! I will! I will!" I screamed. He slid the ring on my finger just before I crushed him in a hug.

∼

Gretchen was reading *Les Miserables* when I came into the bedroom.

"What are you reading?" I asked casually.

She held it up.

"Is it good?"

She shrugged, and sat up on her bed. "It's a really good story, it's just really long."

Even though I had seen the movie, I kept up the charade. "Is it about miserable people?"

"No, more about tragedy, missed chances of love, shows of devoted love. You know, redemption, love . . ."

"I know a good love story for you," I said, leading into my news.

"I can't start reading anything more until I get through this."

Gretchen missed my hint.

"You don't have to read it. You can be a part of it."

I held up my hand.

"NO WAY!"

Gretchen's reaction was what I thought everyone's reaction would be: over-the-top excitement. She screamed. And screamed and screamed. Then I joined in screaming with her.

She was so speechless she couldn't finish her sentences or complete a coherent thought.

"You're getting...?"

"Yes!"

"No way!"

"Oh, my gosh! I'm so in love! I'm getting married!" I flopped back on my bed and punched the air. "I'm getting married!"

"You're getting married!" Gretchen screamed.

"You're getting on my nerves!" Ruby screamed through the wall.

I jumped up and hugged Gretchen. We jumped around, embracing, quietly squealing."

I was engaged to Travis Duckk!

13

SPEECHLESS

My mother, who was never at a loss for words, was at a loss for words.

The phone line went completely silent.

I looked at my phone screen to make sure the call hadn't dropped. Nope.

"What?" she asked again.

"I'm engaged! Travis proposed!" I repeated excitedly. I looked at my ring for like the hundredth time. It was so big and beautiful.

"And you said 'yes'?" If my mother was trying to hide her excitement, she was doing a good job of it.

"Of course, I said yes!"

She exhaled slowly. Loud enough that I could hear. "Don't you think it's kind of fast?"

My mother, the Queen of Positive Mental Attitude, was not looking on the bright side of things.

"But we're in love! It's so exciting!"

"It's *really* fast," she reiterated.

Why did she keep harping on that?

"You and Dad got married quickly. At BYU, I might add. You said it was love at first sight and you just knew, so why is it different for me?" I had a point and my mother knew it.

"I guess I have to trust your judgment."

Was that so hard?

"Just wait until you meet him. You'll understand."

My mother (thankfully) went with the change of direction in the conversation. "When *do* we get to meet the dashing young man?"

"I don't know. We haven't made any plans to come visit yet, it's all happened so fast." Whoops. Did I just admit that? I didn't mean to.

"Have you decided on a date yet?"

"No, not yet. Probably Thanksgiving."

"Sophia Lucia! What's the rush?"

What was her problem? She was always the one obscenely obsessed with finding the good in every situation. Besides, she should talk. She met and married my dad in one semester. I was maybe a month shy of her courtship.

"Mom, you said yourself that when you know, you know. You said it about dad."

"You're going to have all time and eternity to be married, you don't have to decide on a whim to get married."

I sniffed. "It is not a whim, and it's been a month."

My mom softened a bit. "Honey, you don't have to marry the first guy that comes along at BYU. There's going to be a lot of Prince Charmings."

"Wait until you see him. He's beautiful. He *is* Prince Charming."

"Don't you want to date a little more? Experience being on your own a little more…"

I hated it when my mother lectured me. I was a big girl, why didn't she treat me like one? I could make my own decisions, and this was a good decision. Ugh. My mom could be so impossible sometimes.

"What I want to experience is being married to Travis."

"All I'm saying is…"

"That you don't trust me. That you can't stop being my mother long enough to give me some credit." This was supposed to be a happy situation. Why was she not happy for me?

"I want you to be happy. And if you are sure that you are going to be happy, then I can't really force you to change your mind."

Huh. I wasn't expecting that. Then, using one of her favorite lines, I came up with a solution. "Well, look on the bright side, mom, you have a wedding to plan." She would eat that up. It gave her a reason to be *involved*.

"Yes, on to bigger and brighter things, we do have a wedding to plan." And off she went running with lists of things to do, arrangements to make, schedules to schedule and blah, blah, blah. I tuned her out because all I wanted to think about was that I was going to be Mrs. Travis Duckk. Yeah, hated the last name, but loved the guy.

Within a half an hour of hanging up with my mother, my brother called. "Engaged? Really Sophia?" His reaction was a mixture of surprise and disbelief. "Are you completely crazy?"

"You talked to Mom," I said, stating the obvious.

"You don't think she'd keep news like that to herself, do you?"

"Yeah, I know."

"You sure you know what you're doing Soph? You know how RM's are with their raging hormones."

"I know exactly what I'm doing," I said.

I was saying *yes* to my happily ever after.

∿

Telling Boyd and Maxine we were engaged made me anxious. We decided it would be best to do it in person the next Sunday we went there for dinner.

The color drained from Maxine's face. "What?"

"We're engaged," Travis repeated.

Travis's parents were also speechless, but not because they were overwhelmed with joy and excitement.

"Son—" Boyd began, only to be interrupted by Maxine.

"It's too soon. You hardly know each other. It's barely a fling, let alone a relationship!"

This wasn't the hugs and excitement I expected.

"Why the rush?" Maxine continued. Her hand went to her chest. "You're not pregnant, are you?"

Pregnant! That's what she thought?! Even if I was pregnant, three weeks of dating would be too soon to know.

"No!" I said. "We're in love!"

Maxine shook her head. "You kids don't even know what love is."

How would *she* know what we did or didn't know?

"We're not asking for your permission," Travis said. "We're asking for your blessing."

Ooh, good one. Where did he come up with that?

"Don't forget who you're talking to, Travis," Maxine said in a stern voice.

"We just want you to be happy for us," I said, stepping in to calm an impending fight. "That's all."

Maxine's phone rang, and she immediately picked up. "Hello? Hi. No, no, I'm not upset. Travis is here with his girlfriend," she said, then paused. Then she eyed me. "Well, it's a little more serious than I would like." She stood up and walked off.

A little more serious? *Really? Was she* serious? How much more serious could it be? We were getting married. That was serious. I didn't know what bothered her so much. Was it that we were getting married, or was it that he was marrying me?

Boyd leaned forward in his chair, his elbow resting on his knees. "Look, kids. Marriage is hard. Maybe you want to date a little more, get to know each other better, before you decide you're ready to spend the rest of your lives together."

And eternity.

"Dad, we—" Travis started, but Boyd held up his hand.

"You've already upset your mother. Let's revisit this conversation later."

Why weren't our parents happy? Gretchen was the only one who reacted the way I thought everyone would have reacted.

We grabbed our phones and immediately headed for the front door.

"We'll talk later, son," Boyd said before he shut the door.

Travis didn't even say goodbye.

～

WE DROVE HOME IN SILENCE. I didn't know if it was better to discuss what happened at his parent's house then, or wait a day or two until everyone calmed down. Me, included.

I decided I'd wait.

I mentally reviewed what just happened. We literally got in a fight with his parents over our engagement. That wasn't good. They didn't understand we were in love and serious about taking this step. Maybe they needed time to process the unexpected news.

"Call you later," Travis mumbled when he dropped me off at my dorm.

I put my hand on his. "It'll be okay," I said. "I know it will. I love you."

"I love you too," he said and kissed me.

～

TRAVIS CALLED me later that night, fuming.

"What's wrong?" I asked, worried. Was he going to break up with me?

"My parents don't think we should get married. They think it's too soon. They think you're too young."

Hearing what his parents thought infuriated me. "Too young? I'm eighteen. I'm in college. I'm a big girl."

"I told them that."

"Then what is it?" I asked.

"I don't know Fi. I don't know," he said in a soft voice.

I had a hunch. "I don't think your mother likes me."

"Why would you think that?" He sounded genuinely surprised.

"Just a feeling." Among other things. Waves of disapproval that rolled off her when I was around.

"I don't think it's that." He seemed distracted. I pictured him running through different reasons in his mind, trying to find the right reason for them not giving us their blessing.

"Then what?"

"I don't know if any girl will ever be good enough in my mom's eyes."

"She thinks I'm not good enough?"

"It's not you. It'd be any girl. But I don't think it's that. I think it's happening too fast for them. My mom mentioned several times that she thought it was too soon."

My mom brought that up also, several times in fact, but she didn't say she disapproved.

"So?" I held my breath.

"What?"

"Do you think it's too soon?" *Please say no. Please say no.* I didn't want him to change his mind. I didn't want him to back out. I didn't want him to put it off.

"It doesn't matter what they say."

I let out a huge sigh of relief.

He continued. "We're the ones getting married, not them. My parents don't know you like I know you. They don't realize how amazing and breathtaking you are. I don't care what they think. They can't tell me what to do."

"I love you so much!"

It was me and Travis against the world. I liked the way it sounded. I liked the way it made me feel. We could survive anything, with or without his parent's blessing.

I felt like an insurgent in the war for our love.

14

MARRIAGE PREP

Travis and I drove to Vegas for Columbus Day weekend so he could officially meet my parents in person. There had been some quick introductions and short conversations on video chats, but meeting in-person was always better. It also gave us a chance to discuss wedding plans. Up until now, the only thing we'd discussed was when to get married, which was unanimously decided the sooner the better.

Thanksgiving was the obvious choice. It was the closest holiday that gave us a couple of days off. That was easily a unanimous decision.

What was not unanimous, however, was *where* we'd get married.

"I'll call the Las Vegas Temple and see if the Saturday after Thanksgiving is available," I said, talking out loud as I made out a checklist of wedding plans to get done this weekend.

Travis interrupted my train of thought. "About that."

"About what?" I was too wrapped up in my "to do" list to figure out what he was talking about.

"The temple."

My heart stopped. Was there a problem? Did he not want to? Was he not worthy? What could it be? "What about it?" I asked cautiously.

"How do you feel about getting married in the Salt Lake Temple?" He looked over at me briefly, his eyes pleading his cause.

I had two reactions. The first one was instant relief. We still could get married in the temple. My next reaction was confusion. Why the Salt Lake Temple? Wasn't it the girl's choice what temple she wanted to get married in? Of course, it had to be a decision both the bride and groom was happy with, but I assumed we'd get married in the Las Vegas Temple.

"Salt Lake?" My voice expressed my surprise.

This time Travis didn't look at me. "It'd mean a lot to my family if we got sealed in the Salt Lake Temple."

His family? Or his mother? I bit my tongue to keep from saying what I really thought and tried to find out the truth.

"Why would it matter if it was Salt Lake or Vegas?" I asked.

"I went through the Salt Lake Temple before my mission. And my parents were married there. It's tradition. It would mean a lot to my mother if we were married there."

It *was* his mother.

"But..." I was at a loss for words. I always planned on getting married in the Las Vegas Temple.

"Besides, it doesn't really matter *which* temple. It just matters that it's you and me."

It was hard to fight against my own logic, or at least what I thought was logic at the time.

"I don't know, Trav," I said, wanting him to give in.

"Please, Fi? For me? It'd make me really happy."

I heard myself saying, "Okay. I guess it's not that big of a deal." Although I hadn't convinced myself that it wasn't that big of a deal. I hoped my mother wasn't going to think it was a big deal, either. I exhaled. "Salt Lake it is."

He reached across the car, and patted my hand. "That's my girl."

"So," I started, wanting to keep moving through the plans so I wouldn't dwell on the feelings that maybe I had betrayed myself. But marriage was about compromise. And Travis was right. It didn't matter if it was Salt Lake or Vegas, as long as we were getting married in the temple. "Would we take our honeymoon right after the wedding?" I didn't really want to wait until school got out in December.

He gave me a sexy smile. "Of course."

"We'd miss a couple days of school."

"Fi," he said and looked at me. "Let's not rush the honeymoon. I don't *mind* missing school."

I blushed. *Point taken.* I cleared my throat, looking down at my list instead of over at him. "Um, okay, where were we?"

"The honeymoon," Travis filled in for me, then grinned. Obviously, he'd picked up on my anxiety.

I wouldn't look at him, because I'd blush even more. "No, I meant after the honeymoon."

"I'd rather dwell on the honeymoon," he said playfully.

"Cut it out." I swatted him with my pad of paper.

Travis laughed. "I can't help it. You're so cute when you are embarrassed."

"Could we move past the honeymoon and figure out the rest of the details?" Anything to divert the conversation away from the honeymoon.

~

I FELT like a princess as we pulled up to my parent's house in his BMW. Even more so when he got out and came around and opened the door for me. What a gentleman. And I got to have him forever as my husband. I was *so* blessed.

My mom shot out the front door before my feet even hit the ground. "Sophia!" She came running at me with arms wide open. She'd probably been watching out the window. Patience wasn't always her strong suit, unlike her PMA that she excelled in. I inherited her lack of patience, as was easily seen by how quickly we wanted to get married.

"You must be Travis," Mom said, hugging him.

Travis hugged her back. "I am. Nice to meet you."

My dad wasn't far behind my mom and after introductions were made, we sat down and visited. It was nice. Stories were told, laughs were shared, conversations were had and snacks were eaten.

No matter what the question or the topic of conversation, Travis managed to say all the right things.

He said things like, "I wish you'd been my English teacher in high school" to my mom. I could tell by the expression on her face that his compliment just warmed her heart. And "I've never met anyone quite as amazing as Fi," and my dad beamed.

It felt like my parents loved Travis. But how could they not? What was there *not* to love about Travis?

∼

DAN WAS DOWN for the weekend, although he drove down in his own car.

"Since we're all here, we can do a *Star Wars* party," Mom said. She was in the kitchen looking through the cabinets. She must've been checking for certain ingredients.

Travis leaned in. "What's that?" he whispered.

"It's really fun," I said. "We watch the original trilogy and eat *Star Wars*-themed food. Mom makes Darth Vader chips—which are chocolate tortilla chips—and huge cinnamon rolls called Princess Leia buns."

His brows came together. "Sounds kind of boring."

"You don't like *Star Wars*?" I asked. I thought *everyone* liked *Star Wars*.

"Not really." He shrugged. "My mom thought it was stupid, so we never watched it."

"Let's not share that opinion," I said as jokingly as I could.

He didn't give the night much of a chance. He ate the food, but scrolled on his phone through the movies.

When I went downstairs to get more Princess Leia buns, Dan followed.

"Why does he call you Fi?" he asked.

"It's my nickname," I said and told him the backstory.

"But that's not your name," Dan said.

I rolled my eyes. "It's not a big deal."

"Sophia," Dan said, seriously. "He's like a politician."

"Why would you say that? He's great."

"He's so smooth talking. He lays on the charm a little too thick."

I laughed. "You can't be Prince Charming without charm." I loved his charm. "Besides, it's endearing. It's a gift."

"Or a curse."

Obviously not everyone approved of our rush to the altar.

I ignored his comment. "It comes easily to him. Are you sure you're not jealous?" I joked, but there was a note of truth. There is always truth in jest. Dan was graduating in December, was twenty-four, and would probably leave BYU single.

"Even if I met my dream girl today, I'd still leave BYU single. Besides, I wouldn't want to steal your thunder and get married quicker than you."

I gave him a loving punch in the arm. "Don't worry Dan, the force is with you. You'll find your Princess Leia."

"Ha. Ha."

"Once you get to know Travis, you'll love him too."

I was certain of it.

~

"Wedding dress, invitations, engagement pictures, the registry, guest list, receptions, bridal showers, hair, makeup, pictures, luncheon," Mom said, writing down the "To Do" list. "We have one weekend to get it all done."

"It's a lot to do, but I think we can," I said. I *couldn't* wait to get started.

Mom clapped her hands—she was chomping at the bit to work on it too.

Number one on the list: the wedding dress.

The first dress I tried on at the first store we went to was the one I fell completely in love with. (It's a sign!). It was more expensive than my budget, but it was Vera Wang (!) and I had to have it! After all, you only get married once, so why skimp on the fairy tale? The dress was too big, but alterations were easier than ordering the right size. Delivery time was at least six weeks and I was getting married in four.

Mom sighed at the price tag, but silently handed her credit card over. If everything was this easy, we'd be done in no time.

Mom looked at the list when we got in the car. "Okay, next is invitations. Where should we go for that?"

People went places to order invitations? "We'll do it online. But we need engagement photos first."

"When are those being taken?"

"Um...I don't know." I didn't know any photographers. "I haven't made any arrangements."

"Your wedding is in six weeks. The invitations need to be sent out by next week. We need to get on that," she said.

It was like I knew that, but I didn't realize how fast the deadline was approaching. "We don't have to send out physical copies to everyone. We can send out evites."

Mom frowned. "That's kind of tacky."

I didn't think so. That's the way things were done now. But no matter how we sent them, we still needed a picture for the invitation. "Do we know anyone who does photography?" I asked.

"I'll ask around the ward," Mom said. If anyone could find out anything, she could.

"Great."

"Are you already scheduled with the temple? If you don't have an appointment, you can't do any of the other things."

"Travis is handling it." I pulled out my phone and sent him a text.

"Why?"

"Because we're getting married in Salt Lake."

The mood in the car shifted.

"Why Salt Lake? You're from Vegas."

"Because the Salt Lake Temple is his family tradition."

"What about your family traditions, Sophia? It's the bride's choice where to get married."

"And I choose Salt Lake."

After a beat, Mom picked up where we left off. "So, hair, makeup, nails, pictures, and the luncheon won't be done here?"

I could hear the disappointment in her voice. I hadn't thought about how she'd feel if I didn't get married here.

"Let's head home. We'll work on a photographer and the guest list. You should call the building coordinator as soon as possible and get your reception scheduled. Thanksgiving is bound to be a popular wedding date."

Mom and I went home, and while Mom put together a guest list, Travis and I headed to Target.

Shopping for our registry was almost as fun as shopping for my wedding dress. As we scanned barcodes of things we needed, things we thought we needed, or things we just plain wanted to have, Travis generally said, "Whatever you want honey," or "If you like that" or "Okay." Loved it. Registry shopping had to be one of the best kinds of shopping.

The expenses were adding up fast, but you only get married once.

THE WEEKEND WAS A WHIRLWIND, but we got everything done that we could. There was a lot of preparation that goes into a wedding. I was thankful Mom was helping me, because otherwise it might not have gotten done.

We decided on an open house at my parents' the day after the wedding. From there, we'd travel on to California for the cruise.

Since we were on a time crunch, we decided on the menu and Mom said she would take it from there—which she would. She loved planning and it kept her *involved*.

15

PUNCH LIST

Back in Provo, we chipped away at our punch list. We put our housing contracts up for sale. Then we searched for married housing that would be available December first. I had done a little hunting around, getting on waiting lists, but it looked like we might not get into an apartment until January. We didn't have a backup plan. Travis suggested living with his parents, but that was a long commute.

The next weekend, we headed up to Salt Lake for a day of wedding planning with Maxine. I didn't know why she decided to take this on, but I was thankful. There was a lot of planning and trying to balance it with school would be hard. I hoped working on the wedding would bring us together.

Driving there, my phone blew up.

"Who's that?" Travis asked.

"Your mom."

Her texts consisted of links to venues. I'd just barely open the website, and I'd get a text that it was booked.

Maxine: Don't worry. We'll find an appropriate place.

Admittedly, I was a little worried. The date was so close and availability seemed nonexistent.

Next came a barrage of cake pics.

I sighed. I'd sent her a picture of the cake I liked, per her request. "These don't look anything like what I wanted."

Now I was really worried—should I *not* have accepted her help?

"She just wants to be involved, Fi," Travis said.

"I appreciate that, but I don't feel like she's listening to me." She was so pushy, especially about things *she* liked.

"We went to Vegas and your mom helped plan things."

True."I know, but—" It just seemed like his mom was over-involved.

Maxine stood on the driveway, purse on the crook of her elbow, when we pulled in. "I've found the most delightful place," Maxine said. "All of this is last minute, so it's not my first choice in venues, but I don't have enough time to plan properly. I've set up a florist and bakery appointment also." She looked at me. "I sent you the link."

The three of us obviously couldn't fit into her BMW 2 Series Coupe, so Travis drove. I felt obligated to allow Maxine to have the front seat, since she was older than me and might have a hard time getting in and out of the back seat.

"You'll be very happy to know that I was able to get an appointment to be sealed at the Salt Lake Temple. I had to call in a few favors, but we got a two o'clock appointment."

I looked at Travis, confused. "I thought you were going to take care of that."

"I did. I had my mom do it."

I could kind of appreciate his efficiency, but at the same time, it wasn't her responsibility.

The place she found for the reception was an event room at a hotel in downtown Salt Lake. We met with the planner and saw pictures of how it was decorated as part of the package. It was very pretty, complete with twinkle lights, sheer draped fabric and best of all, no basketball hoop.

We decided on a menu for a sit-down meal, Maxine put down a deposit, and then we headed to the florist.

I had pictures on my phone of bouquet ideas. It made it much easier to show the florist than try to explain.

"Peonies and eucalyptus." The florist, Louisa, scribbled on her pad. "I have to mention peonies are out of season in December, so they will be expensive."

Maxine set a bony hand on my shoulder. "Maybe you should choose something more...cost-effective. Or silk flowers."

My parents were paying for the flowers. "It's just for my bouquet, the corsages and the boutonnieres."

"Boutonnieres are so outdated. Maybe eliminate those."

Since when?

"Travis and my parents will have corsages and boutonnieres. If you and Boyd don't want them, we don't have to order them."

It'd save on the flower cost.

Maxine cleared her throat. "It was just a suggestion." She turned to Travis. "What do you think?"

He looked up from his phone. "I don't care. Whatever Fifi wants."

He'd been the same way about the reception location.

"What about the bridal party? Will they need bouquets?"

We had decided to keep it simple. "We're just having a maid of honor and a best man," I said. I had already asked Gretchen, but didn't know if Travis had asked someone to be the best man. Or, at least, he hadn't mentioned it to me.

Louisa made a note on her paper. "Okay. What about decorations for the tables?"

"What can we do with eucalyptus and some sort of flowers like peonies, but not peonies."

"We could use carnations," Louisa said.

Maxine coughed. "We don't want it to look like we're at the Kentucky Derby."

Louisa pinched her lips together for a second. "Eucalyptus makes beautiful table runners and centerpieces. I'll do some research and send you some budget-friendly examples."

"By budget-friendly, you mean cheap?" Maxine asked. "I don't want it to look cheap."

I didn't understand. She didn't think boutonnieres were worth the money, but was worried what "budget-friendly" would look like.

The florist forced a smile. "I can make it as simple or as fancy as you want. It's your decision."

"I look forward to the examples," I said. I gave her my email and Maxine insisted she be included in the email because "she was sensitive to some flowers".

The final stop was the cake shop. Luckily, I had the pic of what I wanted on my phone. I showed the employee taking the order and we ordered chocolate cake with white buttercream.

"All three layers in chocolate?" Maxine questioned.

"Yes," I said.

"What if some guests don't like chocolate or can't eat chocolate?"

It was our wedding and we wanted chocolate cake. I wasn't planning my wedding around what my guests could eat. "They can have cream puffs," I said.

Maxine folded her hands across her lap and didn't respond.

Travis didn't look up from his phone.

The cake lady wrote down the instructions on an order form. Maxine insisted on being the point of contact so she could "take care of the delivery arrangements." It was one less thing I had to coordinate, so I didn't fight her on it.

Maxine broke the silence on the way home. "Are you kids sure you're going to go through with this?"

Did she doubt that we were in love?

"Mom," Travis said, his tone a warning.

"You're just so young—"

Meaning I was young.

"And marriage is hard. I had to quit school to put Boyd through school. We were dirt poor."

"But look how successful you are now," I piped up, trying to insert some PMA into the situation.

Maxine angled her body toward me in the back seat. "We have money because we don't spend money. We worked hard to get where we are now. No one helped us; we supported each other and became successful on our own."

"Of course," I said.

"Of course, I want the same happiness and success in your marriage," Maxine said.

She didn't have to worry about that.

When I'm his wife, I'll make him so super happy he will always remember why he married me.

"Marriage means sacrifice," she said.

Travis gripped the steering wheel. "We're both adults, Mom."

Maxine flipped her perfectly manicured hand. "I know that. I just want to make sure that you're going into this with your eyes wide open."

"We know what we're doing," I said as pleasantly as possible. I was so glad that once we were married, we wouldn't be subjected to her opinions and input. Travis and I would be making the decisions for ourselves and she really wouldn't have a say.

When we dropped Maxine off back at her house, she paused before stepping out of the car. "Fifi, please send me your mom's contact information. That way we can discuss the budget."

"Okay," I said. Since we were going to be family, it only made sense to work on this together, but I had my doubts. Maybe my mom would know how to deal with Maxine better than I did.

The countdown to the wedding was on. Over the next 5 weeks, my focus became everything wedding. We got our engagement photos done and booked the same photographer for the wedding. Invitations were sent out ASAP.

My contract sold within a week of listing it (it's a sign!), but no interest for Travis's.

And Gretchen got her mission call to the New Zealand Auckland Mission.

There were dress fittings, bridal showers and...school, but that went on the back burner. Not that school was that important before. I still struggled with what I wanted to do when I grew up. I didn't know what my major was, what my passion was, what to do with myself. Travis kind of took that all away. My focus was him. My major was him. My passion was him.

And my prayers were answered. I would soon be Mrs. Travis Duckk and I wouldn't have to worry anymore. I mean sure, I'd finish school, get a job (maybe a career?), work for a while and then we'd start a family. So really, I didn't have to figure out what I was doing with the rest of my life because it all kind of depended on Travis. Because once we were married, it would be the solution to all my problems.

~

"Sophia, you do realize you're marrying a family, right?" My mom said. We were driving to my final dress fitting. Gretchen drove me to Vegas for it and a wedding shower. Travis opted out of coming because of homework.

"Yes," I said.

"Well, your future mother-in-law is quite…bossy."

"Yeah. But once we're married, I won't have to deal with her anymore." No more decisions about the wedding and no more decisions about plans or schedules. We'd be our own family.

"Your in-laws will always be a part of your life, whether you like it or not," Mom said.

"I'm hoping it's just because of the wedding," I said.

"Right?" Gretchen added.

Mom smirked. "Don't be so sure."

We rode in silence for a few minutes before my mom started on a different topic.

"What do you most want from your registry?" Mom asked.

"I feel like we need everything, so anything on it will help."

As much as I loved shopping, I knew the wedding cost a lot of money, and didn't want my parents to spend way too much.

"But you have some crazy, expensive things on there," Mom said.

Gretchen snapped her fingers. "I noticed that too."

"Like what?" I thought everything we'd registered for was reasonable.

"Le Creuset pots and pans."

I didn't remember adding those.

"Some speaker sound bar thing that's over five hundred dollars. MacBook accessories, a gaming system, a pebble ice machine," Gretchen said.

Pebble ice machine? *What?* I didn't add that.

I pulled up the registry on my phone. Like they'd said, there were all sorts of electronics and household things that I didn't know about.

Curious, I called Travis and asked him.

"Oh, yeah, I added some stuff. Why not?"

I thought the point of a registry was for people to give us things we needed to start our lives together. I didn't think Nintendo games fell in that category. The registry wasn't a Christmas wish list.

"What about the pots and pans set?" Among other things.

"My mom added that. She said it's important to have good pots and pans."

"*She* added it?" I needed to clarify.

"Yes."

When we set up the registry, we had the gifts sent to Maxine and Boyd's because we didn't know where we'd be living. But that didn't mean she could have access to our registry.

"How'd she do that?" I asked, even though I could guess the answer.

"I gave her the password. It's not that big of a deal."

Maybe it was, maybe it wasn't. But I didn't think it was her business.

Maybe I just needed to talk to her and straighten things out.

After I hung up, I didn't immediately call Maxine. We had just pulled up to the dress shop and I had better things to think about, like my dress!

Trying on my dress put me in a better mood. My dress was gorgeous! It was perfect! I felt like a princess in it!

Standing on the little platform, seeing myself from all different angles, looking perfect, I just knew my wedding was going to be perfect.

16

TURKEY TROUBLE

I stared at the raw turkey, with its pale, goose-bumped skin. My throat constricted and I started to gag.

Could I skip Thanksgiving dinner? Was that an option? It was the morning of, and I had to get this thing cooked.

I stepped back—I had to get away from the scent—turned my head and took a deep breath.

How the...heck...did I get myself into this mess? What the...heck...was I doing?

I didn't know how to cook a turkey!

How did Maxine manage to dump it on me? Maybe that's what I'd wish for when I found that stupid little wishbone: a spine. The ability to say no. To never have to touch a raw turkey ever again.

I never realized how disgusting cooking a turkey could be. I didn't like the smell. The pores on the pale legs looked nasty. Reaching into the cavity of the bird to pull out the gizzards was super gross and disgusting. Then I was supposed to rinse the bird, the cavity, *pat* it dry and *rub* it? Uh, *no*.

I called Maxine to ask her what to do.

"You've never cooked a turkey, dear?" She asked. It was not a question. Her tone made me feel silly and stupid. But I wasn't going to give her the satisfaction of me failing.

After all, how hard could it be? Millions of people cooked turkeys all the time. And if millions of people could do it, so could I.

I turned to my mother next. She gave me general instructions, which I probably should've written down, but didn't. I'd check online, if needed.

I should've looked. Well, at least looked a little closer.

I discovered the turkey came with instructions, but they were wrapped up in all that mesh, and were wet and hard to read. And they ripped when I tried to get them out.

My hands were now covered in raw turkey juice and I probably just exposed myself to salmonella, E. coli, and every other food-borne illness caused by raw meat. I threw all the turkey wrappings away. Good riddance, it smelled funny anyway.

I sort of winged it and went off what I remembered: cook it twenty minutes for every three pounds. Why couldn't they just say six to seven minutes per pound? I could do the math. And if I couldn't, I had a calculator.

I had a fifteen-pound bird. (I wasn't sure how big of a bird I should buy, but I thought I remembered my mom always bought one about this heavy). Ten pounds didn't seem big enough.

I rinsed the bird (yuck), skipped the stuffing (I wasn't putting *anything* inside the bird, especially my hand. I didn't want to ruin my manicure for Saturday), sprayed it down with some butter spritz (for color—like suntan lotion—but for a turkey), and put the bird in its final resting place: my oven.

After all that, I knew *I* would *not* be having any of *this* turkey. No. Thank. You.

I was ready, but the bird wasn't ready. That little pop-up button that announced it was cooked didn't pop up. I checked it every five minutes, opening the oven and poking my head in the oven to get a good look. But each time, the button wasn't up.

I don't know what happened. Maybe I miscalculated the cooking time, or set the oven to the wrong temperature (I thought it said 350 degrees), but I wasn't a hundred-percent sure.

Surely it had to be almost cooked, right? It had been in the oven for the right amount of time.

I set the timer for another five minutes and then my phone rang.

"On my way," Travis said.

"Okay, but come on up when you get here. The turkey is still in the oven."

"Will it be out when I get there?" He asked.

"It should be."

I was positive it would be. How much longer could it cook? I decided that I'd take it out when Travis got here.

The button still hadn't popped up when he knocked on the door.

I whipped open the door. "Hey," I said quickly, and turned my attention back to the oven. The buzzer went off yet again.

Travis stepped in. "Hey."

"Just a sec," I said. I pulled the bird out and set it on top of the oven. After another inspection, the button hadn't moved since last time.

Travis looked at his watch. "Is that bird almost ready?"

I stepped aside and pointed at Tom the Turkey. "What do you think?"

He shrugged. "I don't know. Looks good to me. But it really doesn't matter because we need to leave. You never keep my mom waiting."

Well, dang!

"Now I'm totally stressed out. I don't think it's done."

"It's fine. We'll get there on time if we leave now," he said, with another glance at his watch.

That was the deciding factor. I couldn't make Maxine wait. I already felt like she didn't like me. And Travis and I were getting married in two days. I needed all the brownie points I could get.

So, I did the only thing I could. I took the bird out of the oven, forced the pop-up button up (darn stubborn thing) and covered the lovely birdie in foil. Besides, I rationalized, the foil would hold the heat in and continue to cook the meat for the drive.

When we arrived, no one else was there other than Maxine and Boyd. I was told Thanksgiving at the Duckk household was a huge family affair, meaning lots of extended family. Like the whole flock. Travis carried the bird to the kitchen. "Where's everyone?" He set it down on her granite countertop.

Maxine smiled and put her arms around my shoulders and gave me a squeeze. "Change of plans."

I bought the bigger bird because I thought there was going to be a bunch more people.

"We thought we would keep it intimate with our almost daughter-in-law," Maxine said. She added a wide smile.

"Intimate" didn't make me think "Thanksgiving with Travis' parents".

"We are so excited about you being part of our family," she said. The way she said it made me feel like she should've squished my mouth in one hand. Like old ladies do to babies.

I swallowed hard and tried to smile. "I'm so excited too."

I thought about the button on the bird that had not popped up on its own. "Should we put the turkey in the oven until it's time to eat?"

Maxine glanced at the oven. "No. I have the green bean casserole in there right now. It'll be fine."

"Okay," I said.

I looked around for Travis. He wasn't in the kitchen and I heard the TV in the other room. Football. And then Boyd's exclamation about a touchdown.

"We still have to make the sweet potato casserole. I'll do that while you mash the potatoes."

I waited for more direction. But none came.

∼

AFTER ALL THAT rushing to get there, we didn't end up eating for almost two hours after. Come to find out, none of the sides were done, *except* for the green bean casserole. Not that I expected her to do all the work, but Travis was very specific that we needed to be on time. If dinner was to start at two, Maxine was running *way* late.

I mashed the potatoes, tossed the salads and mixed the punch. While all this was happening, the turkey sat there, waiting for its consumption fate. If I'd known we weren't going to be eating immediately, I would've tried to cook the turkey a little bit longer before rushing up to Salt Lake to get there "on time".

When Maxine finally turned her attention to the bird, it was to carve it.

She removed the foil and carved a slice off the breast. "It looks a little pink. Are you sure this is cooked?"

"It should be," I said. It really should be cooked. It had been in the oven all morning and plus the time it kept cooking while we drove here. It should've been done. Right?

"Maybe it's the lighting?" I suggested. Maxine's kitchen had all this "mood" lighting, being translated as dim lighting.

Maxine made a few more cuts, peeling the meat back and leaning close to examine it.

"We could put it back in the oven," I said. I'll admit, I was hopeful she'd agree. Maybe it did *need* more time in the oven.

Right about now I wished there was such a thing as bronzing sauce for turkey, like self-tanning lotion for pale and pasty humans. Something to darken him up a little so Maxine would stop criticizing him. My poor birdie. He was already being served for dinner, give him a break. Isn't pale the way to go? Sort of like avoiding skin cancer?

Maxine glanced at her watch. "No. We should eat. Let's get the food on the table."

The dining room table was already set with fine china, silverware, crystal goblets and cloth napkins. It was so fancy it felt like a crime to dirty any of it.

"Aren't you going to have some turkey, Fifi?" Maxine asked once we were seated and serving ourselves.

"Uh, no. After touching and cooking that thing, I've lost my appetite for turkey. It was a messy, icky experience."

"Giving birth can be a messy, icky experience, but you still want to hold the baby after," Maxine said.

Where did that weird analogy come from? Holding a baby was a little different than eating the baby.

Travis laughed. Did he find his mother funny? "I hope our babies don't look like turkeys."

Our babies definitely would not look like turkeys. They'd be beautiful, of course.

"What about something else?" Maxine said. "Mashed potatoes?"

While the mashed potatoes *were* good, I had a wedding dress to get into on Saturday.

~

TRADITION in the Duckk household dictated the Christmas tree must go up after dinner, but not before the men took naps, the women cleaned up, and the football game ended.

That tradition certainly wouldn't be *our* tradition.

Everyone napped after dinner. Maxine and Boyd were in recliners, Travis was sprawled out on the couch and I sat in an armchair, wide awake and feeling awkward.

I thought of it as Duckk family down time because everyone had had their fill of tryptophan. But how long could they nap? Twenty, thirty minutes? Then we'd put up the Christmas tree? I could scroll through my phone while everyone slept.

Maxine didn't seem very relaxed. She kept squirming. Finally, she sat up. "I must've indulged too much—my stomach hurts."

"Me too." Boyd patted his stomach. "But it sure was good."

Maxine stood and almost staggered. "I need Pepto Bismol." She reached out, unstable. "Travis, would you help me upstairs?"

Travis hopped off and offered his mom his arm. A few minutes later, Travis returned.

Boyd stood almost immediately after Travis and Maxine turned the corner. "Actually, I might need some myself. My stomach's upset."

Boyd hurried upstairs to join Maxine. I heard their bedroom door shut.

Everything was silent, including Travis. I looked at him, only to find him pale with beads of sweat forming on his forehead. "Honey, what's wrong? Are you okay?"

"I need to use the bathroom." He hurried out of the room and I heard him moan as he shut the door.

This couldn't be happening!

I sat on their stiff, leather couch, alone and deserted in their huge living room, while everyone complained of stomach pains. What should I do? I couldn't very well go check on anyone. Maxine and Boyd were upstairs, behind closed bedroom doors. Travis was behind the closed bathroom door. We weren't married yet. I couldn't peek in to check how he was doing. But I could at least try.

I approached the bathroom door with trepidation. I decided to knock and ask through the door if he was alright or not.

I could hear him moaning through the door. "Ohhh."

I felt stupid and embarrassed. Not only for me, but for him. I didn't know what to do. I didn't want to hear what was going on behind there. But I was worried I'd be caught hovering around the door.

Upstairs I could hear faint moaning, and then...retching. Yuck! There was nothing worse than hearing someone throw up. If anything could induce sympathy puking, it was hearing someone else throw up.

Then I heard it again. Closer. In the bathroom I stood outside of. Travis started puking too.

Retching, gagging, moaning and coughing. Over and over and over again.

Maxine and Travis were both sick. It was like a hail storm of vomit had struck.

I had a sneaking, sinking suspicion everyone had food poisoning.

I sat alone and in silence for an hour, not knowing what to do. An hour. I debated if I should check on them, leave them alone, turn on the TV, or sit there in silence. What was the proper etiquette when you're the guest at a house where everyone has abandoned you in search of a bathroom?

At one point I tiptoed upstairs to check on Maxine and Boyd, but it sounded like someone was throwing up again, and I obviously did not want to interrupt. I tiptoed back downstairs and waited. Soon after that attempt, I tiptoed down the hall where Travis was, and he was still throwing up. It felt like I was invading their privacy as I hovered, uncertain, outside their closed doors.

I went back to the couch and waited, perched on the edge. What had hit them so quickly with such intensity? I Googled the symptoms and all signs pointed to food poisoning.

Finally, a bathroom door creaked open. "Fi?" I heard faintly.

I jumped up and rushed to Travis. I could only see a sliver of his face. "Are you okay?"

"Don't come too close. I'm really sick," he said.

"Honey, I'm so sorry."

"Do you think you could get my mom?"

"Your mom?" Why did he want her? Shouldn't he want me? I was his fiancée, after all. Then I caught a whiff. What he really needed was some air freshener.

"Yeah, I need my mom," he said again.

He sounded like a newly potty-trained two-year-old.

I cleared my throat. "Your mom is still upstairs. She's sick too. Can I help you?"

"No." He sounded crestfallen. Then he suddenly slammed the door.

After almost another hour of sitting there, not knowing what to do, Boyd walked downstairs supporting Maxine.

"We need to go to the hospital."

∼

WE ALL PILED into the car, including Travis, everyone holding bowls in their laps as I sped to the ER. It was a harried, death-defying ride as I weaved in and out of traffic. Maxine demanded that I "get her there", Travis and Boyd puking.

"You're going to kill us all," Maxine wailed.

"I am not dying until I get married," I screamed back, tears streaming down my face. I could think of nothing worse than death before "I do's".

Somehow, we arrived safely to the welcoming, sterile environment of the emergency room. I had never been so happy to be at the ER in my life.

I waited in the waiting room for three hours. Three hours of stressing about Travis, stressing if we would be able to get married, checking my phone for updates from my parents who were driving up tonight.

After three long hours, their diagnosis was confirmed: I had given everyone food poisoning by undercooking the Thanksgiving turkey. Come to find out, pale is *not* the way to go when it comes to cooking turkeys. Pale means undercooked, which means an increased chance of food poisoning. Salmonella. E. coli. You know, all the *run-of-the-mill*, food-borne illnesses. Unfortunately, poisoning your future in-laws with undercooked turkey is not the best way to learn all of this valuable information.

It was *all* my fault. That made me feel *really* good. That made me feel *secure* in thinking I had scored some points with Travis's parents. Negative points.

I got sent home from the emergency room with a photocopied fact sheet about cooking meat, a proper food handling guide, "Don't Eat This Meat" and other, informative pamphlets.

I was also sent home armed with supplies, bed liners, electrolyte replacement drinks, and the suggestion of maybe purchasing some adult diapers. I couldn't picture a dignified way to handle that situation, and decided to pass on the diaper option. Three subjects I decided I never wanted to discuss with Travis or his parents ever again: adult diapers, bowels, or improperly cooked poultry.

To tell the truth, I never wanted to see a turkey ever again.

17

FOR TIME AND ALL ETERNITY

*D*espite Travis, Boyd and Maxine feeling better on Friday, we still had to have an uneasy discussion whether to carry on with the wedding. Against my selfish desires, I offered to postpone it if necessary. They *had* all been terribly sick.

"If we need to, we could put it off a week," I feebly offered, although my heart wasn't in it. Not only did I really want to get married, but rescheduling would be a nightmare—the reception, the photos, the honeymoon cruise. Never mind calling everyone invited to tell them it was postponed.

"I will not have people thinking you are pregnant," Maxine snapped, which probably sapped all her energy.

I was stung by her insinuation. "People aren't going to think that if we put it off for a week. We're still getting married in the temple." Although I didn't know if we could schedule it that easily. "We can tell everyone you were sick."

"Oh, I will. After all, it was *your* doing, dear."

I blamed her response on how lousy she must have been feeling.

I also wanted to remind her that she'd left it on the counter for two hours before we got to carving it. Surely it couldn't have been all my fault? And even if it was, why did she ask me to cook the turkey in the first place?

∼

My day could not have been more perfect. The weather was slightly chilly, but the sun was shining and not a cloud in sight (surely that was a sign, right?).

I considered it a miracle, literally an act of God, that we even made it to the temple. Travis and his parents were pale, but present. It was a good thing our wedding was later in the afternoon, because it gave them most of the day to get themselves together.

As I kneeled across the altar in the Salt Lake Temple, holding Travis's hands, I could see the reflection of him and me in the mirrors behind us. Our reflection was endless. Like our marriage would be. Like our love would be. It would be the two of us, for time and all eternity. We were starting our own life together. It felt so perfect it nearly brought me to tears.

We made it.

We made it to the wedding day.

We made it to the temple.

We made it through all the complicated wedding stuff and now we could finally be married.

As we made our grand exit from the temple doors, Travis put his hand on the back of my neck, under my perfectly coiffed hair and whispered, "You're all mine now."

What a strange thing to say.

Pictures were swift, exact and organized. Our photographer told us what to do, we did it and our sure-to-be gorgeous pictures were done in an hour.

The reception, held early evening and left in the care of Maxine, was actually tastefully done. Except we did a reception line, which I thought was outdated. I wanted to go around to each table and visit with the guests. But Maxine insisted, and it was a way to introduce my parents to people they'd never meet again.

It was held in a nice banquet room in the hotel where we had a room booked for the night. There was a harpist playing, flowers, and an incredible buffet. I was surprised to see a buffet because I thought we were having a sit-down meal. I also noticed that the chicken we had discussed was not there, but was salmon instead. The chocolate fountain was missing, and instead was an ice sculpture cornucopia with cut up vegetables inside. I noticed a few other changes like other foods we'd discussed were not there, there wasn't any raspberry filling between cake layers, and the flower arrangements were silk. But it was my wedding day, and there were other things to worry about.

Like the honeymoon.

The dreaded honeymoon—which was looked forward to with fear and trepidation (and with excitement, of course). At least we'd be on a cruise and Maxine would be nowhere near us, so there was no possibility of her knocking on our door at any time during the honeymoon. Thank goodness.

"Wanna go upstairs?" Travis said quietly in my ear as he nuzzled my neck.

Yes and no. We *were* married! We could have sex! But...*sex*! That was uncharted territory that I didn't want to rush through.

"People will notice."

He gave me a sexy smile. "I don't care."

As much as I wanted to (and didn't want to), we could duck out (pun intended) and check into our hotel room five floors up. But it was kind of hard to disappear when we were the guests of honor.

The send-off came too soon and didn't come soon enough. I was able to quickly say goodbye to my parents and Gretchen before we ran out of the hotel as the guests formed a path with sparklers. I blushed as Travis tugged on my hand and we sprinted to the car. We drove around the block and parked back at the hotel and went and faced the unknown.

18

VOMITROCIOUS

I woke up to rocking. Everything was rocking in the tiny little room with the tiny window that was our cabin.

"Oohh," I moaned, lying face down across the neatly made bed. "I feel awful."

A Mexican cruise for a honeymoon sounded so romantic. But the constant rocking of the ship created the constant feeling that I was about to throw up. Why did people say cruises were so fun? This was *not* fun.

I'd never spent much time on water. Lake Mead was not like the ocean. The ocean ebbed and flowed, rocked and rolled, the up and down motion. I had never felt so nauseated in my entire life. I had to cover my mouth and hold my nose to try to keep the vomit down. But, since my mouth and nose were necessary components to breathing, I eventually had to let go and it all came out. The one thing in the world I hated the most was throwing up. The gagging and retching were disgusting.

And this was only the first day of our honeymoon.

Travis sat beside me, rubbing my back. "I'm sorry, Fi."

"I feel awful."

"How about some Dramamine?" he suggested. "It helps with motion sickness."

"I'll try anything."

"Did we bring some?" Travis asked.

I hadn't considered getting sea sick. I had other things to worry about while packing for my honeymoon. I curled up in a ball. "I don't think so," I moaned. "I hate feeling this way."

Travis stood. "I'll get some. The ship has got to sell it. I'm sure you're not the only one who's ever been seasick."

"Yes, please. And please hurry." I was very whiny, but I couldn't help it.

With effort, I laid on my stomach, balled my fists up and stuck them under me so they pressed into my stomach. That helped a little.

Travis gathered his wallet, keys and put on his flip-flops. "I'll be back," he said.

He forgot to kiss me goodbye.

That's okay. I reasoned. *We'll have the rest of our lives to kiss as much as we wanted.* I smiled despite my sick stomach. That was one of the best things about being married. We could kiss as much and for as long as we wanted.

I must've dozed off, because by the time Travis returned with the Dramamine, it was dark outside our little cabin window.

I lifted my head slightly off my pillow, disoriented. "Where have you been?"

"Sorry. I looked around the ship while trying to find someplace to buy your medicine. It's huge! I checked out the different decks and the pools. There's a gym, a day spa and restaurants. I hope we can drag ourselves away from the cabin and explore."

I could see through my blurry eyes that he grinned.

"Because there is some fun stuff to do on board."

My throat constricted. "I'm sorry, Trav. I don't want to be sick," I said. I wanted to cry. This was our honeymoon. I wasn't supposed to be sick.

"Don't worry, babe, there's plenty of time to enjoy ourselves. You need to feel better first." He gave me a bottle of water and two small, round pills. "These should help."

I sat up, which was a mistake—my head swam—but I drank down the pills like a good girl and flopped back on my pillow. I talked with my eyes closed; keeping them open made the rocking worse. "I'll feel better once these kick in."

And they did.

I slept twelve straight hours.

The next day I felt better. We must have sailed to smoother waters.

Then I stood up, which was a mistake.

"I thought I felt better." I whined. Travis was in bed, facing away from me. He sighed. Was he slightly annoyed?

"Fi, you should go see the ship doctor. We won't do anything on our honeymoon if you're sick the whole time."

As if I didn't know that? As if I didn't feel bad about being sick the first thirty-six hours of our honeymoon? As if I didn't have enough pressure worrying about the honeymoon, then the added pressure that there was a possibility of puking every time I opened my mouth? I didn't need Travis to state the obvious. I was well aware of it. I fell back into my pillow, curled up in a ball and started crying.

Travis didn't notice. He laid there, looking out the cabin window for a good five minutes before he rolled over and faced me. He propped himself up on an elbow. "Hey, honey?"

I wouldn't look at him.

He leaned closer, trying to get me to look at him. "Fifi? You okay?"

"No. I am not okay. I can't stop the rocking motion and you're making me feel bad that I'm sick." I sniffled.

He rolled me over on my back so I had to look at him. "Sorry. I'm not trying to." He kissed me on my lips. I would've liked to kiss him more, but I had the whole opening-my-mouth-was-a-chance-for-vomit-to-escape problem.

He smiled reassuringly. He was so beautiful. He was all mine. I was so lucky.

I took more motion sickness medicine, and fell back asleep.

When I woke from my drug-induced haze, it was early afternoon. Travis sat beside me on the bed, propped up on pillows, watching the TV. Actually, he had nodded off. When he dropped the remote on the floor, it woke me up.

He was obviously bored, which added to my burgeoning guilt.

I got up to use the bathroom and ended up puking in the sink. I hated this! Why did I have to get sick on my honeymoon?

The retching woke Travis. I didn't realize I'd left the door a little ajar. I heard him stand up and stretch. He came to the bathroom door and pushed it open a little more.

"Let's take you to the doctor. They've got to be able to help," he said.

Defeated, I agreed.

He waited on the edge of the bed, watching the TV absently, while I pulled on shorts and a t-shirt and brushed my hair out. My reflection in the mirror was pallid. A far cry from the person I had been two days before at my wedding. Who knew things could go downhill so quickly?

I was so weak, Travis supported me walking there. I hadn't eaten much, but it was a catch-22 situation. If I ate, I'd throw it up. But the lack of food made me feel faint.

The doctor's office had a roomful of people. Apparently, I wasn't the only one afflicted with motion sickness. When I saw him, he gave me a wristband and instructions to get some fresh air and get off the boat when it docks. My visit didn't make me feel instantly better physically, but it did emotionally. I was hopeful.

Travis steadied me as we left. We would get some food (I couldn't wait!) as soon as the wristband thing kicked in and I started feeling better. My spirit buoyed—at least my whole honeymoon wasn't going to be spent in bed, sick.

My buoyancy quickly sank, though, as the woman walking through the doorway while we stepped aside, holding the door open for her, threw up all over the floor, including our flip-flops.

"What is wrong with you?" Travis yelled, looking at his vomit-covered feet with disgust.

"I'm sorry, I'm sorry," she apologized, tears running down her face. "I couldn't stop it."

She spoke the truth. Vomit did have a life of its own—coming up whether you wanted it to or not. I should know.

"That's supposed to make it okay that you puked on us?" He was not quelled by her apology.

"Travis, she didn't mean it," I said in an attempt to calm him down. I wasn't happy about getting puked on, either, but she didn't do it on purpose. And the saddest thing was now I'd have to throw away these flip-flops.

"I don't care. You puked on my feet."

By now the receptionist came out to the waiting room to offer us paper towels.

The paper towels didn't placate Travis any more than the apology. "This doesn't fix it."

At that point, I was sick (figuratively) of Travis's attitude, and embarrassed by his rantings. Get over it! I got puked on too!

I called "thank you" to the receptionist as she disappeared in the back with the lady. I wiped my feet as best I could, and said, "C'mon, let's go shower. Maybe we can finally hit a buffet, because I'm starving."

Travis stopped in the hall; his beautiful face clouded by some emotion I couldn't figure out. "You seem more excited about eating than anything else on this trip."

Was he upset that I was hungry? I grabbed his hand. "C'mon, Trav." I was as upbeat as I could be. "I haven't eaten, or felt like eating, in two days. Yes, I'm excited about eating. But I'm more excited about feeling better so we can actually enjoy ourselves and have a good honeymoon."

I kissed him.

Okay, I kissed him some more. Okay, maybe it was a little too much PDA for the hallway of a ship, but I was on my honeymoon, after all.

The wristband was a miracle. Within an hour, I felt better. I even showered. Even Travis seemed happy that we could actually get out of our cabin. We could finally behave like proper cruise-taking, honeymooning people. We could eat way too much at the buffet, dance, get our picture taken and have an overall good time.

But as the saying goes, "All good things must come to an end."

∼

THE NEXT DAY I felt well enough that we finally got off the ship at one of the ports and onto (wonderful) dry land. I'd never been so happy to have my feet on solid ground—the rocking stopped, the motion in my head ceased, and my legs only felt a little jiggly.

"Sightseeing or food?" he asked, gripping my hand.

"Sightseeing." I hoped once I walked around for a bit, I'd get my "land legs" back. I didn't want to immediately eat and then get sick.

Blissfully, we walked around this little port city, holding hands. *I'm holding my husband's hand.* I repeated the word husband several times in my head. Trying it on for size, liking the way it sounded. I couldn't imagine life getting better than this. But it had to, right? I mean we had our whole lives ahead of us—being able to spend it together, having children (unless morning sickness is like motion sickness, then I might have to reconsider), buying a cute house, having a dog, creating a life together. He and I becoming "us", becoming "we", becoming a family.

"Whatcha thinking?" Travis asked.

"How amazing this moment is," I said.

Other than being accosted by street peddlers trying to sell us overpriced memorabilia (thanks, but we were going to make our own memories), we had a very pleasant time in the city. The weather was so beautiful, the water so blue (I liked it from afar, when I was not actually floating on it), everything seemed perfect. Like a honeymoon should be.

After we had eaten something from a street vendor, at Travis's insistence, ("You have to at least try some of the local food, get a taste for the culture"), I started feeling sick again. The wave of nausea in my stomach, breaking out in sweat. I made sure I hadn't lost my precious, beloved wristband that constantly delivered wonderful motion-sickness prevention medicine in a steady stream into my body. But it was there, on my wrist, where it was supposed to be.

I slowed the fast pace Travis had set. "My stomach hurts," I said, as my stomach gurgled. *Where were we going in such a rush?*

"Not again." Travis said, almost pouting.

I could tell Travis was frustrated. So was I.

"Maybe it will pass," I said, hopeful. "Maybe my stomach isn't used to that kind of food." I didn't want to be sick, again. Yuck.

It roiled.

Uh oh!

What if turned into a case of...diarrhea. That would be *bad*. I could think of nothing worse. Or more embarrassing. Could I buy some Pepto Bismol or Imodium AD on the ship? Maybe Travis would never have to know.

Travis wanted to keep sightseeing, buying up little trinkets, all the while the grip of death tightened its hold on my stomach and intestines. It got so bad I worried about getting sick at any time, without notice. I concentrated on my breathing—in through the nose, out through the mouth—trying to relax and not be sick. I worked so hard at concentrating on not getting sick, I had broken out in a small sweat.

Travis noticed my clammy hands. "Are you all right?" His concern was evident in his expression.

"I feel really bad." My small sweat could no longer be considered "glistening". I was full-on sweating. Profusely.

"Do we need to go back to the ship?"

The ship, the land. It was a toss-up. Neither place was associated with feeling well. But the ship had the bed, and the bed was where I wanted to be, so the ship it was. Plus, I really did want to go home eventually.

I made it to bed without anything escaping my body. I curled up in a ball. It felt like a vice grip was squeezing my innards. Travis went off, again, in search of medicine to hopefully take it all away and make me feel better.

But the thick, pretty pink liquid did not fix the problem. And the taste was enough to make me decide I no longer liked that shade of pink. I still threw up—all over the floor and next to my side of the bed. The food we had eaten that afternoon was not enjoyable the second time around.

Travis didn't like that he had to clean up the mess on the floor. Or have to be the one to rinse out the ice container since that was the only available bowl at the time. I heard him muttering to himself in disgust as he left our cabin in search of clean towels, clean wash cloths, and other supplies to clean up the mess. Somehow, he located a cleaning lady who generously offered to come clean. She was young and I'm sure Travis just had to smile and she was willing to do whatever he asked. But at the time I was too sick to worry about whether Travis was flirting to get his way.

All night long, over and over, I threw up, and heaved and heaved some more and eventually dry heaved because there was nothing left in my stomach to heave. It was not a pretty sight. Or smell. But that aspect of the situation was beyond my comprehension because I was in too much pain. And the only thing I could think about was when I could keep water down so I could take my birth control pill. If morning sickness was anything like this, I'd rather never experience it. I felt awful. I don't think I had ever been so sick in my life.

After several hours of heaving, running to the bathroom, curling up in a ball wishing I was dead (figuratively, of course), Travis reached his breaking point.

"I'm sorry, Fi. I need to get out of here for a few minutes. The smell is awful and I can't hear you gag one more time. It's going to make me throw up."

He left me, after kindly opening the balcony door to let some fresh air in, to suffer my sickness alone.

But really, I couldn't blame him, could I? It had to be disgusting watching your wife puking. Hearing someone puke was almost as bad as doing it yourself. And puke was probably one of the most wretched smelling things in life. I couldn't blame him for abandoning me. But in the back of my mind, I couldn't ignore the little part of me that wanted him to stay and take care of me, no matter what I looked like, smelled like, no matter how sick I was.

Wasn't that part of the marital vow? In sickness and in health, for better or for worse. Oh wait, maybe those weren't in our vows.

I was vaguely aware of him returning at some point. It was dark, so I assumed it was evening time.

"Travis, that you?" I mumbled.

"Yeah," he leaned down, like he was going to kiss me, but then stood back up. He wiped my hair from out of my face. "You might have a fever."

"That can't be. I'm so cold," I pulled the blanket up closer to my neck.

Travis sat down on the edge of the bed, but didn't touch me. "Are you still throwing up?"

"No. Not for a while now," I wasn't sure how long it had been since I had thrown up last, but I was pretty sure I had been sleeping for a while now. But at this point, who knew? Everything was a big, pukey blur. "Just cold."

"Have you taken anything?" Travis sounded annoyed. Maybe I dreamed it?

"No. I'm afraid to stand up." Thinking hurt my head.

"Have you had any water to drink?"

No, I hadn't. Drinking water would require me to stand up and get the water. Standing up resulted in me throwing up, so nope, hadn't had any water. "No," I muttered. "Get me some?"

"Sure." He got up off the bed—I could feel the shift in weight—and opened the little fridge in our cabin. "Here you go, Fi." He placed the cold bottle in my hand. I attempted to take a sip, but spilled it down my chin and onto the sheets.

"Oh." I cried out as the water spread on the bed.

"Geez, Fifi. Watch out."

Did I get him wet too? I couldn't tell. I felt so bad. "Sorry," I muttered as I rolled over to the middle of the bed, getting away from the wet spot.

"I'm going to sleep on the chair over here," I vaguely heard him say, as I drifted off into sleep.

I might have heard him say my breath smelled bad, but I wasn't sure. I wasn't really coherent.

I woke up drenched in sweat. My clothes were wet, my hair was wet, and my pillowcase and sheets were wet. I sat up, kicking the covers off of me, pushing them toward the end of the bed. But wait, I was sitting up. I was upright and didn't feel like I was going to throw up. Wow. I felt better. This was good, right? At least we'd have a day, or so, (I couldn't be sure how long I'd been down) to enjoy ourselves, right? And food. I was starving! I was ready to get cleaned up and go attack the buffet. Yum.

I climbed out of bed and looked for Travis. He wasn't sleeping on the chair. Was he on the balcony? I took a quick look around. Nope, no Travis. Where was he? I opened the bathroom door, thinking I would shower and then try to track down Travis when I saw him. My poor, beautiful husband sat on the tile floor, his head on the toilet seat (the ring, not the lid), clutching his stomach, fast asleep.

I touched his shoulder. "Trav? Are you okay?" I shook him trying to wake him up.

He opened his eyes, barely, trying to focus. Without warning, he turned to the bowl and threw up.

Oh no! Not him too! "Oh, honey. I'm so sorry. You're sick?"

Once he flushed, I wet a face cloth with cold water and handed it to him.

He laid back on the floor. "It started at three-thirty a.m."

"Let's get you into bed," I said. I tried to heft him up by putting my arms under him. He didn't budge.

He resisted moving. "No. I don't want more of your germs." He resisted moving.

Really? He'd prefer to lie on a disgusting bathroom floor than sleep beside his sick wife?

But laying on the floor? Yuck. "I'll change the sheets," I offered.

He nodded. "Okay."

After I helped him to the bed and tucked him in, I looked around. He'd need some sort of bucket. I'd have to find someone in housekeeping to get some sheets, and I'd have to shower and go get something to eat. I was starving.

I looked for the ice bucket. I checked the bathroom, the balcony, around the bed, in the closet. It was nowhere to be found. "Where's the ice bucket, Travis?" I looked in the bathroom, on the balcony, around the bed, in the closet. It was nowhere to be found.

"I threw it away. You threw up in it," he said.

He threw it out? Why didn't he rinse it and have it handy in case I needed it? I shook my head, amazed at his impracticality.

I sat on the edge of the bed. What to do first?

I was stinky and sweaty from my fever breaking, but I really needed to get Travis taken care of. I decided to go find housekeeping to get some clean sheets and a new ice bucket, then I'd shower and find something to eat. I was starving.

Feeling very self-conscious of my body odor, my bed head, and my wrinkled clothes that I had picked up off the floor and thrown on, I went in search of housekeeping.

When I returned—armed with clean sheets and a bucket—the smell of vomit greeted me. Travis had thrown up all over the side of the bed. I sighed. I didn't have much energy, having barely recovered, but this had to be dealt with. I got some towels from the bathroom to wipe up the mess on the floor and bed. Then I covered my pillow so Travis could sleep on the "cleaner" side of the bed until I could get the bed changed.

I went back to housekeeping, leaving Travis sleeping soundly. When I asked for some sort of Lysol or cleaning chemicals, the nice woman offered to come and clean it for me. Okay. Better her than me. She told me she was not allowed to give out cleaning chemicals for liability reasons. Who was I to argue with that? If she wanted to clean up the mess, I wasn't going to stop her. Be my guest.

She was really nice. I felt bad that she had to be down on her hands and knees scrubbing Travis's mess out of the carpet. She reassured me that it happened all the time, and it wasn't a big deal. When I told her we were on our honeymoon, she empathized with me about our plight.

It was while I was coaxing Travis out of the bed and onto the couch that things went from bad to worse.

"Let's move you to the couch," I whispered.

Travis startled. "What's she doing here?"

I tried to quiet him. "Shh," I said. "She's changing the sheets." I helped him get settled on the couch.

"Tell her to leave. Get her out. I don't want her here. I'm sick."

I put my hand on his hot arm. "Relax. Once she finishes, she'll leave. She's almost done."

What was the big deal? He shouldn't be embarrassed. She understood he was sick and worked quickly.

"No. She needs to leave right now."

"Travis—"

"Now! You can finish making the bed."

I hadn't ever seen Travis like this. He was completely unreasonable. *He must feel really bad.* I hoped he didn't get sick too often. I didn't like the ugly side it brought out in him.

"Travis, really," I said as I attempted to reason with him.

"Now I said!" he roared.

I had never seen Travis like this.

The lady straightened and held up her hand. "It's okay. I go."

I followed her into the hall. "Sorry. He's not usually like that."

"It's okay, ma'am." She smiled consolingly, and started to leave.

I held up a finger. "No, no, wait." I went into the cabin, dug out Travis's wallet and took out a twenty. "Thank you," I said, handing her the money. "That was really nice of you."

"Good luck," she said, then left.

I went in, shut and locked the door, then rested against it. I'd never seen Travis like this. Being sick did *not* bring out the charming side of Travis. I hoped his bout only lasted twenty-four hours. I preferred the non-sick Travis over the sick Travis.

It was not a pretty eighteen hours. Travis threw up over and over again. Every time he heaved, I gagged too. But I stayed with him, wiping his face with wet washcloths, holding the ice bucket for him, changing the sheets again. It was really gross, but my poor husband was so sick. It wasn't until he was finally able to sleep for one hour straight that I realized I hadn't eaten anything yet and was ready to pass out from lack of food.

I worried about leaving him. Would he be okay if I was gone for a little bit? I didn't want to wake him up too much, since he was finally able to sleep for a somewhat extended period of time. "Hey Travis?" I wiped his hair off his forehead and kissed it. "Trav?"

"Huh?"

"I'm going to get something to eat. I'll be back soon." I kissed him again on the forehead. My poor honey.

"Hurry," he mumbled.

"Okay," I said. I ignored my appearance as I passed the mirror. I'd been so busy taking care of Travis, I still hadn't showered. I was so hungry I didn't want to take the time to shower. Two weeks ago, I would've died if anyone saw me looking like this. Today, I couldn't have cared less. It had been too rough the last couple of days to worry about appearances. Besides, I was a married woman. Who was I trying to impress?

I went crazy at the buffet—I couldn't help it—I was starving! I probably should've been embarrassed, but I didn't care. There were cinnamon rolls, blueberry muffins, potato salad, pasta salad, roast beef, mashed potatoes, green beans, rolls, chocolate satin pie. The food was endless, and I went back three times without considering I might throw up again. This time from too much food. I brought Travis some saltines, and plain, white rice in case he woke up and was hungry, which was a boring shame with all the yummy food available.

∽

Driving home from California was a bit of a blur. Travis was still sleeping a lot, weak, and mostly out of it. We stopped in Vegas for our open house, which was as good as it could be, considering Travis was not feeling his best. I really just wanted to be back in our new apartment in Provo and start our new life together.

19

WELCOME TO ADULTING

We returned from our not-so-fabulous honeymoon to an empty apartment. There was no furniture, wedding gifts or anything, except for the few boxes we'd hastily packed up and dumped off the day before we got married. It was so barren, old and ugly, it depressed me.

"Huh," Travis said, looking around. "I thought my mom was going to drop off the wedding gifts."

How? "When we weren't home?"

He shrugged. "I gave her a key."

He gave her a key?! "Why?" I asked.

His eyes slid over to me, but his head didn't move. "So she could bring the wedding gifts." He said it slowly, and his tone made it sound like the reason was obvious.

"Is she going to give it back?" I asked. The last thing I wanted was his mother dropping in unannounced.

"Why wouldn't she?"

I shrugged. "Just making sure." I could think of many reasons why she'd keep it. The main one being she liked to be *involved* in her son's life.

It was still early enough that we could drive to his parent's house to get the gifts, but we were exhausted. We'd been in the car for over twelve hours (thanks to traffic in California and a car accident in the Gorge between Mesquite and St. George).

And, having been sick the last week, I didn't have any energy. I'd forgotten there wasn't a bed for us to come home to.

"What should we do?" I asked. "I can't get in the car again tonight...I just can't."

Travis sighed and ran his hand through his hair. "I'm with you on that one, babe. Let's get a hotel and figure things out tomorrow," he said.

"Can we afford that?" I asked.

"Yeah. We've got all that wedding gift money."

True. And sleeping at a hotel was much, much more appealing than sleeping on the floor. "Okay," I agreed.

∼

THE NEXT DAY we went furniture shopping.

We needed everything: mattress, box spring, a bed frame, a dresser, a couch, a TV, a kitchen table.

And off we went, exploring other furniture stores that were a little less "practical."

First stop was Pottery Barn. I loved everything I saw: the style of the furniture, the feel of the fabric, even the scent of *whatever* that hung in the air. This was what I wanted our old, ugly apartment to turn into. A page out of the Pottery Barn catalog.

The only drawback was the six to eight weeks for delivery. Still, it was tempting. Because their accessories were more affordable for our budget, we picked up a few things. Our compromise was to keep looking for furniture, but I could accessorize with Pottery Barn stuff.

The paper bag with handles carrying two chunky, wooden candlestick holders and a whitewashed vase swung from my left hand. I felt better about our apartment already. My right hand held onto Travis. It was nice having a rich husband. Oh, wait. Since we were married, I guess that made me rich too.

We wandered around a larger furniture store, falling in love with all the beautifully staged furniture as the gentle music lulled us into tranquility. We added more items to our "must-have" list.

After hours of sitting on beds, laying on beds, bouncing on beds, comparing features, we bought a mattress. It was our first major "grown-up" purchase as a married couple and it was over a thousand dollars.

Travis stopped in front of a four-poster bed. "What do you think?"

"It's nice," I said.

"Should we get it?"

I clutched the full-sized, yellow piece of paper that was our receipt. "Travis, we can't buy everything." I swallowed down the panic of the moment. "Maybe we should skip the bed frame and stick to the mattress set. It can be on the floor until we buy the bed frame."

"But if this is the bed frame you like, I want you to be able to get it."

We paused to admire it a little more.

Sitting on the edge of the beautifully made bed, complete with linens, a quilt, a plush velvet throw and piles of throw pillows, made it harder to resist Travis's line of reasoning.

But I didn't *love* it. "I liked the Pottery Barn one better. Let's save up for that. Or, we can buy the bed frame and wait on the kitchen table."

Travis almost sounded put out. "What will we eat on, Fi? The floor?" Travis sounded put out.

Picnicking came to mind, and it had a romantic quality to it. We did get a picnic basket as a wedding gift. "I don't know, we could get trays."

"That's really classy, honey. Should we buy two more for when my parents come to visit? We could eat dinner on the trays while we all sit on our mattress on the floor."

I silently walked away, wounded. He caught up to me quickly. "I'm sorry."

I said nothing.

He continued. "We can't do without the necessities. We need a kitchen table. I *want* you to have a kitchen table. I don't want you to do without."

"Let's think about it," I said, as a peace offering. But the furniture shopping didn't get any easier.

"Look at that," Travis said, as a leather sectional caught his eye. It was dark brown, with a reclining chair on each end. It was big, bulky and masculine.

"There's no way that's fitting in our apartment."

He pointed. "How about that sofa and loveseat over there?"

I followed him as he walked toward it.

He stopped at a black leather sofa and loveseat.

What's with all the leather? I hated it before I even looked at the price tag, which was almost two thousand dollars. "This is really expensive. Maybe find something that isn't leather?" I suggested.

"Leather will last longer," Travis said.

"But it's ugly," I said. I pictured light and airy: coastal blues for furniture and whites for curtains and accents. Not this man cave stuff.

"It's not ugly, Fi. It's classy."

"And expensive," I emphasized again. "Maybe we could get one. Like, just the love seat." It was cheaper than the sofa.

"Where will people sit when they come over, Fifi? The floor?"

Who were all these people he planned to entertain?

"I can't picture my parents sitting on the floor," he said.

He had a point. But as I did the mental math, adding up the price tags, the total screamed "too much."

But then we found a sofa I fell in love with, and my resolve wavered a little. Okay, a lot.

It was microfiber, and blue like the waters we should have seen on our Mexican cruise, but were too busy puking to do so.

"Let's forget a love seat and get this," I suggested. "It's big enough that if your parents, or anyone else, comes over we can all sit comfortably."

"You don't want the pair?" Travis questioned.

Of course, I wanted the pair, but knew better. "Hon, our apartment isn't that big, and neither is our budget. Let's get the mattresses and the couch. Everything else we wait on."

"We won't always live in our small apartment. My mother said to make sure we're comfortable. So, I say bed frame, mattresses, couch and an armchair. We don't all want to be jammed on the couch if we have company."

I was about to protest, when Travis added, "And we need to look at the flat screens. I'm not living without a TV."

I didn't want to live without a TV, either. We made our way to electronics, arguing about the size of TV we *needed*. In the end, we left without being proud owners of any furniture.

We the bought the furniture and the TV too. I gulped as I watched Travis hand over the credit card and thought about the debt we'd just acquired.

My dad's practicality kicked in and I started freaking out. I hadn't ever bought "big ticket" items and they were expensive!

We tried IKEA, on the suggestion of Maxine.

I sat down on one of the slip-covered love seats. It wasn't as beautiful as the blue couch, but it wasn't bad and the price was right.

Not only did we buy the couch, but an armchair, a TV cabinet, a kitchen table and chairs and a bed frame and a couple of plants. Individually, the prices were affordable, but everything we bought added up to big bucks. I questioned if we could afford it, but Travis said we could, so we swiped the card.

And we had to pay for delivery because there was no way we could fit it in the BMW.

I left the store conflicted. I was so excited to furnish our apartment, but I also had a pit in my stomach. I felt...*uneasy*. I *liked* to shop. I wasn't used to being the voice of reason. I felt like the parent, the *adult*, telling Travis "no".

∼

BOYD AND MAXINE came down to visit us that weekend, bringing with them the wedding gifts.

Maxine took in our small apartment. "What have you guys been doing? Everything is still in boxes."

It was, but until our furniture was delivered later that day, there wasn't much we could do. So, we'd been hanging out at the hotel. It was like the honeymoon we hadn't had.

"Now you'll have plenty of things to do," Boyd said, pointing to the boxes by his feet.

"I had to get these to you kids. They were starting to interfere with my Feng Shui. Too much clutter," Maxine announced. "How you're going to make it all fit is beyond me, but that's your job."

"You can set those over there," I said, and pointed to the far corner.

She set the bags down inside of the doorway. "I decluttered my kitchen and brought you some things I thought you could use. Utensils, Tupperware and some old pots and pans."

That was nice. I was surprised by her thoughtfulness. I peered inside the bag and spied some well-worn takeout food containers. They probably should've been tossed instead of gifted. There was also a Teflon saucepan with a scratched-up bottom. I forced a smile. "Thanks."

Maxine plopped into the computer chair in the kitchen. "I can't carry another thing," she said, sounding breathless. "There's more in the car for you to grab."

Travis, Boyd and I emptied their car while Maxine relaxed.

The gifts filled up the living room and I couldn't wait to open them and find homes for all of them. I immediately sat on the floor to open the gifts. Travis helped but in a passive way, saying the appropriate "ooh's" and "aah's", but was really more interested in watching the football game on TV.

I looked around, searching for one item in particular. "Where's the vacuum? Our registry said it had been bought."

Maxine put her hand to her chest, her nails now a deep, glossy purple. "About that. We had a little emergency while you were gone."

"What kind of emergency?" I asked.

"Our vacuum abandoned us."

I looked at Travis for some help. Did he know what Maxine was talking about? He was busy with his phone.

"Like ran away?" I asked. Vacuum cleaners didn't abandon people.

Boyd chuckled, but stopped immediately when Maxine threw him a look.

"Like died on us. Just quit in a cloud of dust." She wiggled her fingers in the air. "Right before friends were arriving. So, I used yours. I figured you wouldn't mind, given the nature of the emergency."

An emergency was when someone was breaking into your house, or even when everyone had food poisoning on Thanksgiving. It didn't apply to vacuuming.

"But..." I started then stalled. I had so many questions. Was she going to keep it? Give it back? Expect us to bring it every visit? Were there other gifts she'd taken?

She swept her hand to the side. "Don't worry, I'll replace it."

"With a new one?" I blurted out. She wouldn't give us an old one or a used one. Would she?

"Fifi, of course it'll be new," she ~~cackled~~, I mean, laughed. "You worry too much."

I wanted to ask when we'd get it, but felt like the subject had been closed.

"Now that we have that resolved, there's something else we'd like to discuss," Maxine said.

That didn't sound good.

"After much consideration," Boyd started, resting his hand on Maxine's shoulder, "we've decided it's time to take the BMW back."

Take it back? Wasn't it Travis's?

"What?" Travis burst out. "Why?"

It wasn't *Travis's car?!*

"We're trying to scale back our material possessions," Maxine said.

Really?

"Think of it as a wedding gift. We are giving you financial independence," Boyd said.

My parents gave us a red KitchenAid mixer. I liked that kind of gift better.

"That's not a gift!" Travis blurted out.

It was a cruel inconvenience.

Maxine looked directly at us. "Oh, but it is. No one helped us when we were first married and we figured it out. And we have complete confidence that you will too."

Not only did they take away the car, but told us they would no longer be paying for his college education. Or supporting him in any way now that he was married. When they left, they took the car with them.

"That's not your car?" I asked as soon as they left.

His head dropped. "No. It's my mom's old car. They let me use it."

He never mentioned that.

"A little forewarning would've been nice," I said, angry. What a horrible thing to do to us. Okay, I understood we had to be responsible adults some time. Getting married seemed like a natural and obvious point in one's life to cut the apron strings and go out and make our own way in life. But they could've handled it differently. Say, a little sit down while we were engaged to make sure we understood what we were getting into with the financial aspect of married life.

It's like they put a pin in our balloon.

Travis was silent for a few moments and then unclenched his fists. "We can do it," he announced. "We can stand on our own two feet."

We literally would, since we now had to walk everywhere.

One thing my mother taught me was how to pull myself up by the bootstraps. Okay. We were on our own, it was sink or swim and we were going to swim. We were going to stay afloat on the sea of financial responsibilities.

20

FINALS

*T*wo weeks into married life and Travis made an announcement. "I've decided to change my major."

His proclamation came one morning while lingering in bed. We both had classes to get to, but hanging out at home was so much more appealing in our newlywed bliss.

Schoolwork in general had become a struggle. It was hard to concentrate. It was so boring, especially since we had hours and hours at our disposal to spend together. The last thing I wanted to do was study. I craved romantic time together—candlelit dinners and intimate conversations.

Isn't that what married couples did?

But with the end of the semester fast approaching came papers, projects, deadlines and finals. It really put a damper on our honeymoon phase.

"Oh, yeah?" I propped myself up on one elbow. "To what?" I thought he'd joke and say something funny like love, or you, or some other cheesy, but romantic, thing. Like a doctor of love.

"Law."

Where did that come from? "Like lawyer law?" I needed to clarify.

"Yeah."

I propped myself up on one elbow. "Like goodbye Dr. Duckk dreams, and hello Travis Duckk, Attorney at Law?" I blinked back my surprise, instead of scowling in confusion. I thought medicine was his *passion*.

He rested his arm behind his head, which flexed his muscle. "Yeah, like my dad."

"What about your credits? Isn't it going to be like starting all over again changing your major in the middle of your junior year?" Travis didn't have a whole lot of credits toward his major—or former major now—but it was at least a semester's worth, maybe two. "Will any credits transfer to your new major?"

"No, but, it's okay. It's not that much more schooling anyway." Then he shrugged, as if he hadn't just added two extra years of schooling to our lives. Just. Like. That.

"Huh." I wasn't quite sure how it'd all equal out. I waited for him to explain further, but he didn't.

"I've already changed my class schedule for next semester. It didn't work with my job, so I quit."

I sat up, alarmed. "You quit?"

He stroked my forearm. "Yeah, but it's not a big deal. I'll find something with more flexible hours."

I gulped down the panic rising in my throat. "Are you sure?" I'd been casually looking for a job, but had only found a temp telemarketing job that would've hired anyone with a pulse. It was located on Center Street. When coworkers whispered it was like the portal to Hell, they weren't joking. It was literally the Worst. Job. Ever. I had so many people hang up on me. But it was only temporary until I found something better.

"Yes. No worries. The good news is I've already switched out any pre-med classes for pre-law. I'm ready to jump in with both feet."

I voiced my thoughts. "You didn't tell me you were thinking about switching."

He sat up. "Do I need your approval?" His voice took on an accusatory tone.

"That's not what I meant, Trav. I'm just surprised. I mean, this is the first I've heard of this. I thought medicine was your passion." I wasn't trying to argue; I was genuinely surprised.

"Well, passions can change. If I want to be happy with what I'm doing the rest of my life, I want to make sure it's something I'm passionate about. With law, I'd be dealing more with concrete facts instead of listening to people whine and complain all day about their aches and pains. Law would be more intriguing, more challenging, more...."

More years of school I'd have to support him. It was reality, not a complaint. His decision added another year of living in Provo, putting off having a family, putting off my education (whatever that may be, whenever I discovered *my* passion). I didn't want to share my objections because they sounded selfish. But we were married and it felt like a decision we should've made together. Or at least have a conversation about first.

"What kind of law?"

He yawned. "I don't know. I haven't figured it all out yet. But definitely law."

It took a few minutes to wrap my head around this sudden life-plan change.

"I guess your grades in your med classes aren't going to be that important then," I said. Maybe we wouldn't have to spend so much time studying.

"No, they're not." He smiled.

We went out to breakfast instead of going to classes that morning.

∼

ONCE THE SEMESTER WAS OVER, we turned our attention to something more exciting: Christmas!

I loved Christmas! Christmas was my favorite holiday. I loved everything about Christmas. I loved remembering the birth of the Savior and what that means to me. I loved the spirit of the season, how everyone is so kind and thoughtful. I loved the lights and the decorations and the Christmas songs. I loved the gifts. I loved giving gifts, I loved getting gifts, I loved the whole concept of gift giving.

It was the day after finals and we were going Christmas shopping. I waited in the living room while Travis finished getting dressed after his shower.

Our doorbell chimed and I found an Amazon package greeting me. I ripped it open before Travis made it out of the bedroom. It was a red KitchenAid blender from my mom for Christmas. It matched the red KitchenAid mixer she had bought us as a wedding gift.

Travis looked over the scene. "Why are you opening your gift? I thought we were going to bring our gifts up to my parents' house."

"Aren't we going to do Christmas morning here and then go to your parents'?" I couldn't imagine dragging all our gifts up to Salt Lake on the bus for the sake of opening gifts on Christmas morning.

"But my mom plans on us being there Christmas morning, Fi. It's tradition."

I didn't want that to be our only tradition.

"We see your parents every weekend." Did we have to spend every holiday with them too?

"You don't complain about doing your laundry there for free when we visit them, *every weekend.*"

"This is different. This is a holiday," I said. "Or we could go to Vegas. The weather will be great. I'd love a break from the cold and snow.

"You'll see your parents when your brother graduates. That's a special occasion."

"But that's April." I wanted to add a pout, but was trying to be mature.

"There's long weekends," he said.

Had he forgotten how stingy BYU was about giving days off? Yes, we got the occasional long weekend, and sometimes a day for spring break, but that was it for winter semester.

He continued. "And we can go visit in the summer, after spring term is done."

Had Travis been to Vegas in the summer? With temperatures

soaring upwards of 110-115 degrees, Vegas was *not* the place to visit in the summer. Winter, however, was, on average, a nice daytime temperature of 60 degrees. I was sure it'd be all sunshine and short sleeves.

I finally caved and agreed to spend our first Christmas together at the Duckk's. Once we got through that, we could finally go shopping. I had to decide on what to get Travis for Christmas. Shopping was a little less fun knowing we were going to the Duckks'. But we did buy a small pre-lit Christmas tree and some ornaments. Even with all the shopping, I didn't come up with much to buy Travis.

What could I get for the man who has everything? I finally settled on a photo book of our journey of love. Who didn't love a book of memories? Our professional wedding pictures hadn't come back yet, so I used snapshots from our phones, a few Polaroids, and others people had taken and tagged with our #travandfifi hashtag. I also ordered his mother one, leaving out the more intimate comments.

∽

Later that afternoon, when I was walking back from getting the mail, I noticed the door to the neighbor's apartment open. I knocked quietly on the door, planning on introducing myself.

"Hi," I said when a girl appeared. She had long brown, wavy hair, and was a few inches shorter than me. "I'm Sophia Duckk. We live next door."

"I'm Megan," she said, "and my husband Jack is around somewhere." She leaned in closer and said quietly, "You got a bird name too?"

"What do you mean?"

"Peacock. That's my married name." She rolled her eyes. "I'd take a generic name any day. Smith, Jones, Johnson. Anything."

I burst out laughing and knew we'd be fast friends. "Don't tell my husband, but I hate my new name," I whispered.

"Do you think the manager made us neighbors as a joke?" She

said in a low voice. "Because we have bird names. It couldn't be a coincidence, could it?"

Ooh. She liked conspiracy theories like me. "You're probably right. The manager has a sick sense of humor. Fowl, in fact."

We laughed until we cried. Maybe I wouldn't miss Gretchen so much, who was now at home until she left on her mission in January.

"But get this, it gets worse. My husband's first name is Jacques. Jacques Peacock. It rhymes."

"Why would a mother do that to her child?"

"She's French. Maybe she didn't get that it would rhyme?"

"Does he go by Jacques?" I asked.

"No, thankfully not. He goes by Jack. But it still rhymes."

"That is unfortunate." I pointed to my apartment. "Want to come in and have a Diet Coke? Or whatever you drink."

"Diet Coke," she said, smiling. "Music to my ears."

With that, we were friends.

21

THE MOST WONDERFUL TIME OF THE YEAR

Megan and I were in my apartment, enjoying a Diet Coke when there was a knock on the door. *Amazon? USPS? UPS?* I wasn't expecting any visitors or packages.

I opened the door to a girl I had seen in passing. She held a plate of brownies covered by Saran Wrap. "Sophia?"

"Yes," I said.

She reminded me a little of Gretchen—petite with shoulder-length brown hair. "I'm Nicole. I'm your ministering...person."

"Hi. Want to come in? Megan and I are visiting." It only made sense to invite her. That's what ministering people did—check on members in the ward.

"Thank you, but no. I just wanted to drop these off. I put my number on the note. If you ever need me to do anything for you, let me know."

I took the offered plate. "Thank you. Are you sure you don't want to come in?"

She shook her head. "No. I've got to hurry to class. But I wanted to meet you."

"Okay," I said and held the plate up. "Thanks for the treats."

As soon as I shut the door, Megan and I grabbed a brownie.

"These are really good," Megan said between bites.

"Mmm hmm," I agreed.

My phone vibrated and lit up. Maxine's number appeared on my screen. I swallowed hard and coughed.

"Oh crap! It's my mother-in-law."

"Is that good or bad?"

"Bad. Where's Nicole when I need help?" I joked.

Megan spewed bits of brownie out of her mouth as she laughed.

I considered my options: let it ring and eventually it'd go to voicemail, or answer it and deal with her. I couldn't decline it—she'd know, and the other options weren't great.

Megan went to the kitchen and grabbed a paper towel. "Send it to voicemail," she suggested quickly.

"Then she'll know I declined her." I'd better just answer it. "Hello?" I said, trying hard to sound upbeat.

"Hello-oh! We need to make plans for Christmas," Maxine crooned.

"Travis and I haven't figured it out yet. We'll probably head up sometime in the afternoon on Christmas Day. I haven't checked the bus schedule yet." I added the last part to remind her how inconvenient the bus was. In fact, I hated it.

I could hear Maxine "pfff". "Oh no, that won't do. We always eat breakfast together. Then we open gifts and eat Christmas dinner around two. I think it's best you come for Christmas Eve."

I internally groaned. "That sounds like an all-day event."

"It's tradition," she clarified.

I cleared my throat, my pulse quickening. "Travis and I are a family now. We want to start our own traditions."

"How does Travis feel about that?" she asked.

I could tell by her tone I'd better tread lightly. In fact, forget the treading lightly. I'd better retreat quickly or it might be the grounds for familial World War III.

I caved. It was moot to ask Travis. He wanted to go to his parents. "I guess we could come."

Maxine was quick to hand out an assignment. "Would you bring deviled eggs?"

I was surprised she asked me to bring anything after what happened at Thanksgiving and how she carried on about it. "Wouldn't it be better if I made them at your house?"

"Oh, I'm talking about the Christmas Eve dinner party."

"Christmas Eve party?" I repeated.

"Yes. It's tradition."

"What time are you expecting us to get there?" I thought eight o'clock was suitable.

"Early enough to help me prepare. You are a part of the family now."

I hung up and sighed. "And just like that, we're roped into Christmas Eve *and* Christmas Day at the Duckk's."

"I'm sorry," Megan said. "Sounds like you need another Diet Coke."

I needed a little bit more than that. I needed a spine.

~

THE AFTERNOON HAD BEEN SPENT PREPARING trays of food, and hanging last minute decorations and twinkle lights. There were a pair of cleaning ladies furiously cleaning the large house.

I entered Maxine's huge kitchen carefully holding my deviled eggs. I had arranged them on my nicest plate, attempting to make them look aesthetically pleasing, but the bus ride had been a little bumpy. By the time we were at the house, the eggs were on their sides playing possum. I carefully flipped them back over on their backs so the filling wouldn't fall out. I'd piped the filling with a frosting tip to make my eggs look fancy. Then I sprinkled the tops with a little paprika (for color) and pepper (for taste), and *voila!* A deviled egg even Martha Stewart would've been proud of.

I was proud of them, but quite sick of them. I tried five different recipes before I decided on one. I still felt the need to impress my in-laws.

"Here's the deviled eggs," I announced when there was a pause in the conversation. I set the plate on the granite countertop.

She turned to greet me. "Oh, yes, the eggs." Maxine sounded dismayed as she eyed them. Was she hoping I would forget to bring them? "Did you make those?"

"Yes," I said, then realized what she meant. I should've lied and told her they were store-bought.

Heck, I had even called her for her recipe, which she wouldn't give me, nor would she come right out and say she didn't want to give me her recipe. What was the big deal? There were only so many ways to take egg yolks, mix them with mustard and mayonnaise and add some relish. So really, what was the big deal over the stupid eggs?

"You made them?" Maxine confirmed.

"You asked me to." I nodded and watched as she glanced at the eggs. Was she deciding whether or not to brave eating them? If she didn't trust my cooking, why did she ask me to bring food? "The bus ride was hard on them," I added on a whim.

She recovered quickly and went into hostess mode. "Do you need a serving platter for those?"

I smiled widely, trying to hide the growing frustration. "That would be great." Was she genuinely offering me her platter for serving simplicity, or was she pointing out my lack of couth by not using a deviled egg plate?

"If I had known you were going to need it, I would've gotten it down earlier," Maxine said. "It's very difficult to get out of the cupboard." She pulled a chair up to the counter.

Was she actually going to climb up on her fancy chair, in her "Christmas outfit", and stand on the countertop to get the silly plate down? Unlike my mom, Maxine didn't wear hideous Christmas sweaters. She was dressed to the T, black pants, chiffon shirt with crystal buttons. Her heels looked like Italian leather. She had her familiar brown linen apron on.

"Oh no, Maxine, please. That's too much effort to get a plate. It's really not necessary."

"Deviled eggs must be served on the proper plate. You must. Otherwise, they slide all over the plate and look terrible."

Like I already discovered on the ride up. "At least have Travis get it. I'm afraid you'll fall and break your hip climbing up there."

"Exactly how old do you think I am?"

I assumed, for my sake, that was a rhetorical question.

Travis was called and easily retrieved the platter. As he did, his t-shirt untucked, exposing his taut stomach.

It was a nice view.

Travis handed me the plate and went back to whatever it was he was doing and I finished helping Maxine get ready.

With thirty minutes before the party started, I wiped my hands on a towel and looked around. "Are we good?"

Maxine's eyes swept over the spread in front of her. "I think so. Thank you for your help."

"You're welcome," I said, sincerely. We had been busy enough that there hadn't been much conversation.

She walked to an area of the kitchen that had a desk nook and picked up a flat, wrapped gift. "I wanted to give this to you."

It felt like a picture frame. Had she framed one of our wedding pictures? I hadn't ordered any larger prints yet, so I really hoped Maxine had.

I gripped the gift in one hand and hugged her with the other. "Thank you."

When I went to the bedroom to change, I ripped open the gift, anxious to see what it was. It wasn't a wedding picture at all, but a framed poem about a girl picking up washed-up starfish. The whole point was the girl couldn't rescue every single one, but with every act of kindness, she made a difference to the starfish.

Was this Maxine's olive leaf? Was this her way of saying that small acts of kindness on my part made a difference to her?

Was she putting our past behind her?

∽

CHRISTMAS EVE DINNER at the Duckk home was a large, festive occasion. Extended family was invited (some had to have been Travis's cousins because they looked about our age, or a little bit older), the dining room table was decked out with Maxine's finest china, and dinner itself was touted as a feast. I secretly wondered if they were going to serve some sort of duck dish—you know, Duck a l'Orange, Peking duck, roast duck—any sort of duck. Because that would've been hilarious. To me, with the last name we had, the only way I could deal with it would be to have some fun with it. But I doubted Maxine, or any of the rest of the Duckk flock, would appreciate my sense of humor.

I felt like I was the unspoken guest of honor since Travis and I had just gotten married. This was their chance to show me off. Maybe things would finally click with his parents and things would go smoothly. I readjusted my attitude from not wanting to be there to making the best of the situation. If I kept a positive mental attitude, I might actually enjoy myself.

After the whole family was seated around the table and the food had been blessed, I noticed the eggs weren't on the table. Or on the sideboard. Or anywhere.

I quickly went to the kitchen and discovered the eggs were tucked in the back of the bottom shelf of the fridge. I took them out and made a point to walk around the table offering them to the guests.

I paused when I got to Maxine, wondering if she'd accept one or pass. She sniffed, then gingerly reached out and took one and set it on the edge of her dish, not touching any of the other food.

Maxine spoke. "Let's hope we don't have a repeat of Thanksgiving." She looked directly at me.

Maybe her gift wasn't meant to bury the hatchet. Otherwise, she wouldn't be throwing me under the bus like that.

"What do you mean?" asked the woman beside her whose name and relation I couldn't recall.

"Fifi cooked our Thanksgiving turkey, or *didn't* cook our turkey, for that matter." She let out a shrill laugh. "We all got food poisoning. It was the most awful thing to have happen right before the wedding."

"Oh, no. I hadn't heard about that." Aunt Rebecca (?) said.

Maxine's hand went to her chest. "It was horrible. I thought I was dying. And right before the wedding. I was so sick I thought we'd have to postpone the wedding."

As if the wedding was *her* special day.

My cheeks burned. "I didn't mean to do it," I said. I turned to Travis, who sat beside me, expecting him to stand up for me, or at least put a stop to Maxine's demoralizing story sharing.

He was busy helping himself to mashed potatoes.

Maxine waved away my defense. "Oh, Fifi. You *know* we love you."

"Not everyone can cook like you," Boyd said to his wife. At first, I thought he was trying to tone down Maxine's insult, but really wasn't.

Travis still said nothing—he was stuffing his mouth with my deviled eggs.

"Good job, Fi." He nodded approvingly, reaching for another egg.

"Not as good as your mother's eggs, though?" Maxine challenged.

Travis made an absurd face. "Of course not."

What was with all this competition? I wasn't trying to outdo his mother and her precious, stupid, deviled eggs.

"Well, don't eat too many. Just in case . . ." Maxine gave him a warning look.

I remained silent the rest of the meal, trying to tamp down the growing anger. There were enough people around and so many conversations going on, that my silence went undetected.

After almost ten minutes, Travis took notice. "You're not eating much."

"I've lost my appetite."

"That's too bad. Dessert is always really good."

"How can you sit there and eat?" I asked, incredulous.

His eyes darted left to right. "Easy. Why?"

Had he missed my public humiliation? I opened my mouth to speak, but someone asked him a question.

AFTER DINNER AND DESSERT, everyone gathered in the living room to visit. It was a tight squeeze to fit everyone in and chairs were brought from the living room to accommodate more people. Maxine had a basket full of gifts or party favors (I wasn't sure) and she walked around handing them out.

I chose to busy myself in the kitchen, using cleaning up as an excuse to avoid any more socializing. And I could have seconds on the heavenly red velvet cupcakes with the most amazing cream cheese frosting without feeling guilty.

Two girls who looked about my age walked in the kitchen, opened the fridge, and each took a bottle of sparkling water.

"So, you're Travis's wife?" The one with the long, silky brown hair that fell almost to her waist asked.

"Yes. And you are?" Had I met them at the wedding? I had been introduced to so many people, I didn't remember everyone. And I had been preoccupied about the upcoming honeymoon.

"I'm Liz and this is Tara." She pronounced it Tah-ra.

Tara was taller than Liz and had dark blond hair that fell in waves to her shoulders.

"I see he won his prize," Tara said.

I furrowed my brow. "Prize? What do you mean?"

"Travis was always a bit of a dating snob, always too good for us," Liz said.

I was confused. "Aren't you his cousins?"

"Second cousins, once removed."

Once removed, twice removed, who even knew what that removed stuff meant? But no matter how removed, they were still related. "Isn't it only legal in, like, Rhode Island, to marry your cousin?"

Cousin Liz rolled her eyes. "I didn't necessarily want to marry him."

"Just date him," Tara added. She elbowed Liz and then the girls giggled.

"You wanted to date your cousin?" I asked slowly. There had to be some sort of inside joke that I was missing. I couldn't take their words at face value.

"Second cousin once removed," Liz reiterated.

"Still. He's your cousin." Yuck!

They giggled again. "Yeah, but he's hot."

"But he's your cousin," I repeated more slowly.

Tara flipped her hand as if dismissing the subject. "We're kidding."

But they weren't. Even if the state didn't frown on it, wouldn't their families?

The other cousin shrugged. "And he never wanted to be set up with any of our friends."

"Oh." I nodded slowly. Sour grapes?

"We were never good enough to even hang out with him. He always had cute friends too."

Friends would've been okay. But not cousins.

Tara spread her hands open toward me. "But look. He obviously got his trophy wife."

How exactly should I respond to that? It wasn't a compliment—more of a dig. Was I being too sensitive? Overreacting? It was hard *not* to be when your husband's cousins were confessing their little crushes on him. It was weird. And wrong.

Instead of responding, I stuffed a cupcake in my mouth, gave them sort of a half wave and quickly walked away from them, rolling my eyes once I was out of sight. Maybe this family had some skeletons in their closets.

The list of things I'd be asking Travis once I got him alone was growing.

"I'm going to grab one of the things Aunt Maxine is passing out. Sometimes she gives out Bath & Body Works," Tara said, dismissing herself.

"Grab one for me," Cousin Liz said.

There was one full minute of silence until Liz returned with two flat, wrapped packages. They looked vaguely familiar.

Tara handed Liz her gift, then put hers on the counter dismissively. "It's nothing good," she said. "Just some dumb poem about a starfish."

～

I brought up his cousins as we got into bed that evening.

"What's up with your cousins?"

"Which ones?"

"Tara and Liz."

"They're weird. Like stalkerish creepy."

I was relieved he didn't enjoy their little crush on him.

Then I broached what happened at dinner. "And why didn't you defend me?"

Travis looked at me, his expression completely clueless. "Defend you?" He really *had* missed it.

Tears filled my eyes. "At dinner. Your mom announced I poisoned everyone at Thanksgiving."

Travis pulled me close and squeezed me tight. "She's playing with you, honey. You need to realize that. But don't worry, Fi, I still love you even if you did poison us all." He grinned at me, as if that made it all better. If I hadn't been so angry, it probably would've worked.

"That's not funny." I playfully punched him in the arm, which led to more playful banter, as much as was acceptable in my mother-in-law's house. But secretly I wanted the punch to hurt. Kind of like how Maxine's "playful" remark hurt me.

"And the she was freaking out about whether my eggs tasted better than her eggs," I explained.

Travis immediately cut in. "Don't worry about that, Fi. My mom's joking. She likes to know everything is wonderful. If I tell her it is, she leaves me alone. Besides, your eggs *are* better."

"But it made me feel bad."

He looked me straight in the eye, with a penetrating look I couldn't hold. "Do you remember on our first date, Fi, what I said at the restaurant?" He tilted my chin up so I met his gaze.

Of course, I remembered it. I remembered many things about that night, but not all of the conversation. "You said a lot of stuff."

He held my arms so I couldn't turn away. "I said I wanted the night to be perfect. Even if I had gotten food poisoning, it still would've been a great night because I got to spend it with you."

I remembered that and was happy he also remembered what he'd said that night. "It's the same thing, Fi. My mom can say whatever she likes—it doesn't change how I feel about you. You're amazing. You're breathtaking. And I am the luckiest man alive."

How could I stay mad?

22

MERRY CHRISTMAS TO ME

I was a little surly when I woke up the next morning. I still wished we could've spent our first Christmas together alone.

But tradition called...

Breakfast was French toast. And then we opened our stockings, in turn. It was a little bit of a process since the Duckks took one thing out at a time, showed it off, said thank you and pulled out the next thing.

It was the same thing with the gifts. All attention turned to me as I was the first one to open my gifts.

Maxine gave me a really old book, *The Art of Homemaking*.

I held it up for inspection. "Thanks?" What was I supposed to say about a gift like that? I could understand if I liked vintage books, or was worried about "homemaking". Was there a Target gift card hidden inside and this was some weird way of wrapping it?

"By the looks of things, I figured you could use some help." Maxine smiled widely before continuing. "That was the homemaking bible in my day. I had to search several Deseret Industries to find a copy because it's out of print."

By the looks of the cover, it was not only out of print, but out of date.

"Daryl Hoole was the Martha Stewart of our day," Maxine informed me.

"He was?" Why was a man writing a housekeeping book? Was that much of a thing back then?

"*She* was."

"Martha Stewart's a woman, right?" I asked. I didn't know much about Martha Stewart other than I'd used her recipe for deviled eggs.

"Yes. She also has some homemaking books."

I wasn't sure how to respond. Grateful? Excited?

"Thanks?" I said, questioning her motive. I was pretty sure she was suggesting I wasn't up to her homemaker standards. Was I supposed to care about that? Or be excited about a book that smelled like it had been in someone's musty basement for decades?

"You're welcome!" Maxine enthused. "I'm sure it will help with all your homemaking needs."

Or Pinterest would, because this book was going right back to DI.

I set the book beside me. The next gift was a box-set of ChapSticks, all original flavor (bleh! They smelled awful), a plastic caddy filled with cleaning supplies ("they're so expensive," Maxine added), some fuzzy socks, a mug and a Bath & Body Works candle. I even liked the smell.

For Travis, Maxine went overboard.

She got him a one-hundred-dollar gift card for an electronics store.

"Thanks, Mom!" Travis said.

"Make sure you use that for yourself," she told him.

She got him some clothes from Abercrombie and Fitch (fitting for his looks), but the t-shirts were medium, and he wore a large. She seemed a little out of touch for someone so worried about her son's well-being.

She got him a large bottle of original Old Spice aftershave. I had thrown the other one out on the sly because he never used it. When I asked him about it, he said his mom gave it to him, but he hated the scent. And *I* hated the way it smelled. Now we had more. *Great.*

She saved the biggest—and best—gift for last. Although it was for both of us, Travis went ahead and opened it.

It was a vacuum cleaner. And not the one we'd received as a gift.

"To replace the one I took," Maxine said.

It was the cheapest one available and didn't have good reviews, which was why I didn't register for it. I looked at the bright side—I'd return it.

Maxine clasped her hands together and beamed. "This will make life easier."

Roughly translated, that meant me. It was becoming increasingly obvious that cleaning was considered "women's work" in the Duckk family doctrine.

"You'll get that little apartment cleaned up in no time."

Our apartment wasn't that dirty. We barely had any furniture and aside from the dishes, everything else was picked up.

"At least if I was doing it," she added.

She had a cleaning lady! She didn't even clean her own house! I couldn't hold my tongue any longer. "This isn't the same one."

Maxine glowered at me.

Travis sprang into action. He jumped up and hugged his mom. "This is great. We'll definitely use it. It's really nice."

"Try it out," Maxine said, then stood and stepped on the box, crushing it.

Travis assembled it quickly, snapping on hoses as Maxine read the instructions out loud. Once together, it was handed over to me where I got to "put it to the test".

Could I return a vacuum without a box? If not, maybe I could sell it on Facebook Marketplace.

My gift to Maxine and Boyd was a photo book about Travis and me. I had spent more money than I'd intended, but I wanted it to be something they would cherish and display. I wanted it to be really nice.

"Oh, this is nice," Maxine said as she examined the cover, then set it beside her. "What else?"

She didn't even *look* in the book. Was she getting me back for not opening her book? But this was a personalized photo album, not some old musty thing.

Travis had gotten her a *huge* Godiva chocolate gift basket, a Mont Blanc pen, and a spa gift card.

A spa gift card?

I wouldn't mind going to the spa.

I hadn't seen any of these before. I definitely would've noticed the massive gift basket if Travis lugged it all the way here on the bus.

I leaned over and whispered to him as Maxine admired her basket of chocolate (dark, of course) goodies. "Where'd all this come from?"

"I ordered it online and had it sent here. I wrapped it last night," he whispered back. I had gone to bed earlier than him, mostly because I was socialized out.

"Why?"

"What?" he asked, clueless.

"Why did you buy her more stuff?" Stuff we couldn't afford. "I made the book."

"A book is not enough, Fi." He made it sound like it was a preposterous idea, just giving his mother one thing for Christmas. "My mom likes lots of gifts. It's the tradition in our family."

I got a moldy old book and she got a couple hundred dollars-worth of chocolate that we not only *couldn't* afford, but she didn't *care* that we couldn't afford it. I was a little incensed. And my moldy old book made for really good kindling.

23

DOWNHILL

I gripped the vacuum while we rode home on the bus, making sure it didn't roll away. Travis broke the silence. "That's a nice vacuum my mom got us."

Us? Did that mean he'd use it too? He hadn't vacuumed yet since we'd been married.

I shrugged.

"You didn't have to make her feel bad by saying what you did," Travis said.

"But we already have one."

"This one's better."

"Why?" I asked, genuinely curious. We'd gotten a vacuum as a wedding gift from the Target registry. Maxine knew because she watched us open it when they'd brought all our gifts to our apartment. Why would Maxine would buy another vacuum?

"She only buys the best," he said.

"Huh," I said. I registered for the vacuum my mom used. It worked well and she never complained about it.

"You saw that when you tried it."

Vacuuming for ten minutes with a brand-new vacuum didn't prove anything. New things always worked great.

I shrugged. "I guess." It honestly wasn't worth pursuing. It'd just lead to a fight.

I looked at the two shopping bags beside him, full of gifts not from me. "How can I compete with what she got you?"

He put his arm around my shoulder and squeezed it. "It's not what she gets me. It's not a competition. And even if it was, you'd win every time. Being married to you is the best gift of all."

As a belated Christmas gift, Travis got me some of my favorite lip gloss, a Kate Spade purse and a $100 gift card to Target.

I considered using the gift card to buy some knives for target practice.

∼

About two hours after we got home from Salt Lake, Maxine texted Travis.

Maxine: We were able to switch our timeshare weekend to this weekend. Want to join us skiing in Park City?

"We should go," he said. The excitement was evident in his voice.

Ooh! Park City. I'd never been there, but heard it was really cool. But, then, reality set in. "Can we take a bus to Park City?" And why didn't they ask us this morning?

It was the first of many questions. Or, at least, if it wasn't confirmed, could've mentioned it was a possibility? If we had known, I think we would've stayed and just gone with them.

"There must be a bus that goes there. It's a ski resort. Or we could Uber."

How much would that cost?

"Let's do it," Travis said with finality. "It'll be fun."

I'd never been skiing. The thought scared me, but also invigorated me. Not being the most coordinated person, and having grown up in the desert, I'd never tried it. But it looked like fun. To be able to effortlessly glide down the mountain on the pure white powder had a certain appeal.

"And, they're paying," he added, as if that made it a no-brainer.

Was it safe to assume it was really no strings attached? I assumed (if it was safe to do so) that if they owned the timeshare, we wouldn't have to "pay to stay".

"Are you sure there's like, no hidden costs or anything?"

"No," Travis said, and scoffed a little. "They're my parents. They've never charged me to go skiing before."

I had a little niggling thought. "That was before you were married. We can't expect them to pay for our vacations." And they had just taken away the car.

"It's a tradition, Fi. We always go skiing over Christmas. I really don't think they will charge us."

Travis's reassurance did not reassure me. Doubts popped up in my mind as I packed. I wasn't thrilled about spending more time with his parents.

Travis was in charge of the travel arrangements, which he put off until the last minute.

The bus trip would've taken four hours to get there. The train wasn't much better. Travis asked his parents if we could take the bus to their house and carpool with them, but they had already left. We ended up taking an Uber, which was really expensive.

"That's all we're paying for, Fi. My parents will pay for everything else."

I still worried. There had to be something I was missing. Maxine wasn't this altruistic.

No, there weren't any hidden costs, but there was a hidden price to pay. It was privacy. The condo was a one bedroom with a sleeper sofa. Guess what we got? Yup! The sleeper sofa.

"This is weird," I whispered fiercely to Travis.

"Why is it weird?" he asked. "I always sleep on the sofa."

"But we're married." If he thought there was going to be any hanky panky happening on this weekend getaway, he was wrong.

"That's the way it is," Travis said.

Come to find out, they purchased this condo when he left for college, and, I quote, *it made sense to only buy a one bedroom.*

We should've gotten our own place. I checked on my phone for condos, hotels, Airbnbs—anywhere we'd have an actual bedroom—and almost died when I saw the rates. There was no way we could afford anything, except for, like, pitching a tent in the snow.

The couch would be *just* fine.

~

I WOKE up to pots and pans clanging in the kitchen. Maxine was up for the day and cooking away.

I sat up, yawned and stretched.

"Good morning, sleepyhead," Maxine called out.

I looked beside me at Travis, who was still dead to the world.

I scrambled out of bed, clutching my clothes and hurried to the bathroom. Despite wearing flannel pajamas, it still felt weird to be braless around my in-laws.

Once dressed, I joined Maxine in the small, galley kitchen. "Anything I can help with?" I approached the question with a bit of anticipation and dreaded her answer. But it wasn't like she could assign me to cook another turkey, right? Especially since this was breakfast.

"I don't think your forte is in the kitchen, honey. Maybe you could set the table."

She was only scrambling eggs and making pancakes. How hard was that? But I was okay with not being asked to help.

The conversation during breakfast naturally turned to skiing.

"Have you skied before?" Boyd asked me.

"No," I admitted with reluctance. Based on my track record with anything involving coordination and physical activity, like, say, P.E., my educated guess was I would not pick up skiing.

Travis was by my side, encouraging me. "Come, Fi. It'll be fun."

"I took to it like fish to water," Maxine said.

Maybe it would be okay. But who was I kidding?

I'd be like a fish *out* of water.

I let out an uncomfortable laugh. "I'm not athletically inclined."

Maxine huffed. "At least try."

"No, really, it's better if I don't . . ." My attempt at refuting was lame and seemed futile.

Maxine exhaled loudly, shook her head and walked off.

Why was she so bothered? Who cared if I skied or didn't ski? They hadn't purchased me a ski pass that would go to waste. I wasn't interfering with her time to ski. Did it matter if I joined them on the slopes or hung out at the spa? Really?

In the end, they got their way. Of course. It happened all the time with Travis—he always got his way.

I was bundled up, fitted with snow boots, skis, poles, ski goggles, gloves, the whole nine yards. Internally, I was protesting. It seemed a little bit ridiculous to me. I felt ridiculous. I looked ridiculous. The whole situation was ridiculous.

"Shouldn't I take a lesson, or something?" I asked, with genuine concern.

"Do you think you need a lesson?" Travis asked.

Absolutely! "Yes."

"I guess we could check into it," Travis said.

"You'll come with me, right?"

Travis exhaled. "You're kidding me, right?"

"Well, no. I thought..."

"If I have to stand around waiting for you to figure it out, it's less time for me to be on the slopes."

I didn't realize it'd be such a big deal.

I forced a smile. "It's okay. I'll go by myself."

Travis held my hand. "Fi, I really think you'll catch on. It's not that hard."

"You do?"

He nodded. "I do. What if I just teach you?"

My resolve crumbled. "You know how?"

"I'll be beside you the whole way down the mountain."

"Okay," I agreed. I bet he'd be a great ski instructor.

I had a sinking feeling as the ski lift took me higher and higher up the mountain.

Seeing my feet dangling in the air did not put me at ease. "Trav, this seems really high."

He patted my knee. "You'll be fine. It's pretty much a straight shot downhill. Just keep your skis like a slice of pizza."

All I really wanted to do was go to the spa, get a massage and a facial. But no, instead I was out here on the side of a snow-covered mountain, staring down the face of death.

Downhill was an appropriate term. Things began going downhill the moment we got on the ski lift. I just didn't know how bad it was going to be.

"I really should be starting on a bunny hill." This mountain didn't look very "bunny" to me. "Or a beginner's slope or whatever it's called." I looked back behind us. "Or I could get back on the ski lift."

"Really Fi, you'll be fine. It's not that hard to pick up. Keep your skis like I told you, then you start shifting your weight side to side and you'll get it."

It sounded so simple. Maybe it was that easy? Maybe I was mistaken about my natural ability to ski. Living in Las Vegas, there wasn't a whole lot of skiing happening in the winters when it snowed once a decade. But having a positive mental attitude drilled into me my whole life, I thought, maybe I should give it a chance.

Simple? Simple? Who was I kidding? I tried to gracefully ski off the lift onto the landing like the couple ahead of us did and got all tripped up on my skis and ended up stumbling as soon as I stood up off the lift. Travis almost had to drag me out of the way of the chair. Naturally, I was embarrassed. But I also had images of getting my ski caught on the chair of the ski lift and going back down the mountain tangled up in the chair, dangling precariously by my foot all the way down.

I used Travis's arm to steady myself, "I'm really nervous, Trav. I don't think I'm going to live long enough to make it to the bottom of the hill." *Mountain* was more accurate. We were really high up.

Travis smiled at me, put both of his hands on my face and said gently, "Fi, we just got married. I'd never put you in danger. I love you too much to kill you." Then he laughed.

I continued with the joke. "Well, if you're not trying to kill me, I guess I'm willing to give it a chance. How hard can it be?"

Oh! My! Gosh!

What was I thinking?! Clearly my brain was frozen because I was not thinking straight. Skiing down a mountain, for the first time in my life, with no lesson, no experience, and little more than the advice of "just keep your skis like a slice of pizza" was not the most brilliant thing I could have done.

Travis got me going cautiously down the hill, my skis carefully pointing toward each other to give me some control. Not much control, but supposedly some. Travis picked up speed and gracefully swished ahead of me. Just a little at first. I spread my skis wider, to go a little faster, not wanting to be left behind, not really knowing what I was doing. My mistake.

Travis took that as the green light that I felt comfortable and he skied past me.

I picked up speed, but not necessarily as gracefully as Travis, who was getting farther and farther ahead of me. It was a constant fight for balance and I struggled with shifting my weight while going in the right direction. All those skiers in the Olympics make it look easy. Lies, all lies! It was not easy!

What was easy was how quickly I lost control. I picked up speed, not heading in any particular direction, other than downhill, staggering trying to maintain my balance.

Forget control, speed, steering. I was out of control and I gave up trying to look graceful and ski correctly. I just wanted to make it to the bottom of the hill upright. My panic grew as I picked up speed. People weaved in and out in front of me, around me, surprising me as they whooshed past. What I should have done—as I was later informed—was sit down. *That* would have been nice to have known at the time.

Instead of sitting down, I fought to stay upright. Another unseen skier zoomed past me, spraying snow at me. I startled, lost my balance, hit a bump and headed for a tree.

Scared of crashing into a tree, I overcorrected, lost my balance and fell. But I didn't just face plant to bring my ski of terror to an end. I bounced, rolled, and avalanched downhill, my skis twisting my legs in awkward positions. I was sure I would break a leg, or two, or possibly die. I should've stuck to my original plan and avoided skiing altogether.

I pictured my downhill descent as something you'd see on those funny viral videos, where you see the person flailing down the mountainside, out of control. and taking out bystanders and buildings before finally coming to a standstill.

Much to my surprise, I was still in one piece, all my bones intact. My ankle was twisted, but my pride hurt more than my ankle. I fumbled to release the skis and angrily threw them off into the tree line.

I didn't care if I returned the rentals. My in-laws could pay for them. After all, forcing me to ski was their brilliant idea in the first place.

Two guys skiing by came to an immediate halt when they saw me stranded in the snow.

"Do you need some help?" Nice Guy Number One asked.

"I'm not quite sure what I need," I answered, annoyed with the whole situation. "This is my first time skiing and I got separated from my husband, and . . ." My throat tightened. He had abandoned me.

"What are you doing skiing down a level two trail? This is for more experienced skiers."

Figures.

"I went down the trail I was brought on. Now I just want to get to the bottom and never ski again."

Nice Guy Number One grinned a smile worthy of a toothpaste commercial. "C'mon, it's not that bad."

"I'll be a viral skiing disaster video before the hour is up."

Both men laughed.

"Do you want help down?" Nice Guy Number Two offered.

I frowned and shook my head. "I'm going to abandon the skis and walk the rest of the way."

"It's a long walk."

"But at least I won't die."

The Nice Guys laughed. "What if we ski you down? We'll each hold on to one arm and get you down in safety. Just snow plow."

"Snow plow?"

He showed me. It was the pizza slice.

Sounded good to me. The sooner I could be done with this ordeal, the better. "Okay," I agreed.

"Where are your skis?" Nice Guy Number Two asked.

"I chucked them in the woods." I nodded in the direction I had thrown them in my mini meltdown/temper tantrum.

Nice guy Number One slipped his skis off so easily, jogged the short distance into the trees, grabbed my skis and was back with them in hand. So graceful, even in ski boots. Something I could never dream of. Something I would never have to worry about because I was never stepping foot in skis again. Ever.

They stood me up. They strapped my boots on and we were off, down the mountainside. Nice Guy Number One on the left of me, and Nice Guy Number Two on the right of me, arms interlocked with mine to keep me under control.

Thank goodness for them because I might have never made it down that mountain.

Once at the bottom, they helped me dismantle all the contraptions. "Can we help you with anything else?"

"No, thank you. I need to go find my husband so I can kill him. So, I might need an alibi."

They laughed. "Well, good luck," Nice Guy Number One said, shaking my hand, but waiting for my name.

"Oh, yeah, uh, Sophia. I'm Sophia."

"I'm Brad and this is Zack."

I almost wanted to hug them. It literally felt like they had saved my life. "It's nice to meet you. And thank you."

"No problem. We like saving a damsel in distress. And your husband, he's a lucky guy."

"Not if I kill him," I said with a mock smile. Then added, "Figuratively speaking, of course," just so they wouldn't really think I was psycho.

We all laughed, then they gave a wave. "Well, see you around."

"No offense, but I hope not. I'm not doing that again," I said truthfully.

"Okay, so we won't see you around," Zack said.

"Thanks again," I said sincerely.

I ran through my choices of what to do. I could wait where I was and hope Travis found me. I could look for him, but the chances were slim that I'd find him among all the skiers. But I was really mad, so it might not have been the best choice. I could look for Maxine and Boyd, but I couldn't guarantee I'd be any nicer to them than I'd be to Travis, so that wasn't the best choice either.

I did have the key to the room. That's what I'd do. It'd give me time to calm down.

Travis came to the room about two hours later. "There you are. I've been looking all over for you. Where'd you go?"

Really? I figured he'd been skiing and assumed he'd run into me. Never once did he try calling me.

"Like you care. You went speeding off down the hill, leaving me on my own. If it wasn't for two guys who stopped and helped, I might've never made it down."

"I would've caught up to you. And who were these guys?"

"Who cares? All that matters is they helped me after I nearly crashed into a tree and now I'm here and I'm done skiing."

"Are you sure? You don't want to try again?"

"Seriously?" I asked.

He sat next to me. "I thought you'd pick it up. The first time I skied I stood up and was fine."

"I'm not you. Having two left feet makes it hard to hop up on skis and take off."

"I'm sorry, Fi. I'd really like to ski a little bit more, but I'll stay here with you if you want."

I softened a little. I'd calm down more hanging out in the condo.

Did I really have to tell him? Obviously, I wanted him to stay and make me feel better. I wouldn't mind a little alone time with him.

I shrugged. "I'm not going to make you stay."

He left. His track record for sticking around so far was not so great. He went off on the honeymoon, and now he was off to the ski slopes.

I hated to admit it, especially to myself, but I was disappointed. I didn't want to deprive him of a good time, but a little more attention would've been nice. But we were just getting used to being married and being part of something bigger than just ourselves.

He returned armed with a bouquet of red roses and chocolate. Dark chocolate. Why didn't he remember I liked milk chocolate? But I guess in the end, it was the thought that counted.

"I'm sorry I was being insensitive," he said.

I just looked at him. Anger still bubbled below the surface. I wanted to lash out at him. I was mad that I was pressured to ski, that I was abandoned on the mountainside with no skiing experience. I was mad he left me alone in the condo.

The next day was another skiing day.

I tried to get out of it, but the Duckks all ganged up on me. Duckk attack, or Quack attack, or something. I felt a little ~~pecked on~~, I mean, picked on.

"You're not skiing today?" Maxine said the next day.

"I thought we realized yesterday that I'm not much of a skier," I said. Hadn't we been over this last night? This was one thing I wasn't going to budge on.

She put her hand to her chest as if this was the most shocking news ever. "Why even come?"

Why did we come? So many reasons *not* to come. The words *resort* and *getaway* deceived me.

"Because we're family."

For better or for worse. Or so I'd heard.

24

HAPPY NEW YEAR

*O*ur plans for New Year's Eve was a party at Shane and Amy's—some friends of Travis's that I'd met briefly at our wedding reception.

"You remember the tall guy I introduced you to. We were mission companions and roommates?"

I mentally searched through who I'd met, but couldn't put faces to their names. The only one I remembered for sure was Jake, his best man, who I met just before the wedding.

"I guess I'll remember tonight when we go. Are we supposed to bring anything?" The invite had been texted to Travis, so I didn't know the details.

"I don't think so," Travis said. "We could pick up some drinks or chips."

I didn't want to show up empty handed. "Good idea."

"Should we run to the store now?" Travis asked.

I looked at my laptop.

I shook my head. "Nah. Why don't you go? I need to pay the bills." Some were due *today*. "Just don't spend too much."

Once he left, I flipped open my laptop, determined to bang out this unwanted task. I paid everything due—and thankfully—there was enough, but our balance was less than expected.

I scrolled through the charges. There were almost daily purchases at the food court on campus. Travis bought lunch almost *every day* in December.

I sat back and rubbed my eyes.

Adulting was soul-sucking.

And the "financial gift" of independence kept on giving. It gave me stress, heartburn and made me cranky.

I stared at the screen. Beside me was a notebook listing our bank balance and our bills. Travis's contract hadn't sold yet and that was a big chunk of change.

We needed jobs!

Travis came home, with five bags of chips and a couple of cases of soda.

What the heck?

I looked at the receipt. "You spent that much on *snacks*?" I asked.

Travis scowled. "Why are you mad? We talked about this."

True. I took a deep breath. "I thought you were buying one bag of chips."

He shrugged. "They had a deal if you buy three. I thought we'd want some for ourselves. And I got you some Diet Coke because you were out and we can bring the Coke to the party."

It made more sense once he explained it.

"Sorry," I said. "I just paid the bills and there's not a lot of extra money." I rubbed my temples. I could feel a headache tugging at the edge of my eye. I decided to save the "eating out" conversation for later.

"Why don't you show me," Travis said. The voice of reason.

For the next hour, we hashed out a financial plan. It was too late to apply for financial aid and we realized we both couldn't attend school. Since Travis had a major and more credits, he would continue school. I'd take a leave of absence, work next semester and then see if we could afford two tuitions. If not, I might have to quit and go back to school when Travis finished. It was the most logical plan. Other married couples did it.

"How are we going to pay for your school?" I asked. And why were we just thinking about this now? "Can we borrow money from your parents?" Even though it went against all my convictions.

"Is there any money left from the wedding gifts?" Travis countered. He looked around the room and then back toward our bedroom. Did he think we had a secret stash of money under our mattress?

I shook my head. "We have some. But we spent a lot on honeymoon shirts, pictures, and souvenirs, then shopping and eating out since we returned."

"Oh," he said.

I waited a beat, internally debating what I would say next. "You said you'd look for a job," I said. I hated bringing that up; I didn't want to be a nag. But a second paycheck would help, however big or small it was.

"I'll start tomorrow."

I perked up, feeling the slightest amount of weight lifting off my chest. "That will definitely help."

∽

AMY AND SHANE lived in a tiny, basement apartment complete with a musty smell and spiders.

It was jam-packed and it was warm. I clung by Travis's side, not saying much—it was hard to socialize.

Once the party thinned out, we had a chance to visit with Shane and Amy.

"How did you guys meet?" I asked Amy. She was beautiful, with long chestnut brown hair. It was thick and shiny like a horse's mane. Shane was equally attractive—though not as attractive as Travis.

"We were in the same ward. He was on the men's volleyball team. I had a huge crush on him." She smiled. "I'm a sucker for an athlete."

I smiled. I could relate. I was a sucker for gorgeous and charming.

"We dated all last year, got engaged in April and got married in August. We just found out we're having a baby."

"It all happens so fast, right?" I shrugged and smiled. "We met in September, engaged on Conference weekend and married right after Thanksgiving."

"We got engaged Conference weekend too. Probably a popular time for it. Everyone feels spiritual and inspired." A sheepish smile snuck onto her face. "He proposed in front of the Salt Lake Temple. He'd brought pennies to throw in the fountain and make wishes. It was so romantic."

Romantic? Actually, it sounded *familiar*. Sort of *exactly* like how Travis proposed. Coincidence? I didn't think so. I didn't believe two guys who'd been roommates came up with the very same proposal randomly and on their own. Memories of my proposal suddenly felt tarnished.

I forced a smile. "Yeah. That is romantic." Had her engagement ring been tied to a satin ribbon, with a shiny penny glued to the other end? I wanted to ask what Shane had said, word for word. I wanted to know how much of our formerly romantic proposal was original material from Travis and how much was shared material from Shane's proposal.

Did they plan it? Discuss it? Did Travis steal Shane's idea or the other way around? Did they come up with it together? Maybe they thought it was funny to copy each other's idea, like an inside joke. *Ha. Ha.* I was still disappointed that Travis didn't do something original.

"Fifi?" Amy was leaning down, looking at me.

"Sorry. What?" I got a little lost in my conspiracy theories.

"How did Travis ask you?"

"Kind of like you guys. Travis asked after Conference on Temple Square." I spared her the details. Maybe out of loyalty to her being a woman? Maybe because I wasn't sure who had the original idea? Maybe I didn't want her to feel betrayed, like me? Maybe none of the above? But it was hurtful that two roommates happened to use the same wedding proposal. Maybe I was jumping to conclusions and I'd have to get the real story from Travis later. Maybe it was a coincidence.

Was it, though?

"Travis is so happy. And you're beautiful. I'm happy for you guys." She was sincere.

Pride kicked in. There were always plenty of things to brag about when it came to Travis. "Yeah, he's great, isn't he?"

"He always has a compliment. That's what I like about him. If I wasn't so taken with Shane I might've chased after Travis. He's quite a catch." She sort of smiled and swatted my knee.

"Huh."

"Just kidding. He's like a brother to me. You got a good guy."

Apparently not good enough to come up with his own proposal.

It could've been totally innocent and I didn't know the full story yet. It'd make for good pillow talk. Or, maybe not so good pillow talk. We'd find out later tonight.

I got lost in my thoughts as I waited for Travis to catch up with his friends. He eventually was ready to go.

As we walked out, there was a framed ribbon with a penny glued to it, by the front door. Forget pillow talk, we were going to talk while we walked.

Once outside, Travis surprised me by ignoring me. He stomped off, his steps punching prints in the crisp snow.

Why is he so upset?

It made me momentarily forget my grievances.

"Are you mad?"

"You didn't spend any time with me. You were either talking to Amy or sitting on the couch looking annoyed."

"I thought you wanted me to be friends with Amy. You and Shane looked like you were catching up; I didn't want to interfere. I wasn't ignoring you."

Why would he think that?

He kept his forward march. "We're supposed to be each other's best friend. Not running to any and every girl to gossip with them."

"Gossip? I wasn't gossiping." I was gathering critical information.

"I expect you to be by my side."

I stopped. "You expect me?" That raised my hackles. "Do you care to rephrase that?"

He also stopped and turned to me. "That's not what I meant, Fi. I'm trying to say I'm proud to have you by my side and we should look united. We're married."

I took a deep breath. *Calm down.*

"Okay," I said, wanting to diffuse the situation.

With the mood he was in, now was definitely *not* the best time to ask about the plagiarized wedding proposal.

Maybe the wedding proposal wasn't that important.

What was important was that we got married. Maybe the end justified the means.

I caught up to him. "It's not that I don't want to be with you. I'm just not used to hanging out as a married couple."

"That's it?" he asked.

"Yes. And I love you." I reassured him.

I didn't bring up the proposal question that night. It wasn't the right time. If there was one thing I'd realized since I'd been married, it was that timing was everything.

25

'TIL DEBT DO US PART

"*Maxine*" popped up on my phone screen. My heartbeat quickened.

I gripped the phone, letting the ring tone play on, as I decided if I wanted to answer it.

"Scam Likely?" Megan Peacock asked, watching me.

"Worse. My mother-in-law." I was supposed to like my mother-in-law, right? I mean, she gave birth to the man I loved, and since I loved him, she must've done something right.

Megan nodded. "Oh," she said, her lips making the shape of an "O".

"Yeah," I said. "She stresses me out. I feel like she is always silently judging me."

My phone stopped ringing and seconds later dinged to let me know I had a voicemail. I continued. "It's easier to not answer, and listen to her message." I said as I put the message on speaker phone.

"Hello, Fifi. It's Maxine. I thought it'd be nice to do lunch on Friday, 11:30. See you then."

"Guess you have a lunch date," Megan said.

I thought through my schedule. I had nothing on Friday. Dang! "I wish she'd check with me to see if that works."

"You could always have plans."

I nodded. "I'm thinking up an excuse."

"What about—" Megan started, but was cut off when my phone rang.

This time it was Travis. I picked up on the first ring.

"Hi, honey!" I said.

"Hey. Just talked to my mom. She's coming to visit on Friday."

"I just got her voicemail."

"That's why I called—to make sure you knew."

"Yes. Are you going to skip class?" I asked.

"I can't, Babe. It's the beginning of the semester and I need to go."

Disappointment flooded through me. I needed him as a buffer.

"I'm sure she'll want to see you," I said, hoping to change his mind.

"I know, but I can't," he said. "I've got to get back to studying. Love you."

"Love you too," I said, my voice flat. I ended the call and slipped my phone into my pocket.

"Sounds like you have a lunch date," Megan said, breaking the somber mood.

"With my mother-in-law. Without my husband."

Megan made a cringey smile. "That sounds bad."

"She stresses me out. And every time I tell my husband that, he says something like, *Oh, it won't be that bad*."

"Can you cancel as it gets closer?" Megan said.

I considered it. Maybe I would. "We'll see."

Megan gave me a friendly jab. "I expect a full report, either way."

∽

I DIDN'T CANCEL. And I couldn't convince Travis to join me. Instead, I frantically made plans for the lunch I didn't want to have.

"What does your mother like to eat?" I asked Travis, looking for suggestions. If I couldn't get out of it, I could at least impress her. I wanted her to *like* me. It could also be a chance to clear the air. Maybe then she'd be less condescending. And maybe I could relax when I was around her.

"I don't know." Travis rolled his eyes. "Sandwiches, soup, salad. I don't know. She's not picky. She'll eat whatever you put in front of her."

His "insight" didn't help. I pored over my cookbooks (all three), stopped at the bookstore, perused at the library and searched Pinterest. I checked the cute, homemade cookbook Gretchen gave us as a wedding gift, for something that would be perfect. If Travis had narrowed the options down to say, Pasta Salad, or Soup, I might've felt less overwhelmed deciding what to make her.

I settled on chicken alfredo with asparagus and penne pasta—it sounded really good.

I rushed around the grocery store that morning, regretting that I agreed to this. One stupid lunch and I was completely stressed out. I wished I didn't care about impressing Maxine. I wished I had chosen something different for lunch. The ingredients were pricey, and this one meal had eaten into our food budget more than I planned. I picked up a small succulent to put on the table. It was money I didn't need to spend, but I wanted a little something to brighten my day.

I hurried home to do some last-minute cleaning. Travis had cooked bacon for breakfast and there was grease splattered everywhere. I didn't want Maxine to think I was a poor housekeeper and that we lived in filth.

Maxine's car was already in the driveway when I returned, sweaty and out of breath from my walk home. But she wasn't in the car—she was sitting on my couch.

"How'd you get in?" I asked as I opened my front door.

I felt violated, having her in my house when I wasn't home.

"Travis left his key under the mat. He didn't want me to wait outside."

Travis hadn't mentioned this. Had Maxine snooped around our apartment to pass the time? Did she open the fridge, the closet, the medicine cabinet, my journal? I had snooped around her bathroom, but didn't want her snooping around my stuff. I decided not to do that anymore.

I looked at my watch. It was 11:20. "How long have you been here? We agreed on 11:30."

"I arrived five minutes ago. Don't worry, you're not late."

I wasn't worried about being late. I worried Maxine had been here for longer than five minutes and that she had a key to our apartment.

I kicked into hostess mode, thinking getting busy would relieve the tension in the air. Maybe only I felt tense, but I needed something to focus on. I cleared the dishes on the counter and stacked them in the sink.

"I meant to have this cleaned up. I thought I'd have more time before you got here."

"Do you need some pointers on cleaning?"

Really? "Thank you. That's very kind of you, but I already know *how* to clean. What I meant was I didn't have *time* to clean." Then I busied myself so I wouldn't have to talk to her. If lunch proceeded this way, I'd have to find some way to politely kick her out of my apartment after an hour.

I threw the frozen alfredo mix into the microwave and then filled a pot with water to cook the pasta. "I'll get this going. Lunch will be ready in twenty minutes." Then I started to set the table.

Maxine stood up, with her purse over her shoulder. "How about we go out to lunch?"

I stopped what I was doing. "But I'm making lunch."

She smiled widely. "Don't worry about cooking. Let's just go out for a girl's lunch. Make it easy on you."

Why hadn't she suggested that on the phone? I wouldn't have spent money on food, I wouldn't have spent hours deciding what to cook, I wouldn't have made the meal, I wouldn't have stressed myself out cleaning the apartment. And I definitely wouldn't have killed myself trying to make a good impression. I had other things to do than worry about my mother-in-law's visit. I still had homework to do before finals.

"I can't afford it. I spent over our food budget this week." I hoped she'd get the message that it was because of her.

The microwave dinged.

"My treat," she said.

She still didn't want to eat my cooking.

"How about Italian?" I suggested as I took the food out of the microwave and put it into the fridge.

"Let's do Mexican." Maxine had obviously already decided.

We drove in silence the five minutes it took to get to the restaurant on Center Street.

Once we were seated and our drinks arrived, I decided it was now or never. I would confront our uncomfortable relationship.

"Hey, Maxine, I want to clear the air." I was quaking in my boots. "Somewhere along the line we had a miscommunication about our relationship..."

"Oh, I think we're very clear about our relationship," Maxine said calmly. It was a weird calm.

"Maybe it was the turkey disaster at Thanksgiving..."

"I don't hold that against you." Maxine smiled.

No, she didn't hold it against me, she just would never again eat my food, ever. And okay, I could let that one go. At least for now, since I knew I wasn't a great cook. But if it was still being brought up in ten years, we might have to revisit the conversation.

"Well, whatever it is, I feel like there is tension between us. We're family now, we both love Travis, so I don't want any conflict." Like my trip down the mountainside, it felt like so many things had avalanched in our relationship, I was no longer sure what had gone into making out relationship feel so disagreeable. But I could at least try. I could try to amend, try to be better, try to make more of an effort to embrace their family traditions.

"I'm his mother, I gave birth to him, and as long as you remember that I am the most important woman in his life, we're on the same page."

I blinked. Any earlier resolve to address the conflict in our relationship spontaneously combusted. My mouth opened to say something but I closed it instead. Did I hear her right? She was the most important woman in his life? What the heck? Her unabashed confession was unexpected. I expected we'd kiss and make up and if things weren't really better, we'd at least pretend they were better.

"I...um..."

"And speaking of pages, I believe this is yours."

Maxine took out an envelope and slid it across the table to me. It was already open.

"What's this?" I asked, picking up the letter.

"It's your credit card bill."

We had a credit card?

"You might want to change the address so it starts coming to your apartment. Now that you're married, you have to be responsible for your own finances."

I took the statement out of the envelope and felt the color drain from my face. I even think my heart stopped beating for a moment.

$8,793.96.

Really?

I felt sick.

What in the world? This was our bill? How? I didn't understand.

I skimmed the bill, looking at the charges. The pre-honeymoon hotel, the trip to/from California for the cruise, the post-honeymoon hotel, Christmas, Park City, and the furniture were all listed.

"Travis said you were paying for the honeymoon," I managed.

There was a smug smile on Maxine's face. Was she enjoying my reaction?

"I don't remember agreeing to that."

"But..."

Her look was one of supreme satisfaction. It was as if she caught us doing something wrong. "You can't keep living like your parents are supporting you, now can you?"

It wasn't even me! I wanted to scream. *It was Travis!*

He led me to believe they'd gifted us the cruise. Travis didn't say we were paying for the furniture—not that I expected someone else to pay for it—but Travis said his mother had said we needed to get this stuff. I wouldn't have bought or agreed to the bed frame, sofa, or huge flat-screen TV. I would've been happy with my mattress on the floor, a tiny loveseat and a 13" TV Instead of a credit card bill we had (unintentionally) racked up in one month of marriage.

I set the statement on the table, trying to control my reaction. "That's not as bad as I thought," I said as calmly as I could manage. No, it wasn't. It was way worse! But I wasn't going to give Maxine the satisfaction of thinking we were failing. Screwing up. Being irresponsible. Not able to do it on our own or as well as she and Boyd had.

Why would she want to make me feel bad? This was not a competition of who was more successful as newlyweds. I would've thought she'd be on our side, rooting for us to win, being our biggest fan. But instead, I sat across a table from her, pretending not to be shocked at the huge credit card bill.

I'd lost my appetite and wanted to ditch Maxine. I didn't want her paying for lunch because I didn't want to feel like I owed her anything. My stomach wasn't feeling so well, anyway, after seeing that bill. I really wanted to get up and leave, and not give Maxine the satisfaction of seeing me squirm.

So, I did the only thing I could do. I ordered shrimp. I was allergic to shrimp. Not so allergic that I'd go into anaphylactic shock and stop breathing. I'd get hives around my mouth and my lips would itch. I figured it was better than outright lying and making up an excuse to leave. Besides, we'd had this lunch date planned for a week, far too long to have accidentally forgotten something on my calendar. Suddenly I was thankful we weren't eating at my apartment. Then I would've had to think of some way to get her to leave, and I'd never been very good at lying. At least this way I could go home and eat by myself.

I was good and itchy before I said anything. "Something's wrong," I announced, touching my lips.

Maxine looked up from her food. "Why dear, you're having an allergic reaction. Your face is swelling."

My face? That hadn't happened before. But then again, I had only had the reaction once before, two years ago at the nightmare prom. I dug through my purse to find a mirror, and sure enough, my reflection was different than expected. Not only were my lips swollen, but I had hives—big hives—the size of nickels, all over my face. My eyelids were swollen and I was puffy.

I freaked out, not knowing what to do. The last reaction hadn't been this fast or this severe. What if I didn't make it home in time to take Benadryl? Would water help? I frantically reached for my glass, thinking water might help wash some of the toxins out or at least dilute it.

The water did nothing, since all I managed to do was spill it on myself.

"I'll call 911," Maxine told me, phone already on her ear, hand in the air signaling the waitress.

An ambulance pulled up a few minutes later, along with a firetruck. I would've been fine with just one. Three paramedics came in, one carrying a large backpack and two pushing a gurney. I hoped I wasn't going out on that gurney; it was bad enough that everyone around was watching.

"Have you had a reaction to seafood like this before?" the EMT asked as he administered an EpiPen shot.

Maxine listened closely.

"No," I kinda-lied.

I mean, I *had* had a reaction a couple of years ago, but it *hadn't* been like this. If I'd known it was going to blow up (literally) into such a mess, I wouldn't have resorted to such drastic measures.

"You might want to carry an EpiPen with you in case you have another reaction," the EMT said. "Each one could get progressively worse."

"You really don't have much luck with food, do you?" Maxine laughed.

"Yeah, I guess it's good we didn't eat the food I had prepared at home. I might've killed you."

I was beyond pleasantries. I had been slighted for the lunch I had slaved over, been blindsided by a huge credit card bill, shot by an EMT, and insulted about an honest mistake. I was done being nice. I stood up and headed for the door. I could walk home. Who needed her so-called "hospitality"?

"You can't go," the EMT said.

"I can't?" I asked. Why not?

"You have to go to the hospital after an EpiPen shot."

I exhaled slowly. This was a bigger deal than I thought. I should've just suffered through lunch.

"We can take you in the ambulance, or she can take you." He pointed at Maxine.

I couldn't afford an ambulance.

Maxine drove me to the hospital and insisted on escorting me in. I insisted I was fine and waited until she left before I left. I really *did* feel fine. And I didn't need a hospital bill added to our already huge credit card bill.

I walked home and called Travis on the way.

"Hey," he said, his voice full of concern. "Are you at the hospital? My mom just called."

Should I be thankful or upset that he heard the news from Maxine? "No. I'm already heading home."

"Want me to come get you? I would've left class if you'd called me sooner."

"Everything happened so fast, there wasn't time to call you. But I'm okay."

It was mid-afternoon when I made it home.

"Hi." Travis greeted me at the door.

The scent of chicken alfredo was in the air, meaning Travis had already eaten. I hoped there was some left for me. I obviously didn't get to finish lunch and was starving.

I dropped my purse on the tile by the door and kicked off my shoes. "I'm tired."

"My mom called to check on you."

"She could've called me if she wanted to know how I was doing," I said.

"She knows my number better."

I was sick of his mother. "Lucky you."

"Why are you so . . ." he shook his head, as if there were no words to describe my behavior. "Argumentative?"

"I had an allergic reaction today and then your mom calls to tattle to you."

"She wasn't tattling, she was concerned."

If he had seen the look of superiority on her face as she slid the credit card bill across the table, he would understand why I didn't believe she was concerned. "Could we not talk about it?"

"Sor-ry." Travis didn't hide his irritation.

I took a deep breath; we needed to start over. "I'm sorry. I've had a bad day. Your mom gave me our credit card bill, and..."

"Our credit card bill? What credit card?" Did Travis not know it was our financial responsibility now that we were married?

"The one you always use."

Travis's brows came together. "But they always pay it."

Exactly what I thought. I exhaled loudly. "Not this time. It's almost nine thousand dollars. I'm a little freaked out. I don't know how we're going to pay that."

His eyes widened. "Nine thousand dollars? Do you have it with you? Can I see it?"

I dug through my purse. "Sure."

"I'll talk to my parents. It'll be okay." He smiled reassuringly, pulled my head to him and kissed me on my forehead. "I'm sure it's just a miscommunication."

I wasn't sure it was. The charges were ours. I was also under the impression, obviously a mistaken one, that his parents had given us "permission" to furnish our apartment on their dime.

Travis pulled me to his chest and hugged me. "Don't worry, we'll figure it out."

The credit card bill occupied my mind. We'd accidentally overspent, but we could move on, not spend like that ever again and be in debt for the next ten years.

I sure hoped so.

But we had each other. And we were in love.
Love could conquer anything.
Right?

26

A GOOD JOB IS HARD TO FIND

I scowled at my laptop screen, and I swear, it scowled back. Maybe it was just my reflection. I sat back, blew out a long sigh and brushed my hair from my face. Finding a good job in a college town was harder than I thought. It was almost cutthroat. As cutthroat as Christians could be without intentionally doing harm to another. Provo was a town with an overabundance of people, an overabundance of skills, and an overabundance of talent. Somehow, I hadn't considered how oversaturated with applicants the job market would be.

I mean, I had the soul-sucking part-time telemarketing job already. But I hated it. One could only take so many hang-ups and nasty comments a day. I needed something better, something with more meaning. Something that didn't make me hate my life twelve hours a week.

Stupidly, I thought I could saunter into a job interview and walk out with a job.

I couldn't even get an interview.

The job postings website updated every morning, I'd apply, and follow up with a call the next day. It wasn't unusual to be told they had already accepted their fill of applications, or already hired someone. Or, I simply didn't hear back.

If I did get an interview, I had too much experience or not enough experience. Somehow my love of shopping did not translate into actual job experience for being a buyer at a department store, or even a manager at a clothing store. I needed to revamp my resume and get creative. Not working was not an option.

∽

THE JOB SEARCH continued to prove fruitless and my motivation and PMA fizzled.

I remembered when Gretchen read the incredibly boring book, *Pilgrim's Progress*. She talked about the slough of despair. It was a muddy, murky puddle that hindered Pilgrim's progress.

That was literally how I felt—stuck in a thick, disgusting mud that I couldn't get out of. The only thing I could do was keep moving forward. First step: find a second/better/full-time job.

I finally found another part-time job at a clothing store close to the mall. It was geared toward teenagers, but technically, I was still in that demographic. I had to take a bus there, but I chose to count my blessings that I was employed. And it was the only thing I could find that worked with the schedule of my first job.

The timing was always stressful since there was only a small window of time between clocking out and getting to the bus. If I missed the bus, I was late to my next job. But my mother had taught me well, I could look on the bright side, right? I loved clothes, so working in a clothing store and getting a discount was a good thing. And doing telemarketing surveys was a good thing because...well, it wasn't, but I got paid.

At the "mall" job, I had the pleasure of getting (that's a very heavy sarcastic *getting*) to work with Hanna and Shanna. Yup. Those were really their names. They were best friends (of course!) and had just graduated high school (barely!), were total mall rats (as if!), and were attending Utah Valley University (like that matters!). Every sentence uttered ended with rising inflection. Can you just hear the attitude? Somehow, we *always* worked the same shift.

~

BY MY SECOND week of working there, I finally felt like I knew what I was doing. What I was doing that particular day, was meticulously folding a stack of shirts on a plastic guide.

"Like, oh, my heck," Hanna announced.

"Total babe coming our way," Shanna whispered. They giggled like high school girls. But, then again, I was in high school last year too.

I craned my neck from behind the mound of clothes to see what was going on.

It was Travis. Why was he here?

Before I could say anything, Hanna approached him. "Hi," she said in a low voice. Was she was trying to sound alluring?

Shanna stepped in front of her. "Can I help you find anything?"

Travis smiled slowly, looked around the store, but still hadn't seen me. "Actually, you *could* help me." He looked back at the two competing mall rats and paused for effect. I wasn't sure what he was doing, but he had to know he was dealing with Hanna and Shanna. I complained, I mean, talked about them all the time.

"I'm looking for . . ."

The girls leaned closer toward him.

"My wife." He grinned, then watched their reactions.

Hanna curled her hair around her finger. "Your wife, or a wife? 'Cause, like, I'm available."

My inner sarcastic voice responded in like tone. *Rilly? Like, are you like, kidding me? Did they forget to, like, do a ring check?*

Travis shook his head. "No, thank you. *My* wife would be just fine. You know her. Fifi."

Hanna frowned and Shanna groaned. The disgust was evident. Apparently, the mall rats disapproved of something. "Fee...Fee's your wife? You're her husband? No way."

I ruined the fun by bursting out laughing. And accidentally snorting. But I couldn't help it. Watching Hanna and Shanna ogle my husband, only to find out he was *my* husband, was too funny.

"Hi, babe!" I said, being overly happy as I approached him.

He pulled me to him and kissed. "Surprise."

"What's the occasion?"

"You are much more interesting than class, so I skipped and hopped an express bus. I got to meet your...friends." He looked over at the "twins" and raised an eyebrow.

I'm not lying when I say they were drooling. They were apparently stunned, watching the scene unfold, their mouths hanging open. Literally spit was forming at the corners of their mouths, starting to make its way for the chin. It was *very* amusing.

"If I'm skipping class, then you should skip work. It's only fair," Travis said. "Can you suddenly get a headache, cramps, or something girly? I miss you."

If only it *was* fair. "I can't. But I could skip the next job." Who liked telemarketers anyways? They annoyed people.

Travis glanced at his watch. "How long before you're off?"

"Forty-five minutes."

"I'll go look around. Maybe I'll see something I need to buy for you."

I giggled.

He leaned in and kissed me. "I'll be back."

He gave an awkward half-wave to the mall rat twins. "Uh, see you...around?"

Hanna awkwardly waved back before abruptly stopping. "Hopefully soon."

"We love you. I mean..." Shanna called out, then trailed off before shaking her head. As if she could just shake that mistake right out of her hair. "Love Fifi." She smiled, slid her glance to Hanna, probably realizing how stupid she sounded. "We love her."

We all took in the beauty of watching Travis saunter out of the store.

They turned on me the moment he was out of ear shot.

"Oh, my, gosh! You didn't tell us your husband was a babe! Does he have any brothers?!" Hanna gushed.

"Or friends? I'd take friends too," Shanna panted.

I couldn't picture either of them dating Travis's friends. Would that mean we'd have to, like, hang out, and pretend to like each other? Like, no. Way!

Travis returned forty minutes later carrying a small Kate Spade bag. Inside was a pair of gumdrop glitter earrings.

"We can't afford these," I said automatically.

"It's already taken care of," Travis said.

They were pretty.

I wasn't going to ask what he meant in front of the "twins", so instead I hugged him. "Thank you! I love them!"

They swooned at how romantic he was. I swooned at how romantic he was. We all swooned.

I checked my phone for the time. "Hey guys, do you think it'd be okay if I clocked out five minutes early? Last time I missed the bus." A few minutes wouldn't be that big of a deal, would it?

"Like, sure. We don't care," Hanna said.

I was still unsure. "Should I call the manager and ask? I don't want to get in trouble."

"Why would you get in troub-bul?" Shanna said. "I've, like, had to do it before and he totally didn't care."

"So, it's cool?" I asked, cautiously. I hadn't worked there long enough to know exactly how big or small of a deal it really was.

"Or we could clock you out. It's like, no prob-lem-o," Shanna said.

Okay, like the way she talked was like, rilly annoying.

"Maybe I should come in five minutes early next time, to make up for it?" I asked.

"Oh, pul-lease," Hanna said. "It's five minutes. Go. You don't want to miss your bus."

We didn't miss the bus.

What I did miss was how overly willing they were to encourage me to leave early.

∽

For my next shift at the clothing store, I made sure I clocked in five minutes early. Granted it was only five minutes. What was the big deal? The big deal was that the supervisor was there, waiting for me.

"Sophia, you left early yesterday," he said.

Apparently, he was not a supervisor that had problems with confrontation. I could tell by his tone of voice that he was not happy.

I gulped. "Um, yeah, sorry. I was going to call you, but Hanna and Shanna said they would tell you. I didn't want to miss my bus."

"Hanna and Shanna are not your supervisor. You don't report to them, you report to me."

I got this pit in my stomach and my heart began to race.

This wasn't going well.

At all.

I backtracked. "I know and I'm sorry. I came in early to make up the time today, and . . ."

He continued studying the inventory report. "And now you can get your things and go. You're fired."

He didn't even have the decency to look at me when he fired me!

My mouth dropped open. I stood there, speechless, as the words sunk in. Finally, after what seemed like forever but was probably only ten seconds, I spoke. "Fired?" I repeated. "I understand I left early, but they said they would cover it and . . ."

He cut me off. "Hanna and Shanna said you left and said nothing to them. You didn't even clock out. Five minutes or five hours, you don't have the authority to change your schedule how you like."

I wrung my hands together. "Really, this is a mistake. I'm sorry. I should've asked first. Can you give me a warning or, or . . ." How had it gotten so out of hand?

His steely eyes met mine. "I need dependable, respectful associates. Obviously, you think you're the boss and can do whatever you like. So, no, I can't give you a warning. You no longer have a job." He walked off to the back room.

Really?

I was stunned. I'd never been fired in my life. Granted I'd only had two other jobs, both in the summer, one being babysitting. But fired for leaving five minutes early? I didn't realize Richard was so strict and unreasonable.

"What's up?" Hanna said, walking up behind me. Shanna was right beside her.

I glanced at my watch. 10:03. They were three minutes late.

I turned to them, looking for back-up. Surely, they could vouch I was a good employee. There were smug smiles on their faces.

Oh!

I got it! Now I understood the overly helpful, overly encouraging attitude of "don't worry, it's not a big deal". They made it a big deal. They weren't my friends. They caused much ado about five minutes.

Sure, they were immature. But why had they done this?

I gathered my purse and keys and sunglasses from behind the counter, then walked to where they stood. "So, *girls*, guess what? I got fired."

Shanna bugged her eyes. "Seriously? I can't believe Richard would do that."

Fool me once, shame on you. Fool me twice, shame on me.

I imitated her tone. "I *know*! I can't believe it, either."

"You know Richard," Hanna piped up. "He's always making *such* a big deal out of ev-ry-thing."

I crossed my arms. "I guess I don't know Richard. Or you two, for that matter."

"What do you mean?" Shanna asked.

"Silly me, believing you when you told me it wasn't a big deal."

Hanna's eyes widened and she shook her head.

Shanna's hand went to her neck. "We didn't think it was," she said.

I pointed an accusatory finger back and forth between them. "So, you two had nothing to do with it?"

I knew the answer. I wasn't an idiot. They had everything to do with it. I just didn't know why. And I wanted to hear them say it.

"Like, no. Of course not!" Hanna said.

I didn't expect a confession. I expected maybe a claim about a misunderstanding. Or a mistake. Maybe they'd simply forgotten to clock me out. Maybe they were covering their own backsides so they wouldn't get in trouble. I got all that. But if it was a mistake, wouldn't they apologize?

I waited, but neither one of them said a thing. Obviously, they weren't going to.

My instincts were right.

I took a deep breath.

Okay, I could be the bigger person. I could walk out of here with my head held high, without unleashing the rash of mean thoughts and ill will I wished to wish upon them. "Well, good luck."

Hanna pasted a fake smile on her face. "Don't worry, Fifi. You'll find another job."

"Yeah, all you have to do is bat your eyes, flip your hair and smile," Shanna added with a giggle.

I studied them, confused. Is that what they thought of me? Not that it *mattered* what *they* thought of me, but did I really appear to be a person who could simply get my way with a little flirting?

Huh.

Yes, I had always been given a lot of attention because of my looks, and yes, I liked that attention, but did that give people reason to hate me? Wasn't I a good person? I didn't think I was stuck-up. Maybe a little stuck on my appearance, and Travis's too, but was it wrong to take pride in my appearance?

I didn't want them to think they had gotten the better of me, but I didn't want them to get away with it, either. I said the first thing I thought of.

"Well, what goes around comes around, and Karma's a witch, so good luck."

With my stuff clenched to my chest, I spun on my heels and marched out. I held my head so high, my neck hurt.

Immediately, tears filled my eyes and my throat constricted. I wiped my eyes, not wanting to break down publicly. I hid behind my sunglasses, even if tears rolled below the frames.

So what? I'd lost my job. It'd be okay. I just needed to find something else. I still had the Portal-To-Hell job, even if I hated it. But I could hold on a little longer.

Through blurry eyes, I made it to the bus stop.

I mentally ran the numbers. My income was just enough to pay our rent, food, and utilities. What little was left over we used for date night.

I thought of our list of unpaid bills. How were we going to pay them now? Or pay down the credit card balance that had barely changed, despite the payment I made last month? There was nothing extra to pay that down.

And what about rent for Travis's contract? We hadn't sold that yet.

What were we going to do?

I considered our options and tapped them into my phone notes so I could discuss them with Travis.

Travis could find a job.

We could ditch some of our streaming channels.

~~Eat out less.~~

We barely ate out. I brought dinner to Travis every night up on campus. I packed him his lunch every day, that way he wasn't spending money buying it on campus.

That was all I came up with. There had to be more. Maybe Travis would have some ideas.

Was this what adulting consisted of? Busy lives, stressing about bills, responsibilities and making ends meet? Dreading another bus ride, or missed bus, another credit card bill, another visit to his parents?

His mother always wanted us to come visit on Sundays. It would have been a whole lot more convenient if we had a car to drive. Not that we could afford it.

This did not feel like happily ever after.

∼

Since I suddenly had a couple of free hours, I called Travis. Maybe I could meet him on campus for lunch. Plus, I needed a little pep talk. I could've called my mom and spilled the story, but I didn't need *that* peppy of a pep talk.

"Hey, babe. What's up?"

If I told him immediately that I was fired, I'd start crying again. I convinced myself it was better to do it in person.

I cleared my throat. "Want to meet up for lunch?"

"Sorry, I can't."

My disappointment sank lower. "But I've had a horrible day."

"It's not that I don't want to see you, but I have a ton of work to get done before class."

Now was not the time. I sighed. "Okay, fine. I'll see you tonight." I hung up without waiting for his goodbye. I shouldn't be too upset with him—he *did* have class.

I rested my head against the window of the bus, which was probably a huge, gross mistake. But I didn't care what kind of germs—or *things*—might be on it. I was *drained*. I watched as we drove past restaurants, store fronts, and apartment buildings. If I thought about anything other than the scenery passing by, I'd most definitely cry.

We passed Deseret Industries. I thought about self-medicating with some retail therapy—cheap retail therapy. But after what just happened, I couldn't justify spending money on more stuff. I'd put it off for another day.

And like my mom always sang, "The sun will come up tomorrow."

27

REALITY CALLED...IT WANTS YOUR ROSE-COLORED GLASSES BACK

I worked all afternoon on a plan.

I called my dad and he walked me through the basics of a budget. We discussed recurring bills, paying down debt and prioritizing needs and wants.

Sad to say, my wants way outnumbered my needs. High up on the "Wants" list was hair product, acrylic nails, and pricey purses. Travis would probably add Diet Coke to that list, but that qualified as a need.

I suddenly understood what my parents meant by priorities. I used to think if I spent too much money on makeup at Sephora and then ate cheap ramen noodles the rest of the week, that was prioritizing.

Being financially independent was a daunting task, but I knew there were ways we could trim our spending.

A knock at the door interrupted me. Megan? Amazon? Secretly I hoped for either. Anything would be a welcomed distraction.

It was Nicole. With another plate of brownies. Brownies were good. I could eat some brownies right now.

I stepped back. "Hi. Come in."

Like last visit, she declined. "I'm in a rush, like always. But I wanted to let you know I'm thinking of you and if you ever need anything, let me know."

Right now, I needed brownies. They would do. "Thank you," I said and accepted her offering.

I texted Megan.

Me: Got more brownies from Nicole. Want some?

Megan: Have class. Save me one?

Me: Sure. I wonder if Nicole will actually ever visit.

Megan: At least she comes. I haven't seen my ministering person.

Good point. Maybe Nicole was sincere in her offers. Even if she wasn't, she sure made good brownies. I ate most of the brownies and hid the rest for tomorrow.

~

I WAS EXCITED and felt empowered when Travis came home that night. Armed with the knowledge my dad had given me and the PMA my mother had drilled in me, I was ready to do this. We were going to take control of our money and our financial destiny.

After discussing my job loss during dinner, it was time to make plans. I made sure we were good and comfortable before starting the discussion.

"My dad suggested we come up with a budget," I said.

"A what?"

Travis was not riding the same wave of financial independence as me. I, on the other hand, had been surfing the internet all afternoon gathering knowledge.

"A budget," I repeated. "We should sit down together and figure out a budget."

"Oh yeah? Why?" Travis wasn't challenging me. He didn't understand why it was necessary. I heard it in his tone.

Did I really need to explain why?

"We need a plan to pay off the credit card bill." I thought that was obvious.

He sunk into the couch and flicked on the TV. "Oh yeah. I guess so." His lack of excitement didn't dissuade me. I clutched a legal pad and sat down beside him.

He clicked through some channels.

Obviously, I'd have to persuade him that we needed at least the same amount of commitment for this to work. I plowed forward, full speed ahead. "First, we should prioritize how we spend our money. Wants versus needs."

He settled on a sports channel, then frowned a little. "We don't buy anything we don't need."

I looked around at our apartment. There were plenty of things we didn't need here. Yes, it was true. We wanted all of them, but did we *need* them? I was not to be deterred. *This* was something we needed to do. All this stuff we'd gone into debt for hung over my head, giving me heartburn and headaches everyday while I slaved away at my minimum-paying job.

I grabbed the remote and shut the TV off.

He tried to get the remote back. "Babe, I was watching that."

"I just need a few minutes, I promise," I said gently. "Then you can watch whatever."

He sighed loudly and threw up his hands as a sign of submission. "Okay, okay. What were you saying?"

I sat poised with my pen, ready to write. "Let's make a list of our expenses, then list the extra stuff."

I had already made a list, but made a split-second decision to not share it. We needed to do this as a couple.

"Like what? Bills?"

"Yeah, like tithing, rent, food, utilities, bus pass, entertainment."

Travis glanced longingly at the TV and then back at me. "Okay."

He wasn't into it, but we *needed* to get a handle on our finances.

"Anything else you can think of?"

Travis was silent. I glanced over at him and he was scrolling on his phone until he pulled up the remote for the TV. *So* glad he was *so* interested.

He settled on a channel and scrolled through the shows. "Nope, can't think of anything."

I took a deep breath and then carefully broached a touchy subject. "What if we went to Salt Lake every other Sunday instead of every Sunday? It would save a lot."

Travis didn't miss a beat. "That's not an option. Besides, we buy a monthly bus pass."

True. I scrambled to justify my suggestion. "Time-wise it'd give us more time together but still see them."

He paused a basketball game long enough to make eye contact. "No."

I swallowed and forced a smile to my face. "But we need to compromise. I'll cut back on my Diet Coke. That'll save some money, right?"

"That's a no-brainer, Fi. You drink too much of it anyway. If you stopped drinking it altogether, we'd probably save fifty bucks a month. Besides, water would be healthier."

"We're talking about money, Travis, not my health."

"Still." Travis softened a bit, cocked his head sideways. "Thanks for being willing to give up something you love. I just feel it's important to visit my parents. I know it's a lot of time, but it means a lot to me, Fi. It means a lot to have you come with me."

How could I argue with that? I melted a little.

He shut off the TV and I leaned into him on the couch. He put his arm around my shoulder and kissed me on the cheek. With his other hand he reached over and took my hand. I looked at our fingers intertwined.

See. Compromise was good.

"I'll stop getting my nails done." I offered, even though I loved acrylic nails. "I can paint my own nails."

I could be an example of self-sacrifice. It took three hours at work to pay for a set of acrylic nails. Did I even need to worry about my nails? I could spend less on cosmetic, superficial stuff to make our budget work.

How well did the press-on, DIY nails work?

Travis held my hand up and inspected it. "But I like your nails. They make your fingers look long and elegant. It feels really good when you scratch my back. You should keep them."

"I'd love to keep them, but I don't really *need* them."

He kissed my hand. "Add a gym membership to the list."

I gave him an appraising look. "But you look really good just the way you are." He was hot when he was shirtless.

"If you want me to stay looking like this, I need a gym membership." He lifted his shirt to show me his abs. "This doesn't just happen. I have to go to the gym to get this way." He dropped his shirt.

"I'm all for you working out. How much does it cost?" I leaned forward to the coffee table, ready to jot down the number.

"I don't know." Travis wrinkled his brow. "Like fifty bucks a month?"

I must've accidentally scowled.

"What?" he asked.

"BYU charges that much?"

Travis shook his head. "I'm talking about a real gym. Not on campus."

Was the BYU gym a fake gym? Isn't that where all the school team athletes worked out? "But on-campus would be cheaper." And better. There were standards at BYU. The men were separated from the women, unlike a "real" gym. Women wouldn't be wearing skimpy workout clothes trying to pick up men. Maybe they would, but it'd be in their BYU issued gym clothes.

"I don't like campus," Travis complained.

"You could give up your bus pass for a gym membership," I suggested, knowing full well he'd reject the idea.

"I said that is not an option," Travis snapped, suddenly angry. "I don't see what the big deal is."

How did we go from a civil conversation to an angry outburst? Over a gym membership? Or was it because I wanted to cut down on visiting his parents?

"The big deal, Travis, is that we're living on minimum wage, we owe eight *thousand* dollars. We're never going to pay it off if we don't budget our money."

I was the one working. He still hadn't found a job. Had he even looked for one yet? And because of that, I felt *all* the weight of that debt on *my* shoulders.

"Sometimes you take all the fun out of everything." Travis raised his voice.

When did I become the big bad money police?

"I don't like it either," I said loudly.

As soon as the words were out of my mouth, I realized I shouldn't be yelling at him. We could deal with this a lot more civilly if we weren't yelling at each other. So, I took a deep breath. A deep, cleansing breath. "I want to be able to pay the bills," I said calmly.

There. Look at me. I was the model of propriety. I was a mature, financially responsible adult, having an open and honest discussion with my husband. Wow. When did I become this mature adult?

Travis interrupted my "aha" moment of maturity. "I know," he said and snapped his fingers. "You could stop buying all these plants. They all end up dead, anyway."

I shouldn't have taken it as a personal attack when he brought up the plants, but I did. Plants didn't cost that much. Besides, wasn't it nice to have something green and alive in our apartment? Our apartment was so ugly to begin with.

"Not buying new plants isn't going to save all that much money or solve the problem."

Travis shrugged. "Maybe you can find a better paying job now."

I was taken aback. "At least I have one." Forget nice and calm, he was attacking our means of support.

"What's that supposed to mean?" Travis was defensive.

"You had a job," I yelled. "We had extra money. Then you quit!" My frustration couldn't be suppressed.

Travis threw his hands up in the air. "I have to study, Fi. That's how I'm going to get a good job after graduation."

He wasn't studying before this conversation started. He was watching TV. "That's fine, Trav. But until you get that good job after graduation, if you choose not to work, we can't buy everything we want."

His phone rang. It was probably his mother. He never seemed to have anyone else call him. He silenced his phone.

"And another thing," I said, his phone ringing reminded me of more expenses. "We probably should get cheaper phone plans."

"Actually, it's time to get a new phone." Travis crossed his arms across his chest, his phone still clenched in his hand, as if he was challenging me—daring me to argue with him.

There was nothing wrong with his phone. It worked fine, the screen wasn't cracked, it still held a charge. "Why? Is that one broken?" Did he not get what we'd been talking about? We needed to cut back, not spend more.

"No, I just want a new phone." He shrugged, like it was no big deal. "The new ones are really cool."

Really cool? That was his basis for justifying spending that kind of money on a *phone*? Seriously? I wasn't going to be the only one sacrificing in this deal. "Well, I'd like a new purse, but I'm not going to buy one because we need to pay the rent. So how about you keep the old phone since it still works?"

"What? Does something have to be broken to get a new one?" Travis's voice didn't hide his irritation.

"It does now," I said.

He chucked the phone across the room into the concrete blocks that made up our living room wall. It shattered into pieces. "There. Now it's broken." He purposely stepped on a piece of the case on the floor as he scooped it the phone and walked out the door.

"Grow up!" I screamed in frustration once the door clicked shut.

That went horribly awry.

Tears of frustration welled up in my eyes as I clenched my fists and dropped onto the couch. I scrubbed the tears off my cheeks.

I considered going out after him, but I wasn't sure where he went.

But I also wasn't in the mood to smooth things over with him. He wasn't the only one frustrated.

Besides, where could he go? He didn't have a car.

And it wasn't like I could call him to find out where he went. His phone was in pieces.

He returned almost two hours later. I'd been curled up on the couch pretending to watch TV, but I really spent the whole time listening for his footsteps on the stairs.

He had a bunch of carnations—his peace offering. He sat beside me and handed me the flowers.

"I'm sorry, Fi."

I set them on the coffee table and sat up.

He took my hand and rested his elbows on his knees. "I'm not used to sharing decisions. I'm not used to living on a budget. I hate that I can't go out and buy something if I want it."

"I hate it too," I said quietly. Life would be a lot easier if we could afford to buy whatever we wanted. But we couldn't. I hated that we fought over stuff like this. I hated feeling like I lectured my husband about finances. I hated having to be the one that always said "no" or to practice self-discipline. I hated feeling like I was the adult in this situation. I wanted to go out and frivolously spend money on useless stuff just as much as he did. Why did I have to be the bad guy when it came to money?

28

NOPE

"How about we try having a baby?" Travis suggested the next morning

I was still waking up. I hoped I'd heard him wrong. "A baby? Don't you mean a puppy?" Was this some sort of make-up solution to our fighting? I would've preferred it if he said something else, like "How about I make breakfast?" or "Don't worry, you never have morning breath."

"Well, yes, I'd like to have a dog someday too, but maybe we should have a baby."

I rubbed my eyes and yawned. "I can't even keep the plants alive. And they're not human." I didn't excel at keeping living things alive.

He propped his pillow against the headboard. "I'm serious, Fi. All joking aside."

I also sat up. "I'm serious too. I don't want a baby."

His chin lifted slightly. "Why?"

"Because." *Was he serious?* Did I really need to justify why *now* wasn't a good time to have a baby?

"Because why?"

I rolled onto my side so I could have the conversation face to face. "My job sucks. We have a lot of debt. How would we pay for a baby?"

He reached out and rubbed my shoulder. "It's not about the money, Fifi. It's about starting our family."

"With what money? You have years of schooling ahead of you. If I'm working and you're going to school full-time, who's going to watch the baby?"

"My mother could..."

I tensed. "What? We'll send the baby on the bus to Salt Lake every morning?" I didn't want a baby and I definitely didn't want his mother watching it.

"She'd probably be happy to help out, but what I was going to say is she can't wait to be a grandma."

"That's great, but I can wait. It's not her decision."

"I never said it was. I just know how happy it'd make her."

And how unhappy it'd make me. I wasn't ready.

"We'd make it work," he said.

I was pretty sure "we'd make it work" meant I'd be the one left trying to figure out how to make everything work. And Travis would continue being a full-time student. No thanks. Too much stress.

"Trav, hon, it wouldn't work. I couldn't do it. I don't want to do it. Not now, not yet."

Travis scowled. "It's not all about what you want."

I could feel the embers of an argument stirring. I backed off. "Honey, I want kids, just not right now. We are literally poor college students. Let's get through school and get a real job before having kids. Maybe even have real insurance. What if I get really bad morning sickness and feel like I did on the cruise? I can't function feeling like that. You'd have to work and go to school. Why rush into babies? We have our whole life ahead of us."

"Shane and Amy are doing it," he said.

I inadvertently laughed. "We're *not* having a baby because of peer pressure."

"They're finding a way to afford it." His words sounded like a challenge.

I was done arguing. "Good for them." I would secretly take my pill for the next three years if that's what it took. I was *not* ready to have a baby. "They also got scholarships and Pell Grants. We got nothing."

"We can apply for those."

The more he justified his reasoning, the more decided I became. "All this to have a baby? There's not only the baby and the doctor bills, there's formula..."

"You'd breastfeed," he said, as if the decision had been made. What if I didn't want to breastfeed? I thought I did, but what if, in the end, I didn't?

"And diapers..."

He waved it away. "We could use cloth. Be environmentally friendly. Wash them ourselves."

I burst out laughing. Where were all his crazy ideas coming from? "We are not using cloth diapers. Unless you plan on changing that baby and doing all the laundry."

"You could sell something on the side, like Amway. Make some money and get a discount on the diapers."

I became more and more frustrated. I had no interest in multi-level marketing.

"So, work and sell Amway just to have a baby? Ha. Ha. You're funny. The Portal-To-Hell job is not going to support a baby." I tried a new tactic, one that I probably should've suggested in the first place. "Don't you think maybe we should pray about this?"

He spread his arms wide. "What's to pray about? The Lord wants us to have families. You know, multiply and replenish the earth."

"But we need to be able to provide for that family."

He scowled and flipped the covers off of him. "You worry too much."

Someone had to. "Trav, I want to have kids, just not yet."

"Think about how cute it would be."

It probably would be very cute. Especially if it looked like daddy. Our babies surely would be model material. Maybe, baby. My resolve wavered a little. But still, I didn't want Travis to know that. He'd take full advantage of it. I didn't want to rush into kids. We were still getting to know each other. I liked our alone time. I was a little selfish of that, even to the point where I didn't want to share our time with his parents.

Besides, I was only eighteen.

"Can we wait a month or two?" I asked.

Or a year or two?

"I want more time to think about it," I said.

"You're always so serious. Think of how fun it'd be trying."

Trying to make my life more difficult did not sound like fun.

"We could just move up to Salt Lake," Travis said suddenly.

"And commute?" That didn't make any financial sense.

He straightened. "No, no. Listen. What if we moved in with my parents and I transferred to the University of Utah? Then we could save money on rent, have a baby and probably even have the car back."

"Travis, we need to get your parents out of our life, not move in with them."

"What do you mean by that?"

"We need to be independent." Autonomous. Maybe even get into some marriage counseling since it felt like all we ever did was disagree. "We need to figure out how to take care of ourselves before we have a baby."

Travis flashed me his seductive smile. "C'mon, Fi. Let's have a baby. We'll figure it out along the way."

I didn't respond. I hated everything about what he had just suggested. There was no way I could agree to that.

∽

I TURNED to Megan Peacock for her opinion.

"Travis wants a baby and to move in with his parents," I said, popping open a Diet Coke, sitting in her living room.

"Do you want a baby?"

"Nope."

"And how about living with his parents?"

"A hard no. How about you guys? Do you want a baby?"

"Nope. No way." She shook her head emphatically. "My sister got married at nineteen, got pregnant on the honeymoon, and had three kids by the time her husband finally graduated. Their oldest kid was nine years old. They lived in married housing for like, ever. I am determined to get my degree before I get pregnant."

I sighed. "So, I'm not an evil, wicked person for not wanting to get pregnant as soon as I get married?"

Megan snickered. "I think it's worse to have a baby if you can't afford it. You have to be able to feed it, you know."

I clapped my hands once. "Exactly my point! Why doesn't my husband get it?"

Megan and I looked at each other and then busted out laughing.

"I'm realizing that my husband views things very differently than I," Megan said. "And I think with something like a baby, you both need to be on the same page."

"Yeah, we need to get on the same page," I agreed.

Her advice made so much sense.

We needed to get on the same page on so many different pages. It felt like we weren't even in the same book.

29

MELTDOWN

The not-having-money issue made Travis grouchy. He seemed to be on the war path, picking apart anything and everything, then apologizing later for it. I also seemed to have an inclination to want to rip Travis's head off at every little infraction of careless money spending.

I tried to make Travis lunches, so he wouldn't buy it on campus. We were trying not to spend frivolously.

I decided to make a nice, homemade dinner, bring it up to campus and spend time with him while he studied. It'd mix things up from the boring dinners and be a peace offering for all the fighting we'd been doing lately.

I settled on risotto.

It sounded so good. Creamy.

I found a recipe on Pinterest and went to work.

It was complicated, though, with lots of stirring and I developed an instant aversion to it, vowing never to make it ever again. I also burned the whole bottom layer of rice and the bottom of the pan.

I plopped what was not burned into a Tupperware container (mustard yellow, a hand-me-down from Maxine's 1970's collection) to bring up to Travis.

Since risotto was so much work, I figured that could be the focal point of the dinner and I could "compliment" it with some side dishes —say a can of chunk light tuna—arranged tastefully on the side. Or at least served in a complimentary olive-green Tupperware container. I added a sprig of cilantro for a touch of class. Even if the risotto didn't taste good, at least the presentation was nice (as nice as could be with the Tupperware I was using).

I licked the spoon after portioning it out. It was good. *Really* good. So good I couldn't stop eating it. I forced myself to stop when I got dangerously close to the burned layer.

But there are some things a good bowl of risotto and a sprig of cilantro cannot fix. Such as, say, a husband in a very foul mood. And a wife who brought dinner up late, being detained by the necessity of constant stirring of a silly rice dish made with cheese and broth.

Travis saw me and scowled. "Where have you been?" He demanded.

I stared at my dear, sweet, love-of-my-life husband.

After the complicated instructions, stirring too much, not stirring enough (obviously with burning the bottom), and the overall mess I made in the kitchen, I was out of patience. "Making dinner. Risotto doesn't make itself," I answered, annoyed.

Travis pinched his lips together. "Riz-what?" He straightened and stacked the books scattered around him on the table.

Was he making space to eat?

"Risotto. It's a rice dish. It's very yummy." I pushed the still-warm container toward him. Condensation had formed along the top as proof it was just made.

He pulled it toward him, knocking the plastic spoon off that I had placed on top. "I was expecting you forty minutes ago. I'm starving."

Tomorrow I'll pack him a little baggie of Cheerios with his school lunch. Apparently, he spontaneously regressed to a two-year-old when hangry.

"Sorry," I said, not feeling apologetic. Instead, I felt wounded. But once he tasted my dinner, I was sure all would be forgiven.

I waited, watching him take his first bite, which literally, fell right back out of his mouth.

"Hot!" he said.

I thought it would cool by now. "Really?"

"A warning would've been nice, Fi." He stirred the rice around, blew on it, causing the steam to float away in wisps.

I pushed my chair back, putting some space between us. "Well, maybe next time you're in a foul mood, Travis Duckk, you might want to give me a warning."

I smiled at my play on words—fowl, duck—genius!

He tilted his head, looking at me out of the corner of his eyes. "Sorry, Fi. Bad day at school."

It sounded like a half-hearted apology to me.

"For the record, I had a bad day at work and had a bad fight with the burner on the stove. You're not the only one who had a bad day, so don't take it out on me." Normally, I wouldn't have lit into him like that, but between work, risotto, and my moody husband, I was fresh out of patience.

He lifted the spoon slowly and tried another bite. I watched him, expectantly, waiting for him to appreciate the flavor and also my effort after my rotten day.

"It's really...sticky," he said.

Sticky. Sticky?! He was kidding, right? He had the nerve to call my risotto sticky? He must've *really* had the mentality of a two-year-old if he wasn't smart enough to realize he should at least *pretend* to like it —even lie, if necessary.

Then he opened the container with the tuna fish, and even a sprig of cilantro didn't improve the situation. "Tuna? You're kidding me, right, Fi? You didn't seriously bring me a can of tuna and sticky rice for dinner, did you?" He dropped his fork dramatically and pushed the food away, his nose turning up in the air.

He glowered.

He literally sulked.

I was literally married to a toddler.

Oh, boo hoo! Poor Travis, having a little tantrum.

It was a good day to find a spine and decide I wasn't a doormat.

I stood up.

His mouth frowned and his eyes scrunched up. "Where are you going?"

Travis was genuinely confused. Go figure.

"Anywhere but here," I said.

I snatched the two ugly, but full, Tupperware bowls, walked to the trash can and threw them away. They landed with a thud. I stalked back to the table and grabbed my purse.

Travis jumped up and reached for my arm. "Honey. Stop. I'm sorry. I didn't mean..."

I faced him, biting back my anger. "I don't care, Travis. I don't care what you *meant*, or that you had a bad day, or whatever your excuse is. There's a whole other world outside the little microcosm of Travis you live in."

"It's not the food, Fi."

"I don't care if it was the food or if you're hangry. But you are *not* going to criticize me. Find your own dinner. Heck, charge it on the credit card. Then call your mother to tell her about our little fight. Sounds like the making for a pretty good conversation."

I walked away from Travis instead of groveling and blaming myself. I walked home, ate the rest of the unburned risotto, then threw the pot into a trash bag. I dug through the cabinets, finding every used kitchen item Maxine had given us, from pots and pans to Tupperware and spatulas. I didn't care what brand it was—Cuisinart or whatever—it went in the bag. If it came from Maxine, it was going to the Dumpster. The bag landed with a loud clatter and startled the stillness of the night. Startling but satisfying.

Travis slept on the couch that night. I was too stubborn to apologize. I was not wrong. I wasn't going to placate him. And I was not going to be the one to give in.

∽

THE NEXT MORNING, Travis was gone before I got out of bed, making it easier to avoid him. I hoped he was hungry today, since I didn't make his lunch. I rode my wave of justified indignation all morning, mentally daring anyone to cross me, because I was not in the mood to be messed with. I maintained the same level of don't-cross-me-ness at my next job. By the time I got home, my angry energy was starting to slow down. Maintaining that level of anger was exhausting.

I sank into the couch, and leafed through the mail. I froze at the envelope with the scrawly writing on it, addressed to me. It was Maxine's writing. What was it? Travis hadn't mentioned anything about this when I was still talking to him two days ago. Did he know it was coming? What it was, was a bill. Apparently, my dear, sweet, two-year-old husband bought a new cell phone, to replace the one he broke. Not only did he buy an undiscussed cell phone, but he charged it on a credit card—*another* card— that was his mother's account. Attached to the copy of the bill was a little, yellow, sticky note: *I believe this is your charge.* ;)

Seriously? He bought a phone—an expensive phone—and didn't tell me?! Really?! Did he need the most expensive phone? Couldn't he have repaired his old phone? Buy a used phone? Or a cheap phone? How would we pay for the phone? What was he thinking?

I skimmed over the bill. Not only was that charge his, but charges at the food court. Like almost every day he was charging something. Sometimes twice a day!

What. The. Heck!

I was working my butt off at a miserable, minimum-wage paying job. Meanwhile, he was living like mommy and daddy still supported him and that he not only *deserved* nice things, but was *entitled* to nice things. I hadn't bought any nice thing since that first credit card bill came, showing me we'd already bought too many nice things. Why did he think it was okay to spend frivolously when we were literally poor college students?

I took the yellow Post-It note and wrote my reply.

This is your son's purchase. Take it up with him. :)

I taped the envelope shut and marched it over to the mailbox.

Between the risotto last night, his buy-on-the-sly new iPhone, the coy and cutesy note from dear, sweet Maxine, that was really laced with venom, I was done. I wasn't going to kill myself working and sacrificing only to have Travis undermine me at every turn. I was done listening to his voice of reason—or unreason. I didn't want to live in debt the rest of our lives because Travis had no self-restraint and I had no self-respect to stand up to him. I had to stop believing Travis' mindset that we could not only afford to buy everything we wanted, but *deserved* it. Things needed to change. I had to make it happen, because Travis certainly wasn't going to.

Is this adulting?

Rage reigned as I steadily made rash, but necessary, decisions. I had to relieve myself of the heaviest burden weighing on me.

The furniture.

At the current rate, we'd never pay it off.

It had to go.

I'd return it.

Getting rid of the furniture equated to peace of mind. As long as we had a mattress to sleep on, we didn't need any other furniture. Heck, we could go to DI and buy a gently-used couch. We could eat on TV trays.

It was drastic, it was crazy, but it was practical. It would solve everything— less debt and more peace of mind. It felt like the smart, adult thing to do.

It made me actually do it.

I wasn't even actually sure if I could return the furniture. But a few phone calls later, arrangements were made.

In a few days, I would calmly *explain* to Travis the rationale behind my rash behavior. I hoped we would happily and unanimously agree I made a *mature* decision so we could finally get on with our happily ever after.

30

IF I WAS JONAH, I'D BE IN THE BELLY OF THE WHALE

I fully intended to tell Travis about the returning-the-furniture-incident/decision/whatever, but put it off. I still had a week before I *needed* to tell him. I knew he wouldn't agree with me. I also knew not including him in my decision was wrong and would cause yet another fight. And I didn't want to deal with that right then. I was *working* up the courage to tell him. I justified telling him at the last minute. That way, he wouldn't be able to do anything about it and would have to accept it.

But then crisis struck.

It happened while I was praying—begging—for help with a change of heart. See, I didn't want to change my heart. I was having a rip-roaring good time in my reign of hard-heartedness, but I needed to change. I knew that. I needed to ask Travis for forgiveness, and also forgive him. But I didn't want to forgive him because my pride stood in the way. I wanted to stay mad at him. I wanted him to acknowledge he was wrong. But it was wrong *of me* to feel this way.

My marriage wouldn't survive if I held grudges. If both of us insisted "I" was in the right, so obviously "you" were in the wrong, we'd never make it.

My marriage needed to work. I wanted it to work. This was a

bump in the road of settling into married life, right? All couples went through adjustments and had to learn how to give and take. I truly felt, if we could be on our own, away from the opinion and influence of his mother, out of debt and working together, we could make it work. It'd be like a clean slate. But in order to do that, I also needed to have a change of heart.

It was during this one-sided conversation while begging for a change of heart, but still justifying my hard-heartedness, that my phone rang.

An instant answer to prayer?

Travis?

Not quite.

It was my mom.

"Hello-o," Mom said cheerfully when I answered the phone.

"Hi," I said.

"You sound...funny," mom said. "Sniffly."

I *was* sniffly.

Crying would do that to you. I could try to hide it or...lie. "Allergies."

"Did you take anything?"

"Not yet," I said. I needed a good dose of Swallow-My-Pride.

"I'm coming up to Utah this weekend."

Uh-oh.

I gulped. "This weekend?"

Not what I needed at the moment.

"Why?"

"Dan has a job interview on Friday in Draper and is driving up there Thursday night. I thought I'd visit you."

There was no way she could visit and *not* sniff out the tension between me and Travis.

She continued. "Do you have room on your couch for me?"

By then I wouldn't *have* a couch!

I didn't want her here, in the middle of a war of wills, meddling in the name of mediating. Or at least meaning to mediate.

I hoped to dissuade her. "Our apartment is really small, Mom."

"I'll try to stay out of the way."

I didn't even *have* a couch to put her on, never mind patience to deal with her.

"This weekend isn't the best time," I said. I carefully phrased my words so I wouldn't make her suspicious. Anything less than harmony and marital bliss would encourage PMA, and I couldn't handle any PMA at the moment.

"It'll never be a good time if you don't make it a good time—"

"But," I protested, trying to think of a good excuse.

Desperation lent itself to making really poor decisions. Maybe rash was a better word. I had to keep my mom from knowing our marriage was in trouble—she'd blow it out of proportion. Things weren't great at the moment, but I was confident they could return to being great.

"How about I come home this weekend?" I blurted out.

It got worse with every sentence.

"I could drive back with Dan. I'd love to get away from Provo and the snow. Then I could see Dad too."

"Great," she said. I pictured her so enthused that she clapped her hands. "We get you both for the weekend."

I hesitated, wondering if wanted to open this can of worms. "It'll probably just be me." I tried sounding casual.

"No Travis?"

I exhaled. "Nope. No Travis."

"Why not?" she asked.

Her mind was probably spinning.

"He has some papers due. He has to get them done."

"Oh."

I could hear not only the disappointment in her voice, but the doubt.

Mom wasn't satisfied with the explanation.

"He couldn't work on them here?"

"No," I said. *Keep it simple*, I reminded myself.

"Is everything okay, Sophia?"

I choked up. Part of me wanted to tell her, to let it all out. But the other part of me remembered how she warned me against marrying Travis. It was too fast, too soon. She'd been right, but I was also sure Travis and I could fix it.

I cleared my throat. "Just stressful."

"Is there anything I can do?"

Not come? Not lecture me with "I told you so"? Not tell me to try harder? Maybe give us some space. And definitely *not tell me to look on the bright side.*

I forced myself to breath normal and sound upbeat. "Not that I can think of."

There was an uncomfortable silence.

After a beat too long, my mom continued. "Okay, then. We'll see you this weekend."

That was it. I was committed. I was going to Vegas.

Travis and I needed to have a conversation. Then we could put all the bad stuff behind us and move forward. Our fresh start.

I had so much going on and such an overwhelming sense of relief being out from under that cloud of debt, that I forgot to initiate that discussion with him. Sort of.

∽

MY BROTHER PICKED me up from work at the mall Friday afternoon. "My name is Luke Skywalker and I'm here to rescue you," he said and added a half-sweeping bow.

"Do you think Mom is going to want to do a *Star Wars* party this weekend?" I asked, as I settled into his car. I was more tired than excited by the idea.

"What Mom is going to want to do is strap on a lie detector machine and grill you until you spill the truth about why Travis isn't coming."

Dang! "She told you about that?"

"She brought it up to me like a billion times in one conversation," he said.

I let my head loll on the headrest.

"You know she's going to ask until you tell her."

"I know."

I guess if I was a mom, I'd also want to know. I'd want my kid to be happy.

"Maybe we should accidentally break down in St. George and never make it home," I suggested dryly.

"St. George is too close, sis. Mom would be up in a heartbeat." Dan smiled knowingly because he was exactly right.

"I guess."

"So, what's up?" Dan asked quietly.

I shrugged. "Nothing. Travis has school. You know he'll get nothing done if he comes to visit."

Dan accepted my explanation by not asking any more questions. I didn't offer any more conversation and we drove the rest of the way to my apartment in silence.

When we pulled into the apartment parking lot, I pointed to our empty parking spot. "You can park there," I said.

"You sure you're ready for this?" Dan asked as we got out of the car.

A weight sat on my chest and it made it hard for me to breathe. The dread surrounding this visit was starting to mount. "Maybe I shouldn't go."

When I opened my front door, the sense of emptiness smacked me in the face and I remembered why I was ~~running away~~, I mean, visiting my parents. I stepped in. "I need to grab my bag," I said.

Dan followed but immediately stopped. "Whoa. What happened?" Dan asked, his eyes wide. "Did the repo man come or something?"

I stopped in the middle of the empty living room. "I returned all the furniture," I said without looking at him.

"I can see that."

Suddenly my rash decision seemed a little too rash. And I was afraid to own up to my own behavior.

He reached out and gripped my elbow. "Soph. Why?" he asked.

I couldn't hold back the tears. "I was being responsible," I said, dropping my arms by my side. Surely Travis would understand and agree with me, right? If I knew the answer was a resounding "yes" I wouldn't be acting like a five-year-old (I considered myself a few years older than Travis since I seemed to be the only one in the relationship willing to make adult decisions).

"No furniture equals no debt," I explained. No debt equaled peace of mind. "But I haven't told Travis yet."

Dan saw right through my ploy. "That's why you're coming home."

I shrugged. "Yeah. That's part of it."

"Only part of it?"

"Yes." The only part I was willing to tell him. "I'll get my bag." It only took a second since I was already packed. I wanted to be gone before Travis got home from school.

Dan didn't press the issue and made small talk as we headed out of town. It was nice to have something else to talk about than my usual problems. Even hearing about the happenings at home was a refreshing change.

"How'd the job interview go?" I asked, realizing I hadn't asked Dan anything about it.

"There were about fifty other people who were probably more qualified than me, all applying for the same job. I'd be surprised if I got it. For now, I'll keep my entry level, crappy-paying job and live at home a little longer."

"You really don't think you'll get it?" I asked.

Dan shook his head and snickered. "Nope. Pretty sure I won't be getting a call back."

"Sorry," I said. Here I thought that when I got married, things would magically work out. So far that wasn't true. I wondered if my brother thought that once he got his degree, the jobs would magically open up for him. It didn't seem like things were working out for either of us the way we assumed.

∼

It wasn't until we were out of the town of Nephi that I called Travis.

"Hello?" Travis sounded less than enthused.

"Hey, honey." I hoped he didn't notice the caution in my voice. "Where are you?" If he was at the library all night studying, I could put off telling him the "news" and not have to have the discussion in Dan's car.

"Heading home." I could tell by the way he was talking that he was walking.

Crap!

How close he was to our apartment?

"Are you going to be there? Or are you still mad at me and punishing me by going to your parents?"

This was already heading down hill and I hadn't even replied. Double crap! He was going to be so mad when he found out what I had done. "No, I'm still going home. Dan and I are already on the road."

"Mmmhmm," he mumbled into the phone.

Maybe I should prepare him. I took a deep breath. "Um, Trav, I had a little moment earlier this week." It was actually more like a big moment, but no need to make it worse.

It sounded like he stopped. "Like a senior moment?"

My stomach tightened. "No, like a freak our moment. It's kind of funny..."

"Funny like ha-ha, or funny like weird?"

Did I hear keys?

"Funny that you should mention weird..." It was a lame attempt at making a weak joke, but I was shooting for comic relief.

The phone went silent for five very long seconds. "Fi? Where's the furniture?" He had obviously made it home. He didn't sound surprised, he sounded no-nonsense. There was going to be no messing around with him about what I did.

Uh. Oh!

I gulped. "You got home before I could tell you the great news. We're debt free. Yay." My voice fizzled at the end.

I really wanted to fake static and claim we were going through a tunnel. But there were no tunnels on the way to Las Vegas, and we both knew it. And, unfortunately, we hadn't been driving long enough to claim going through the Gorge after St. George.

"You sold all the furniture?" he asked.

"Actually, I returned it." My heart hammered in my throat as I waited for his reaction.

Through the phone I heard the front door slam. "Are you kidding me? You returned all the furniture?"

"Not the mattresses," I managed. As if that was the bright spot in this whole situation.

"What are you thinking, Sophia?" he demanded.

I didn't have to be in the same room with him to know he was furious.

"I was thinking there was no way we'd ever be able to pay off the furniture."

There was a small thud. Did he throw something?

"You don't just get rid of everything," he growled.

"We couldn't afford it. The credit card bill—"

"I'm done, Sophia. I don't want to talk to you anymore." With that, he hung up.

I tried calling him back three times. All three times it went straight to voicemail. On the fourth call, I finally left a message trying to explain my thought process leading up to my actions.

When I ended the call, he texted back.

Travis: I don't want to talk to you. I'm blocking you.

Blocking me? With those two words, it felt like he slapped me in the face.

Way to be mature, Travis.

"That didn't go very well," Dan said gently.

I looked out the window so I could wipe the tears out of my eyes. "Yeah. It's not going very well at all."

31

EXHALE

The weekend visit went as expected, but also unexpected. My mom constantly questioned me about Travis and my marriage. I stuck to my narrative and game plan: deny, deny, deny. It was exhausting.

When I snuck into our apartment Sunday night, I was struck by the starkness of it. Even though I had thought about returning the furniture all weekend, it was still shocking to walk into our bare apartment. It felt like more than just the furniture was missing.

Travis wasn't home, thank goodness. I wasn't ready to face the inevitable conversation we'd have. I was sure he was still going to be mad. I assumed he was at his parent's.

I was still awake two hours later when he slipped into bed.

He laid down, his back toward me. "You're back," he said in a flat voice.

I matched his tone. "I am."

"My mom was hurt that you didn't come up to visit this weekend."

Uh-huh. She was probably happy she had Travis all to herself. "Well, my mom was hurt that you didn't make it down to visit this weekend," I retaliated.

"Maybe you shouldn't have run off to your parents." His tone was snide.

I propped myself up on my elbow so I was looking at him. He remained facing away from me. "Travis. I don't want to fight, okay? I'm sorry. I don't want us to be making snide comments and being mean to each other. I was wrong. I should've told you about the furniture. And I realize that was a decision we should have made together. I'm sorry. I freaked out."

"You think?"

Deep breath. "Travis, I'm trying to apologize. But if you want to keep fighting, I guess I can't stop you."

"I'm going to sleep on the couch. Oh, wait, that's right, we don't have one."

Reconciliation was obviously not going to happen tonight. *Whatever.* I was too tired from beating myself up to fight it out with him. I flipped over to my side, facing away from him, and eventually fell asleep.

I woke up the next morning after a night of very troubled sleep. I needed to apologize to Travis and patch things up.

I propped myself up on my pillows against the wall (our new "headboard") and watched Travis sleep. Looking at him still made my heart skip. He was so gorgeous. Especially now, with his scruffy face and rumpled hair. I wanted to cry—I loved him so much. Why was everything so difficult? Why was marriage so hard?

Our courtship had been so easy. Everything was so exciting, romantic and passionate. Now that we were married and adulting, it seemed so much less passionate and exciting. Like the fire had gone out. Wasn't that the opposite of how it should be? Wasn't it supposed to get better and better? Instead, it seemed harder and harder.

My feelings for Travis hadn't changed. I still loved him. But real life kept interfering with my happily ever after. Paying for his education, paying the rent, paying the utilities, paying down our debt; bills would always be a part of life. But it was *hard*. Working a soul-sucking job, not having a car, cooking and cleaning was *hard*. Life being hard wasn't bringing us together and making us stronger—it was tearing us apart. It made us behave like animals, tearing at each other's throat.

And we had to keep his mother—and maybe even my mom—from meddling.

Tears filled my eyes unexpectedly. I couldn't let pride ruin our marriage. I loved him. I loved him so much it hurt to think of life without him. But we had to figure out how to be a couple instead of two separate, selfish people. There was so much to love, I just didn't understand why it was so *hard*.

I needed to try harder.

I slid down under the covers and snuggled up close to him. I ran my hand over his stomach, feeling his muscles.

He woke up. "What is it?" He was a little gruff until he rolled over and saw me crying. "Fifi? Honey, what is it? What's wrong?"

My words caught in my throat. "I am so sorry. I am so, *so* sorry. I take it back, honey. I take it all back. I didn't mean to be spiteful and return all the furniture. I was so freaked out about the money and . . ." My eyes stung as tears spilled down my face and my throat was tight and burning. "I don't want it to be like this. I don't."

"Shh, shh, Fi. It's all right. I don't want it to be like this, either. We'll figure it out."

I listened to his quiet, reassuring sounds he whispered in my hair and resolved to do better. I resolved to work harder at our relationship. We could get through the rough patch and find our happily ever after.

After he reassured me, I made him a good breakfast. Maybe it was to reassure myself more than anything.

Things seemed to get better after that day. I couldn't say exactly what changed—whether it was my attitude, or his attitude, or both our attitudes. Things seemed to smooth out. Travis didn't seem so put out if I didn't come up to campus to bring him dinner and be with him every night. Maybe alone time had been the key all along—both of us needing some space instead of suffocating each other by being together every free moment we had.

I finally felt like we were melding together, finding the right balance that made us both happy and satisfied as a couple and as individuals.

And best of all, Travis didn't insist on going up to his parents every Sunday.

I hung out a little more with Megan.

For the first time in months, I felt like I could breathe freely.

Strange, I hadn't even realized I'd been holding my breath.

32

WAIT! WHAT?

"This isn't working," Travis announced on Saturday morning, two weeks after the "Furniture Weekend". He leaned against the kitchen counter, holding the loaf of bread.

I thought he was talking about the toaster. "It should. I just used it," I said absently, as I crunched down on my own toast and scrolled through my phone.

He shoved the toaster toward the wall, scraping loudly on the Formica counter. "Not this."

Alarmed, I looked up.

He motioned between where he stood and where I sat at our small kitchen table. "This."

The kitchen arrangement? It was so small we didn't have much choice.

I made the same frantic side-to-side motion. "This, what?"

"This." He motioned again. "Us."

I snapped to attention. I shut off my phone and put down my toast. "Us?" I repeated, not sure I'd heard correctly.

This has to be a joke.

It *was* April Fool's Day. I had plastic wrapped the toilet seat as a prank. Was this revenge?

He crossed his arms and rested against the cabinets. "Yeah, us." His face was hard, his expression set.

I was confused. My eyes scrunched up as I looked at him closer, trying to read his expression. I swallowed hard. "What do you mean?"

"We're not working out."

The ambiguity of his words gave me a small glimmer of hope. "Are you talking about exercise or our relationship?"

His lip curled and his eyes narrowed. "Our relationship, Fi." His arms uncrossed and gripped the countertop.

Where did this come from?

Where is it going?

"Well, it's not like you can break up with me, honey," I joked, trying to lighten the situation. "We're already married."

The disgusted look returned and he huffed. "Fi, why are you making jokes? I tell you there's something wrong with our marriage and you joke about it."

"But what's wrong? I don't get why you think that."

I thought things were improving since the furniture fight. Sure, we argued—maybe a little too much—but didn't all couples argue? Weren't disagreements part of adjusting to married life? I didn't think anything was *wrong*-wrong. There were plenty of things wrong, but none that we couldn't fix. We probably needed a bunch of counseling, too. But we could work through it. In fact, I felt like we had finally found our stride.

He shook his head. "Don't you see it? Don't you feel it? Something has changed."

"What? Nothing's changed." I shrugged my shoulders, still not understanding what he was getting at.

"Things were different when we were dating," he said.

I still struggled to see his point. "Yeah, because we weren't married then. Other than that, nothing's changed." My feelings for him hadn't changed. If anything, I loved him more.

He looked directly at me and our eyes locked. "It has, Fi, it has. You've changed."

I became frustrated. "What are you talking about? I haven't changed. I'm the same person now that I was then."

He shook his head slowly. "No, you're not. You're not the person I fell in love with."

"What's that supposed to mean?" I exploded. "You've known me for a grand total of seven months. I haven't changed all that much." Did he blame me? Like I caused his unhappiness and dissatisfaction?

"You have," he insisted. "You used to be fun, loving. I could tell you were always thinking of me. Now, it's like you barely even notice me."

My mouth dropped open. "I'm not paying enough *attention* to you? Are you kidding me? What are you? Two?" I thought of all the things I did for him—for *us*.

"See," he said. "You're making me feel bad for how I feel."

I shook my head in disbelief. "Making you feel bad? I can't understand why or how you would think I don't pay enough attention to you." My voice rose steadily. "I'm not working that horrible job for fun. I bring dinner up to campus for you. I hang out with you while you do your homework. I type your papers. How am I not paying enough *attention* to you? All I do is pay attention to you!" I pointed an accusatory finger. "How am I not doing enough for you?"

Travis shrugged. "It's different now than when we were dating."

"You're right," I shot back, bitter about his feelings. "We're minus a car and I'm working and cooking and cleaning all the time. Tell me how to be more fun when I'm doing all of that and I'll do it." I threw my arms up. "But right now, I'm a little tied up trying to make your life easier."

How dare he accuse me of not doing enough for the relationship? His accusation was completely unjustified and unfair.

A little smile appeared, as if he had proven his point. "See. You resent me."

Whoa, didn't see that one coming. "Resent you? Really? Are you serious?" That was ridiculous. "I love you and that's why I do it."

He looked a little bit smug as he crossed his arms across his chest again. "Our marriage isn't going to work if you resent me."

"I didn't say I resent you!" I yelled, furious and confused at the same time. Sure, maybe I resented some of the things he had done, but that wasn't fair to make it a blanket statement. But he probably resented me for returning all the furniture. We had both done things that the other didn't like.

He shifted his weight. "You don't have to say it."

"Why don't you believe me when I tell you I don't resent you?" I sputtered, still bewildered.

"Because I don't feel that way. You make me *feel* like you resent me."

I stood, the chair scraping against the linoleum floor. "Travis, that is ludicrous. Why would you ever think or say that?"

"Because you were different before. I don't feel like the person I married is the person I dated."

I took a tentative step forward. "Things were going to change, Travis. You had to have realized that, right? But that doesn't mean that it's a change for the worse."

Travis shook his head. "But it is. You're not fun anymore. Now you just nag me. I can't buy this and I shouldn't do that. I should study. I shouldn't be late for class. All you do is tell me what I should or shouldn't do."

My thoughts stuttered for a moment as I tried to figure out how to respond to that. It was true, but it wasn't my intention. There was a lot of things I said he shouldn't buy. But didn't he understand I didn't like being the person to tell him no? I went along with his every whim when we were first married and it put us into a pile of debt. But the rest of my "shoulds" were meant as encouragement, and sometimes motivation. He really couldn't skip his Friday afternoon class every week and not have it affect his grade. I didn't want to "mother" him, but left to his own devices, he tended to take the path of least resistance. But if he saw it as nagging, I could stop.

"What are you saying?"

Travis stared at the floor instead of looking at me

He glanced at me and then back to the floor. "I'm not sure I love you anymore," he murmured.

"What?" I managed after a moment. My stomach clenched up and my pulse quickened.

"I'm not sure I love you anymore." With each word, his voice became more determined.

Tears instantly filled my eyes, blurring my vision and my heart hammered in my chest. "How can you not love me anymore?" I choked out, shaking my head. Hot tears spilled over and rolled down my cheeks. "We just got married."

He looked at his feet. "You've changed and I don't like it."

I was stunned. How? Why? Why would he say these things? Why would he feel like this? He hadn't said anything like this before. He hadn't even mentioned any doubts if he was having them. I wanted to tear into him and hold onto him at the same time. The pressure in my stomach tightened like it was in a vice grip. My mind shuffled, as if in slow motion, through the possible responses. If he didn't love me anymore...I stopped, not wanting my mind to go there. "What does that mean?" I finally managed. "Like it was all fun and games until you got married and then reality set in and you have to be a responsible adult and all of a sudden it's no longer fun? Is that it?" I demanded.

He shrugged.

"You don't just change your mind like that, Travis." I said angrily, closing the gap between us and getting right up into his face.

He stepped aside. "Well, I have."

I took a deep breath and a step back. I used the edge of the counter to steady myself. I needed to calm down and deal with this rationally. "Can we back up a little? If you feel like something is wrong, maybe we should get some help? Talk to a marriage counselor?" Wasn't that normally the first step? Get some professional help and talk about it.

He snorted. "How's that going to help? Are they going to change you back to how you were before? I doubt it."

I gave into sarcasm. "Maybe they'll be able to change you back to when you weren't acting like a jerk and thinking like a fool."

"It's just different and I don't like how things have changed."

"I don't like you right now. I can't believe you. Where is all this coming from? You don't just change your mind about being in love with me." I looked at him, waiting for him to respond.

He wouldn't meet my gaze. "Maybe I have."

Rage coursed through me and adrenaline pricked at my skin. I gritted my teeth. "Don't you think you should have considered this *before* we got married?" I spat at him.

"I didn't feel that way at the time."

I threw my hands up in exasperation. "So why do you now? It hasn't been that long. Four months is not that long."

He finally looked me in the eye. "I can't be married to someone who resents me and makes me try to pretend to feel something I don't."

"I told you I don't resent you." I yelled. Realizing my yelling was probably not helping the situation, I made another attempt at calming down. "Let's get counseling." I said it as gently as I could. I reached out to rub his arm.

He shook off my hand. "I don't want counseling."

Deep breath. "Maybe we should talk to the bishop?" I was grasping at straws, trying to find something or some way to make him stay.

"Why?" he lashed out. "What is he going to do? Tell us to read the scriptures and pray together? How's that going to change you?"

"Change me?" My spine straightened. "Maybe you're the one who needs to change. You're the one who's unhappy."

"And I wasn't unhappy until I married you," he shot back. "Ever since then it's been downhill."

"Well, thanks. I love you too." I yelled back with as much sarcasm as I could. My thoughts spiraled. He didn't want counseling, he didn't want to talk to the bishop, so what did he want to do? If he wanted me to be fun, I could make a concerted effort. But at some point, he was going to have to realize that adulting and marriage was not always going to be "fun."

"I want a divorce."

He said it so simply, he could have just as well been asking me to pass the salt.

"What?" My heart stuttered for a second. He didn't say that, did he? The vice grip in my stomach gave one final squeeze, making me think I was going to throw up.

"I. Want. A. Divorce."

"Tr...Tra..." I stammered. I desperately wanted to back things up. "You don't mean that."

"I do."

He nodded for emphasis.

"But, but...This came out of nowhere. You don't just announce you're unhappy then tell me you want a divorce." I tried thinking back over the last few months. Had there been clues? Nothing significant that I could remember. "It's not fair to blindside me like that."

"I've been thinking about it for a long time."

"We've barely been married for four months. Don't you think maybe you need to give it more of a chance?"

"I have." His voice took on a pleading tone. "I have given it a chance. And the longer we stay married and pretend we share feelings for each other the longer I'm going to be unhappy."

I couldn't believe him. "You? You think it's all about you? What about me? I'm really sorry you're unhappy, but I think you have the problem and you're blaming me. I thought we were happy. I'm doing everything I can think of to make this marriage work. And then you change your mind and want to walk away."

"It's not fair to me to stay married to someone I don't love." He shrugged and held up his hands like he was helpless. Like he was trying to make himself feel better by getting me to agree.

A thought came to mind. "Is there someone else?" I could barely whisper the words. I could not wrap my head around the thought, the possibility, that maybe there was someone else. Surely, he didn't have time to meet someone else. All he did was go to class and study. And usually when he studied, I was with him. Except for the last couple of weeks. Had he met someone while studying since I stopped going up to campus every night?

Was it my fault for not going up every night? But then common sense kicked in. No, it wasn't my job to babysit my husband to make sure he stayed faithful. But he couldn't have been unfaithful, could he?

"No."

My breath rushed out and I felt my lungs deflate. "Really?" I asked in a small voice, hoping it was the truth.

"No, there isn't someone else," he insisted.

But still. If it wasn't someone else, why would he decide he no longer loved me?

"Travis," I said quietly. I held my hands open in front of me, helpless, scared, vulnerable. If he left me, what would I do? I didn't want that. I didn't want to give up and walk away from our marriage. "It doesn't have to be this way. Really. We can do whatever it takes to fix…whatever it is that is wrong. I don't want to get . . ." I couldn't say the 'D' word. "I don't want to lose you. I love you. Please, please don't do this."

He shook his head. "I'm sorry, Fi, but I don't want to work it out. I can't stay married and be shackled to you the rest of my life."

"Shackled?" My temper flared. I was speechless for a moment. The word was like acid burning me. My hands shook with fury. I clenched them tightly into a ball to try and control it.

"I think I need some time away from you to think without you being around nagging me."

"Nagging you? I don't nag you. You make it sound like I'm a horrible wife. I don't get it, Travis. If you've been feeling like this you haven't let me know."

"I want some space." His hands went out from his side, creating a visual for me. "I want to be able to think without you here. My parents agree."

Bringing his parents into this was the final straw. I snapped. "Your parents? Your parents know about this? I should've guessed. And I bet your mother was right there encouraging you to leave me." She never did like me. She didn't like to have to compete for her son's attention.

Travis pursed his lips and nodded his head. Then he smiled. What was he so happy about?

"My mother always told me nothing good came from Vegas. I didn't want to believe her, but now I think she was right." He seemed to gather courage from his declaration. His voice was steadier, his words more forceful.

My eyes narrowed. "Coming from Vegas has nothing to do with it. I could just as easily say nothing good comes from Salt Lake. After all, look at you."

"You need to accept it. I want a divorce and nothing you do is going to change my mind."

"But, but . . ." I opened my mouth but no words came out.

"I'm done. You're not going to change my mind."

And I didn't.

He left me without as much as a backwards glance, a second thought or a second chance.

33
MAY

34
JUNE

35

JULY

"Rise and shine," my mother said as she burst through my bedroom door and made a beeline for the sole window and pushed aside the blackout curtain with gusto. Then she pulled up the blinds with a loud *zip*.

She did this every morning.

And every morning, as soon as she closed the door, I stumbled out of bed and put the blinds back down.

I think it was her excuse to check and make sure I was still alive, and it was my excuse for exercise. We went through the same routine every day, and every day it didn't inspire me to *rise* or *shine*. There was no *rise* or *shine* left in me.

Today I waited until I heard Mom back out of the garage and the door shut before I made my move.

And then I did something I didn't normally do. I didn't go back to bed.

I caught a glimpse of myself in the mirror as I walked across my room and I actually stopped for a moment to study my reflection. At first, I did a double take, because it didn't really *look* like me.

My hair was matted and greasy. It hung down my back in a lifeless cascade of blah. I piled it on the top of my head, not even trying for a messy bun. It was messy without any effort. My armpits smelled bad enough I gagged. It had been at least five days since I had showered.

I stared at my sallow skin and decided maybe today was the day I'd go outside and get some sun. I could probably use the vitamin D.

Since it wasn't Saturday (or maybe it was. Who knew? I'd lost track) I decided not to shower. On Saturdays, my mom always came in and forced me to take a shower. While I was out of my room, she gathered up my sheets, sweats, pajamas, or whatever I'd lived in that week, and threw them in the laundry. At first, I was mad because I just wanted her to let me be. But recently, I had started to appreciate the fresh scent of Tide. It was like the one good thing in my life.

Somehow my body was tired from staying in bed most of the day most days. I pulled on my bathrobe and quietly opened my door. I listened for a few seconds to be sure I really *was* alone before going downstairs.

I wandered around the kitchen, looking in all the cabinets until I found some Pop Tarts. Diet Coke was chilled and ready in the fridge, as if my mom had been waiting for this moment. I went outside, squinted at the sunlight and sat on the patio swing.

The heat was a shock to my body. When had it gotten so hot?!

Obviously while I'd been hibernating.

I swiped on my phone to check my messages. Nothing. Not that I expected anything. My life had been pretty dead since *That Day*.

The day Travis told me he wanted a divorce was still fresh in my memory, like an open wound. I had run out the front door, and smack into Nicole. I was hysterical, and through the tears, told her what had happened. This was one of those times that I was sure she didn't want to ask if I needed help.

But she did ask. When I told her I needed to go home, she asked me where that was. This time, instead of being in a rush, she packed me in her car and drove me to Las Vegas as I cried the whole way. She had texted me a few times since *That Day* to check on me, but stopped since I never responded. I couldn't blame her.

But the person I really wanted to hear from, I didn't. I hoped for something from Travis—a text, a phone call, a voicemail, anything. But I hadn't. At least, not recently.

Originally, there'd been a few heated calls and Travis said he needed some time and space. That turned into him not answering my calls. A month later, the divorce papers came in the mail. There was no note inside–just some sticky arrows pointing to where I needed to sign.

I still hadn't signed them. I got a text every few weeks reminding/demanding that I sign, but I hadn't. I couldn't. I didn't want to.

I was waiting for him to realize he still loved me. And that he missed me. And I hoped he'd realize we could make it work. Our marriage was far from perfect. I didn't even know if it was good. But I loved him. If we got some counseling, and got his mother out of our marriage, I thought we had a chance.

After five minutes, I was hot and sweaty and went back inside to the cool air conditioning. I looked around, not knowing what to do with myself. But then the doorbell rang.

Nicole?

Obviously it couldn't be Nicole, but the sound triggered my memory. Maybe I'd work up the energy to call her. Or maybe not. I didn't have any good news to share or anything to talk about.

I answered the door, only to find a college-aged kid in a polo shirt and a lanyard around his neck.

"Hi, I'm Todd. I'm from Killabug. Some of your neighbors have been having a problem with cockroaches–"

I cut him off. "Killabug? Is that really the name of your company? And none of my neighbors are having issues. You guys need to think of a new sales pitch."

His hand went to his chest. "There really is a roach infestation. Your neighbor Mary–" he pointed east, "had us spray–"

"Liar!" I pointed at him and yelled. "I don't even have a neighbor named Mary!" I slammed the door without waiting for an answer. Stupid door-to-door salespeople! If it wasn't pest control, it was solar panels or security systems. That job might've been worse than my

Portal-to-Hell telemarketing job. But I had no pity on them. They were lying and deceiving cockroaches themselves.

I marched into the kitchen, ready for another Diet Coke. My eye caught the divorce paperwork, stuck to the side of the fridge with a magnet.

Should I try calling Travis one more time? Maybe by now he'd know he'd made a mistake and–

Ding dong!

Seriously?

I stomped through the house and whipped open the front door. "Go away you liar!"

"Hello, Fifi."

My heart stopped. I blinked my eyes several times to make sure I was seeing clearly. When the person on my porch came into focus, it wasn't Todd from Killabug.

It was Travis.

I wrapped my bathrobe around me tighter, trying to hide that I was still in pajamas. My hand went to my hair to make sure it was still secure. "Travis?" I looked closer at him. He didn't look any different. Still breathtakingly gorgeous.

Was he a mirage? The only way I knew he was real was because sweat trickled down his temples. It was so freaking hot out.

Was he here to visit me? Should I invite him in?

"What are you doing here?" I managed, still unsure if I was really awake or dreaming. Maybe I was hallucinating from heat stroke?

He held up some folded papers. "I need you to sign these."

I shook my head and backed up against the doorframe. "But I don't want to sign them."

His eyebrows lifted and he rolled his eyes. "I need you to sign these." He tried to hand them to me.

I wouldn't take them. "We can work it out, Trav. I know we can," I said, trying hard to think coherently.

He slowly shook his head and looked at me like I was a pathetic little child. "No, I don't think we can. I don't love you anymore and nothing will change that."

His words pierced me. How could he not love me anymore? Did our temple vows mean nothing to him? Did I *really* mean nothing to him?

A movement off to the side caught my attention. I turned to see what it was and realized a woman stood there. A *very* pretty woman. She had long, wavy brown hair, a perfectly made-up face and wore a skinny little business suit and very high heels.

"Who's she? Your new girlfriend?" I asked him and threw a look of disgust her way.

Did he really bring his new girlfriend to his almost ex-wife's house?

"She's the notary. To make this legal," he said.

Notaries made house calls?

Count on Travis to find one—an attractive *female* one—who did.

He held the papers closer to me and produced a pen from his back pocket. "Sophia, just sign the papers. Make it easy on both of us."

"Fine!" I spat at him. "Fine, okay. I'll sign them!" I snatched the papers and pen and dramatically whipped the pages open. This copy also had the sticky arrows for my signature. I scribbled my initials and my name everywhere I was supposed to and threw the stack back at him. They fell on the ground.

He slowly bent down and picked them up. "See. That wasn't so hard."

But it was hard. By signing those papers, I admitted our marriage was through.

We both had to do things for the notary to make the transaction legal, and then the girl left immediately.

Travis wasted no time making his exit. He tucked the papers in his back pocket as he walked away

In a moment of bravado, and a last-ditch effort, I cried out, "But you're going to miss me and be sorry you ever left me."

He stopped and looked over his shoulder at me with a snide expression. "Maybe I will..." his words hung in the air and I had a moment of satisfaction. "But I don't think so." With that he left and didn't look back. A car door shut and the BMW squealed out in a white blur.

I screamed in frustration and slammed the door. I leaned against it and slowly slid to the floor into a crumpled heap. The tile cooled my cheek against my hot tears. It really was over. I had just signed away my marriage. Now I was divorced and my life was over. What was I going to do? Why did this happen to me? How did my happily ever after end so quickly?

I ugly cried, letting the sobs rack my chest, as I wiped my nose on my arm. I didn't care how disgusting it was.

I don't know how long I was on the floor before my mother found me.

She got down on her hands and knees and put her hand on my shoulder. "Sophia? What's wrong?" she asked, her voice concerned.

I blinked as I faced her. "It's really over, Mom. I did it. I signed the papers."

Mom squinted. "For the divorce? Why now?"

"Travis came here—" I motioned to the door—"and made me sign them."

She looked me up and down. "Did he hurt you?"

I blotted my eyes with the heel of my hand. "He destroyed me, Mom! He really doesn't love me anymore. What am I going to do?"

She gathered me up in her arms and hugged me. "You might not understand it now, but everything will be okay, Soph. Everything will work out. The sun will come out tomorrow."

And I believed her. Not because I wanted to, but because I didn't know what else to do.

SUDDENLY SINGLE

Want to follow along as Sophia gets a second chance at love? Check out the first chapter of *Suddenly Single*.

YOU NEVER GET A SECOND CHANCE TO MAKE A FIRST IMPRESSION

This was a mistake.

I mean, why would I be trying to meet guys? I was barely divorced, and I wasn't even completely recovered from it yet. And what if Travis changed his mind?

But here I was at my BYU singles ward opening social two weeks after school started feeling anything but social. I'd been feeling this way since last April when my husband unexpectedly left me. As for being here tonight, my overly energetic roommate Rhonda insisted that I accompany her and our other two roommates to the activity.

"This is your first chance to make a good impression," Rhonda said.

The only impression I wanted to make was the one my head made on my pillow every night.

I could have helped plan this evening, having been offered a calling to serve on the Relief Society committee in charge of this activity. But I turned it down, much to Rhonda's horror.

"What is your calling?" She pounced as soon as I returned from meeting with the bishop on Tuesday night.

"Aren't you supposed to wait until Sunday, after it's announced?"

"Sure, if it was important, like Relief Society president. But she's already been called, so it's not that."

"My calling wouldn't be important?" I suggested.

Rhonda backpedaled. "No, that's not what I meant. I mean, every calling is important—"

"I didn't get one," I interrupted, letting her off the hook.

"What do you mean? They're bringing in, like, the whole ward tonight to issue callings." Rhonda was truly taken aback.

"Nope. No calling. Dodged that one."

"I don't get it. Everyone gets a calling. Unless . . ." She was thoughtful for a moment. "Oh, okay." Rhonda looked as though understanding had just dawned on her. "Ohhhh."

"Oh, what?" I demanded, annoyed by the insinuation.

"You can't have a calling."

I nearly choked in disbelief. She was way off. "It's not that I can't have one; it's that I don't want one. I declined."

"You declined?" She stared at me. "Are you kidding? You're not supposed to turn down a calling. There's a reason you're called to a calling."

I knew the reason. It was to encourage me to be social. But she didn't need to know that. "I'm not picking and choosing callings." I exhaled, trying to be patient. "I didn't want a calling. Any calling."

"You're not supposed to do that. You're not . . ."

I didn't wait for her to finish. "But I did," I said quietly.

There were a lot of things I wasn't supposed to do. Like get married at eighteen and four months later get divorced. I had lived the freshman fantasy of meeting and marrying my eternal companion my first semester at BYU. Infatuation over Travis Duckk helped me escape another freshman blight: the typical "Freshman Fifteen" weight gain.

Travis's last name was Duckk, which, at the time, seemed to be his only flaw. I never liked the name, but I'd thought I was being petty. And it was petty, but I hated going from Sophia Davis to Sophia Duckk. At one point, I suggested keeping my own name, but he was offended. So in the end, I made peace with the fact I would be Sophia Duckk. But name or no name, I'd thought I was one lucky duck.

So here I was, a year later, back in the same position I was last year: suddenly single. The only difference was the baggage I now carried. Having the opportunity to attend another round of opening socials, family home evening groups, and ward activities sounded challenging. Tonight's theme, "speed dating," did not thrill me. Dating wasn't high on my priority list, but neither was getting out of bed, getting dressed, or going to class.

Since the surprise breakup of my marriage, I'd become just a little bit bitter. My brand-new therapist at the counseling center told me it was a natural reaction for dealing with my recent trauma. Trauma, drama, it was all the same to me: I wished I didn't have to deal with it.

Not only did I not want to deal with it, but I also didn't want to tell anyone about it either. I was worried what the reaction would be. Divorced students at the ripe old age of nineteen were probably pretty rare at BYU. I figured it would make people uncomfortable. Why would I want to put myself out for rejection again?

As for this evening, I seemed to be in the minority with my lack of enthusiasm. People were practically buzzing as they took their seats at the tables set up along the perimeter of the room reserved in the Wilkinson Center, or the Wilk for short. The idea was the girls were seated by apartments on one side of the tables, the guys were grouped likewise by apartments on the opposite side of the tables, and we had two minutes to visit with the person sitting across from us. When the buzzer rang, the guys would move down one seat until they had visited with every girl in the room.

Offering minimal information was my remedy for handling this evening's activity. The first set of willing and able young men sat across from us with two minutes on the clock.

"Hi, I'm Taylor."

"Sophia."

"It's nice to meet you."

"You too." I could at least be cordial in my disinterest.

"Where are you from?"

"I'm from Vegas. And you?"

"Cedar City. What year are you?"

"I'm a freshman." I could have and should have been a sophomore. But I'd put my education on hold to work full-time supporting Travis, who was starting his second semester of prelaw. The only things I gleaned from helping him study were some eye strain, a little bit of legal jargon, and hours of reading boring, useless stuff, since he divorced me soon after.

"And you?"

"Sophomore. I just got back from my mission."

"Where'd you go?" A returned missionary usually liked to talk about his mission.

"New Zealand Auckland Mission."

My roommate from last year was currently serving in New Zealand. "Did you know a Gretchen Clark?"

"Sister Clark?" He looked thoughtful. "Doesn't ring a bell."

I didn't know what to ask next, so I said, "Brothers? Sisters?"

"Three brothers, two sisters, and I'm number two. How about you?"

"I have an older brother. He lives with my parents and has a computer software job."

The timer rang, announcing our time was up. "Nice talking to you," I called out politely as he moved with his roommates to the next table.

Here we go again, I thought. I wasn't sure I could make small talk over and over again through fifteen male apartments.

"I'm Jordan," the next one said as he introduced himself. "I'm from Southern California." He looked the part: tan, slightly shaggy blond hair, good-looking, muscular, ultra-white teeth. "You're, like, going to make the perfect trophy wife."

I pictured a trophy with the metal topper slightly crooked, as if it had been dropped one too many times and then donated to Deseret Industries. "Oh, no." I managed a small laugh, trying to hide my surprise at his assuming words. "Don't be deceived. I'm far from trophy material."

"Well, you look pretty perfect to me." He smiled confidently.

"Nobody is perfect," I said softly, resulting in an awkward pause.

"So what about you? What's your major?"

"I'm a Spanish major."

"Spanish, huh? Did you serve a Spanish-speaking mission?"

His face lit up. "Yes, Argentina Cordoba Mission. How about you? Any mission?"

"Nope, no mission."

"How about a major?"

"Nope, no major."

"How about a minor?"

"Nope. Can't say I have that either. I do have a goal to have a major someday, but that means I would have to commit to something." I paused and gave a little laugh. "And I may or may not have commitment issues."

"Does that go for relationships too?"

"Right now, yes." There was another awkward pause. I think it was safe to assume that was not the answer he was looking for.

The timer saved me. Next! I felt like shouting as another guy sat down.

"Hi. I'm Bradley." He was about six feet tall, wiry, hair almost shaved. Being five ten, I had a rule when I was dating to only go out with guys who were taller than me. His deep tan made his eyes look very blue. I wondered if he was a lifeguard.

"I'm Sophia."

He grinned. "Didn't I see you riding a bike a couple of days ago?"

"I'm pretty sure it wasn't me." In fact, I knew it wasn't me.

"Really? I could swear it was you."

I twisted my mouth. "I, uh, don't know how to ride a bike," I confessed.

"You're kidding. You can't ride a bike?"

"Only if it's stationary, like the exercise kind."

"Why?"

"It's kind of a long, embarrassing story." I didn't want to get into my childhood stories.

He looked at his watch. "I've got one minute and five seconds," he encouraged me, then waited.

"Okay." I cleared my throat. "I was learning to ride without training wheels, and I went down a hill, got out of control, crashed into a block wall, and knocked out both of my front teeth. I was so traumatized I refused to ever try riding a bike again."

He smiled. "You're making that up."

I think he thought I was flirting with him, but I wasn't. If I was making up a story to be more attractive to him, it would be something way less embarrassing.

"Do you think you'll ever learn to ride a bike? I could teach you."

I shrugged. "It's not on the top of my to-do list." I had things of higher priority, like recover from my divorce, get over Travis, and get on with my life.

He nodded his head slowly as if processing my response. Before he could suggest anything else, the buzzer rang, signaling it was time to move on.

The evening continued with the same get-to-know-you questions — What's your name? Where are you from? What's your major? Did you serve a mission?—until finally we were at the last round of rotations.

I rested my head in my hand. Reluctant socializing was exhausting.

"You look ready to be done," the next guy said, taking a seat.

"I am." I looked up to see who I was talking with. Out of all the guys this evening, he had the best opening line. Or maybe the most accurate.

"I'm Luke. I'm your neighbor." His voice was warm and creamy, like a cup of hot chocolate. The rest of him was okay too, I supposed. Not that I was interested. He was tall and had brown hair, hazel eyes, straight teeth (always a plus) that were not blindingly white, a nice jawline, and a great smile. He was nice enough looking (again, not that I was looking), but not the stop-your-heart gorgeous, Abercrombie and Fitch model–type Travis was.

"Nice to meet you," I said politely.

"Any luck tonight?" he asked.

His question caught me off guard. It was the kind of question I would have asked. "What do you mean by luck?"

"You know, did you meet anyone interesting? Someone of eternal significance? Isn't that the whole point of this activity?" He raised an eyebrow.

I laughed. "Honestly, I wasn't interested in meeting anyone interesting tonight. My roommate Rhonda"—I pointed my finger at her—"insisted my eternal salvation was at stake if I didn't come."

"And?" He looked amused.

"I haven't had any huge revelations since I came."

"Yeah, me neither." He rolled his eyes and laughed. "Thank goodness, huh? That could be scary."

"It's been known to happen at BYU." I should know.

"Yes, it has. In fact, our roommates look like they're hitting it off." He nodded at Rhonda, pointing out what seemed to be an intense conversation.

"I'll have to ask after." I was glad it was her and not me. She probably was too.

The buzzer rang. "Well, it was nice to meet you, but I didn't get your name."

"Sophia."

"Sophia. I'm sure I'll see you later." He smiled again before getting up from the table.

"Yeah, see you around." That is, if I happened to get out of bed someday.

The activity ended but not without the same, if not more, excitement. Then it was time for treats. Time to pursue some of the more interesting encounters of the evening. Time to cozy up to that cute guy or girl to see how far one could get with flirting. Time for the wallflowers and sweet spirits to at least enjoy a brownie . . . or two.

∽

Rhonda's main priority back home was to analyze the evening.

"Oh my gosh. There are definitely some super cute guys in this ward. That was so fun."

She jumped onto the couch and patted the cushion next to her. "Come on, girls. Sit. We need to discuss."

Sarah, our RM roommate hailing from Denver, Colorado, obediently sat.

Claire, our other roommate, the accounting major, dismissed herself. "I thought the whole thing was kind of lame."

From what I had gathered, which was quite a lot since I was home most of the time, Claire didn't do much other than study.

"Well, come on, Sophia. You, if anyone, should have plenty to talk about." Rhonda scooted over to make room for me.

"What?" I was confused. I didn't feel like anything amazing had happened. I was just happy I'd survived.

"Guys were definitely checking you out tonight." Sarah nodded in agreement.

"Oh," I said dully. "I hadn't noticed." I truly hadn't.

"How could you not notice?" Sarah asked, her eyes wide.

"Quite easily, actually." I said almost to myself.

"Gosh, Bradley Benson practically asked you out right there at the table," Rhonda said.

"Bradley the bike guy?"

"Yeah," Sarah chirped.

Rhonda filled me in. "Bradley-one-of-the-most-sought-after-bachelors-in-the-ward Bradley. He's totally athletic, outdoorsy. He is a river guide down near Moab for whitewater rafting trips, and he rock climbs."

I could see myself on a video on YouTube falling backward off the raft and being left behind. I was so not an outdoorsy kind of girl.

"Good thing I'm not seeking." I laughed weakly, trying to downplay their detailed analysis of his possible interest.

"He's a hot commodity," Rhonda said, and they giggled. Had I been like that last year?

I was relieved when the attention turned to a TV show Rhonda wanted to see.

Claire declined watching it, and I fell asleep on the couch. So much for roommate bonding.

ACKNOWLEDGMENTS

I always have to thank my family first. They are my biggest fans and cheer me on. I love them and am lucky to have them!

Trisha Long has loved my characters as long as I have and appreciate all her help with everything to do with Sophia & Co.

Thank you to Danielle Booker for being my friend and my coconspirator.

Thank you to Michelle Morgan for helping fix all my mistakes. I appreciate you!

ABOUT THE AUTHOR

Sally Johnson has always had an overactive imagination and writing is how she puts it to good use. To date, she has written eleven novels, the latest of which is *Anxiously Engaged*. She enjoys watching classic rom-coms, but movies like *Notting Hill, About a Boy,* and *The Wedding Singer* have inspired her quest to explore real life relationships in humorous but grounded fiction.

She is a native of the East Coast, but currently lives on the West Coast in Las Vegas. When not writing, she taxis her kids around, dog-sits, and thrift-shops like a fiend.

For more books and updates, visit *SallyJohnsonWrites.com*

Sally would love to hear from you on social media!

READ MORE BY SALLY JOHNSON

The Suddenly Single Series

Suddenly Single (previously published as *The Skeleton in my Closet Wears A Wedding Dress*)

Clearly Confused (previously published as *Worth Waiting For*)

The Wit and Whimsy Romance Series

If the Kilt Fits

If the Boot Fits

If the Suit Fits

If the Broom Fits

If the Ring Fits

Standalone Romances

Dear Mr. Darcy

That Thing Formerly Known As My Life

Pretty Much Perfect

Join my newsletter to get all the latest information!

SallyJohnsonWrites.com

Made in the USA
Monee, IL
01 February 2024